THE
KOUGA
NINJA
SCROLLS

M000194901

THE
KOUGA
NINJA
SCROLLS

FŪTARO YAMADA

TRANSLATED BY GEOFF SANT

BALLANTINE BOOKS
NEW YORK

The Kouga Ninja Scrolls is a work of fiction.
Names, characters, places, and incidents are the products
of the author's imagination or are used fictitiously.
Any resemblance to actual events, locales, or persons,
living or dead, is entirely coincidental.

A Del Rey Trade Paperback Original

English translation copyright © 2006 by Random House, Inc.

Map copyright © 2006 by David Lindroth, Inc.

All rights reserved.

Published in the United States by Del Rey Books,
an imprint of The Random House Publishing Group,
a division of Random House, Inc., New York.

DEL REY is a registered trademark and the Del Rey colophon
is a trademark of Random House, Inc.

Originally published in Japan under the title *Kouga Ninpouchou* by
Kodansha Ltd., Tokyo, copyright © 2005 by Keiko Yamada.

This edition published by arrangement with Kodansha, Ltd.

ISBN 978-0-345-49510-5

Printed in the United States of America

Cover illustration by Masaki Segawa

www.delreybooks.com

Book design by Jo Anne Metsch

CONTENTS

MAP OF JAPAN / VII

CAST OF CHARACTERS / IX

THE GREAT SECRET / 3

KOUGA ROMEO AND IGA JULIET / 34

THE WORM AND THE SPIDER / 59

HIDDEN IN THE WATER / 84

A DEATH MASK OF MUD / 108

HELL OF HUMAN FLESH / 135

A LETTER OF CHALLENGE FOR A NINJA WAR / 151

THE CAT EYE CURSE / 168

BLOODSTAINED KASUMI / 193

THE SEDUCTIVE KILLER KAGEROU / 212

THE IMMORTAL PHOENIX OF THE NINJA / 234

OCCULT-PIERCING TIME / 260

THE FINAL BATTLE / 283

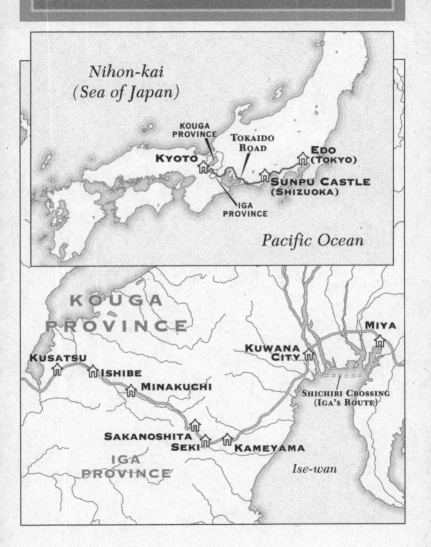

ALONG THE TOKAIDO ROAD

Nihon-kai
(Sea of Japan)

KOUGA
PROVINCE

TOKAIDO
ROAD

KYOTO

EDO
(TOKYO)

SUNPU CASTLE
(SHIZUOKA)

IGA
PROVINCE

Pacific Ocean

KOUGA
PROVINCE

MIYA

KUWANA
CITY

KUSATSU

ISHIBE

MINAKUCHI

SHICHIRI CROSSING
(IGA'S ROUTE)

SAKANOSHITA
SEKI

KAMEYAMA

IGA
PROVINCE

Ise-wan

CAST OF CHARACTERS

THE INNER CIRCLE

TOKUGAWA IEYASU: One of the greatest generals in Japanese history, Tokugawa Ieyasu eventually united all of Japan under his family. He selected one of his sons to officially rule as shogun, but Tokugawa Ieyasu maintained actual control behind the throne.

HATTORI HANZOU (THE YOUNGER): A high-ranking official serving Tokugawa Ieyasu. He is the leader of the ninja of Iga and Kouga.

HATTORI HANZOU (THE ELDER): Father to the younger Hattori Hanzou, the elder Hattori Hanzou instituted a ban on warfare between the Iga and Kouga ninja clans. The elder Hattori Hanzou once saved Tokugawa Ieyasu's life with the help of ninja from Iga Province. Acting under Ieyasu's orders, he also forced Ieyasu's eldest son to commit suicide.

OFUKU: Later known as the Lady Kasuga, Ofuku is an important member of the inner circle of the Tokugawa family. She breast-fed and raised the elder of Tokugawa Ieyasu's two grandsons (Takechiyo).

TAKECHIYO: The elder of Tokugawa Ieyasu's two grandsons, Takechiyo stutters and seems unintelligent.

KUNICHIYO: The younger of Tokugawa Ieyasu's two grandsons, Kunichiyo seems extremely bright and talented.

RIVALS

GENERAL ODA NOBUNAGA: At times an ally and at times a rival to Tokugawa Ieyasu. During the Iga Rebellion, Oda Nobunaga's troops invaded Iga Province and nearly obliterated the Iga and Kouga ninja clans. The ninja clans ended up seeking protection from Tokugawa Ieyasu. Oda Nobunaga has already died at the time this story takes place.

TOYOTOMI HIDEYORI: The ruler of Osaka. Osaka Castle is the last remaining holdout against the Tokugawa family's attempt to unify Japan under their rule. Toyotomi Hideyori's father, Toyotomi Hideyoshi, was also a great general.

KOUGA NINJA

KOUGA DANJOU: The elderly leader of the Kouga ninja clan. His grandson is Kouga Gennosuke.

KOUGA GENNOSUKE: He is in love with Oboro of the Iga ninja clan. Kouga Gennosuke is the grandson of Kouga

Danjou and is next in line to become leader of the Kouga clan.

JIMUSHI JUUBEI: Has an oxlike face, with gray skin and large ears. He lacks both arms and legs.

KAZAMACHI SHOUGEN: Hunchbacked, he has shining red eyes and long gray limbs.

KASUMI GYOUBU: Bald and completely hairless—lacking even eyebrows—Kasumi Gyoubu resembles some kind of strange monk.

UDONO JOUSUKE: He is extremely fat, with a barrellike belly and droopy facial features. Udono Jousuke is the personal retainer of Kouga Gennosuke.

KISARAGI SAEMON: Completely featureless and so ordinary-looking that few can remember what he looks like after meeting him. Okoi is his younger sister.

MUROGA HYOUMA: The blind ninja. He is a high-ranking member of Kouga.

KAGEROU: A beautiful female ninja whose face resembles a tree peony. Kagerou is from a respected Kouga family and she is deepy in love with Kouga Gennosuke.

OKOI: A young teenage woman with a voluptuous body. She is the younger sister of Kisaragi Saemon.

IGA NINJA

OGEN: The elderly "grandmother" and leader of the Iga ninja clan. She was alive during the Iga Rebellion many years earlier. Oboro is her granddaughter.

OBORO: A beautiful female ninja, she has a shining, lovely face that resembles the sun. She is in love with Kouga Gennosuke from the opposing clan. Oboro is the granddaughter of Ogen and next in line to be the leader of the Iga ninja clan.

YASHAMARU: A very handsome young ninja. He carries a black whip. He is in love with Hotarubi.

AZUKI ROUSAI: An old ninja with a white beard, Azuki Rousai often walks so hunched over that his back is parallel to the ground.

YAKUSHIJI TENZEN: This man has purple lips, an expressionless forehead, and feminine features. He is a leading figure in Iga.

AMAYO JINGOROU: His face and body resemble the corpse of a drowned man. Blue mold grows on his skin. He is considered a master assassin.

CHIKUMA KOSHIROU: Carries a huge, two-handed scythe. He was raised from birth by Yakushiji Tenzen and is intensely loyal to him.

MINO NENKI: Has wild, flowing samurai hair, and a thick coating of fur all over his body. He wields a club in battle.

HOTARUBI: A female ninja. A snake under her control is often coiled upon her head like a headdress. Hotarubi is in love with Yashamaru.

AKEGINU: A beautiful, slender female ninja with extremely pale skin.

THE INNER CIRCLE

TOKUGAWA IEYASU
HATTORI HANZOU (THE YOUNGER)
HATTORI HANZOU (THE ELDER)
OFUKU
TAKECHIYO
KUNICHIYO

RIVALS

GENERAL ODA NOBUNAGA
TOYOTOMI HIDEYORI

KOUGA NINJA

KOUGA DANJOU
KOUGA GENNOSUKE
JIMUSHI JUUBEI
KAZAMACHI SHOUGEN
KASUMI GYOUBU
UDONO JOUSUKE
KISARAGI SAEMON
MUROGA HYOUMA
KAGEROU
OKOI

IGA NINJA

OGEN
OBORO
YASHAMARU
AZUKI ROUSAI
YAKUSHIJI TENZEN

AMAYO JINGOROU
CHIKUMA KOSHIROU
MINO NENKI
HOTARUBI
AKEGINU

THE
KOUGA
NINJA
SCROLLS

THE GREAT SECRET

1

THE CASTLE KEEP STOOD IN THE BACKGROUND, SEVEN stories high. From a distance, it looked like a heap of dancer's fans piled atop one another.

Two men faced off.

In the blaze of the sun, the men's bodies turned transparent. Clouds dropped their shadows upon them, shifting the men into hazy shadows as well. They nearly faded into nothingness. An audience watched but they had to squint their eyes more and more to see the men, frequently losing sight of them.

But no one looked away. A distance of no more than fifteen feet separated the men, and within that space a charged air of menace billowed back and forth in waves. Yet neither man held an unsheathed sword—rather, both of them stood empty-handed. If the audience had not just witnessed the shocking display of ninja skills, the watchers would probably not have recognized the deadly energy surging between the two men now.

One of the men, Kazamachi Shougen, about forty

years old, was hideous, with a bumpy forehead and hollow cheeks that contrasted with the shining red dots that were his eyes. He had a round, swollen hump like a hunchback. His long narrow gray limbs had been bloated abnormally at their limits. Every one of his fingers and toes—which poked out from straw sandals—was as large as a lizard.

Moments ago, he had been attacked by five samurai. As they approached him, his arrogant stance said: *You wish to cut me down as if I were a mere novice.* Unimpressed, his attackers advanced in the intimidating *Yagyu* sword-fighting stance. Holding their swords out from their bodies, they looked like scarecrows.

"Aaah!" Two of the five warriors suddenly screamed and staggered back, clutching at their eyes. Without a word, Kazamachi Shougen had attacked them. They didn't understand what had happened, or even how it had occurred, but the remaining three men panicked, and their terror sent them into a furious frenzy. Their swords were already drawn, and they had just been attacked, so in a mixture of shock and reflex action the remaining three waved their swords in the air and charged.

Shougen darted to the side, toward the stone wall of the castle keep. Escaping from the onrushing, poorly manufactured swords, he scrambled up the wall. Amazingly, he did so without ever turning his back to his enemies. Spiderlike, with his back to the wall, he clambered up the huge stone wall using his hands and feet. Or, one should say, his *hand* and feet—his right hand continued gripping his sword. Climbing just beyond the men's reach, he looked down at the three pursuing samurai and smirked.

It only seemed to be a smirk. Something flew from his mouth, striking the three remaining soldiers, who all immediately slammed their eyes shut and stumbled in dizziness. The other two soldiers were still writhing and covering their eyes. His back pressing the wall, Kazamachi Shougen noiselessly crept down. The battle was already over.

The object that exploded from Shougen's mouth was no ordinary weapon. It was a glob of mucus the size of a coin from the *Keicho* reign. From anyone else, it would have been nothing more than phlegm, but Shougen could make his mucus extremely thick and sticky. The five soldiers would be unable to get it out of their eyes for days, not before they had torn out all their own eyelashes in the effort.

Meanwhile, Yashamaru—a youth from the province of Iga—had also been pitted against five samurai.

Yashamaru's handsome appearance far outshone other young men. Dressed in coarse clothing as if he had come from the mountains, he had cheeks the color of cherry blossoms and his black eyes shone. He looked like the ideal image of a handsome young man.

Stepping toward the five warriors, he chose not to

touch the mountain sword that hung from his waist tied to a rattan belt. Instead, he drew out a black ropelike object. This "rope" had immense power: It was incredibly thin, yet had the strength of steel wire. Even a direct chop from a sword could not cut it. During the day, it shone with dazzling brilliance. But once the sun went down, it became completely invisible.

Suddenly, the mysterious rope twisted around a sword and flung it into the air. A sharp, earsplitting groan erupted as the rope came whistling across horizontally. Two soldiers collapsed, gripping their thighs and backs. Yasha-maru used both hands to hurl the ends of the rope in different directions at the same time. He didn't bother to attack the soldiers closest to him; instead, he brought down two soldiers who were ten feet away. He lassoed them around the necks like bellowing beasts.

The rope had been forged through a special technique: Black strands of women's hair had been tied together and sealed with animal oil. A mere touch of the rope upon human flesh had the same effect as a blow from an iron whip. As the rope coiled around the thighs and bodies of the defeated soldiers, their skin burst open as if sharp swords were slicing them. Several dozen feet long, the rope moved like a living creature—spinning, twisting, striking, encircling, and amputating the limbs of its enemies. And yet, watching it revealed nothing of its next movement—it was inscrutable. Unlike swords and spears, the rope could move autonomously, without regard to

Yashamaru's position. Movements of rope and master were unrelated. Enemies had no way to defend themselves, and certainly no chance to attack.

And now, the two mysterious warriors—both of them victors over five attacking samurai—challenged each other, silently, almost magically.

The early summer clouds that hung over the castle keep slowly thinned and dissipated into nothingness. It was as if they were melting in the blue sky. And although it took no more than a few minutes, it seemed to last an eternity. That was the way time flowed . . .

Kazamachi Shougen's mouth twisted into a smirk. Simultaneously, a groan erupted from Yashamaru's fist, and his rope burst forth, striking at Shougen like an unleashed whirlwind. Shougen dropped to the ground. For a second, all those watching seemed to be witnessing the same mass hallucination—it seemed like a gigantic gray spider was scrambling across the ground. It took another second before the observers realized that this was Kazamachi Shougen, and that, instead of being ensnared by the rope, he had escaped. He landed on all fours and, smirking, spat a light blue sticky clump at Yashamaru.

The round, filmy membrane had nearly struck Yashamaru's face when it vanished in midair—lassoed by Yashamaru's rope. Realizing this, Shougen—for the first time—seemed frightened.

Tsu-tsu-tsu. Shougen scampered backward on all fours. With his head hanging upside down, he scurried up the stone tower of the castle keep in one burst. Everyone watching gasped and the sound echoed off the castle walls.

Shougen's body seemed to fly up the white wall, outracing the tip of Yashamaru's pursuing rope. Shougen glided to the top, then disappeared into the shadows behind an ornamental board at the edge of the curved roof. Using it as his shield, he spat a sticky clump downward. But Yashamaru was no longer there. Yashamaru had lassoed his second length of rope around the edge of the roof and pulled himself up. Yashamaru now floated in midair. Shougen scampered away across the bronze roof tiles. But as soon as he outraced one length of rope, Yashamaru threw another length of rope at him. The battle pitted a trembling bagworm shooting out deadly threads against a scampering spider spitting magical phlegm. The airborne death match that raged against the backdrop of dazzling early summer clouds clearly was not a duel between mere human beings. This was a fight between monstrous creatures—far removed from the world of humans.

In the midst of the crowd that watched this nightmarish battle was the elderly lord of the castle. He waved his hand and looked to the side. "Enough. Have them cease, Hanzou. Let's continue this battle tomorrow."

The duel had already ranged over three floors of the castle. The way things were headed, at least one ninja, and maybe both, would end up dead. The old lord of the castle snapped, "This must not become some kind of spectacle for townspeople to gawk at. Sunpu Castle is full of spies from Osaka." The speaker was Tokugawa Ieyasu, lord of the castle—and the man who had nearly conquered and unified Japan.

2

IT WAS THE END OF APRIL IN 1614—THE NINETEENTH year of the *Keicho* period. Within Sunpu Castle, the great lord of the castle Tokugawa Ieyasu watched the strange battle.

He was not alone. There was the shogun, Hidetada, and his royal consort, Eyo, as well as their two children, Takechiyo and Kunichiyo. In addition, important ministers like Honda, Doi, Sakai, and Ii were all sitting close together. Konchiin Senden, the monk Tenkai, and the master swordfighter Yagyu Munenori were also present. The entire family and brain trust of the Tokugawa dynasty were gathered in this room. Osaka was the last part of Japan holding out against the rule of the Tokugawa family. A winter garrison had been established outside of Osaka in October, and it was necessary for Ieyasu to warn against "Osaka spies."

Even so, "foreign elements" had mixed in with the others. Their foreignness was not limited to the fact that they did not match the beautiful surroundings. They seemed foreign from the world of human beings—like icy meteorites that had dropped from the sky.

They were an elderly man and woman sitting before Ieyasu at a distance of about twenty feet. Both had snow-white hair. The old man had shiny dark skin, like leather, while the old woman's skin was icy blue. In spite of their appearances, both throbbed with mysterious energy and looked as powerful as any military general.

Like a gust of wind, the two men who had been fighting rushed inside, hands extended in respect. Kazamachi Shougen stood before the old man, while Yashamaru stood in front of the old woman.

The old man and woman silently nodded, and then stared strangely at each other's representatives, the old man looking at Yashamaru, and the old woman looking at Kazamachi Shougen.

"You must be exhausted." Speaking equally to both sides, Ieyasu looked in their direction and then added, "What do you think, Yagyu Munenori?"

"I'm afraid that I would offend you if I spoke." Yagyu Munenori hung his head. Yagyu Munenori had recently been sent to Tajima Province to act as captain of its forces, but previously he had taught sword-fighting for the Tokugawa family.

"I thought I was already familiar with the skills of the ninja," he continued. "I had no idea that they could reach this level. Rather than blame my students for being defeated, please blame their instructor." A bead of sweat trickled down his forehead. "Even though the ninja are from my native province of Iga and from the neighboring province of Kouga, they had been a secret from me. I have failed, and I am deeply ashamed."

Instead of criticizing Yagyu Munenori, Ieyasu nodded his head. "Hanzou presented me with a remarkable display."

Hattori Hanzou, who had remained standing in order to serve Ieyasu, clasped his hands and bowed. A great self-satisfied smile spread across his face.

"Hanzou," called Ieyasu. "Bring two cups of sake for the leaders of the ninja clans, Danjou from Kouga and Ogen of Iga."

As Hanzou glided toward the old man and woman, Ieyasu turned his head to look at those seated around him.

On one side sat Takechiyo, his eldest grandson. Next to him was Ofuku, the woman who had breast-fed and raised him as a second mother. There was also the captain of the Aoyama garrison, and Tsujii, Sakai, Honda, and others—

On the other side sat the shogun Hidetada and his consort, Eyo. Next to them was the second-eldest grandson, Kunichiyo. There was also the captain of the Asakura garrison, and Ii, Konchiin, and others—

With deeply downcast eyes, Ieyasu pondered those

around him. Those present stiffened in response. The Tokugawa succession had to be decided. As the great Tokugawa Ieyasu began to explain his surprise decision, it was clear he had chosen to take an enormous risk.

Would the third shogun be Takechiyo or Kunichiyo?

IEYASU WAS seventy-three years old.

He was ready to unleash his final assault upon the hold-out city of Osaka.

Toyotomi Hideyori ruled Osaka. At Ieyasu's suggestion, Toyotomi Hideyori had begun construction of a great Buddhist hall in Kyoto to honor his deceased father, the imperial regent Toyotomi Hideyoshi. In April, they began casting the massive bell. All of Osaka strained under the massive expenditures involved in building the Buddhist hall. That fell in line with Ieyasu's farsighted plan. As soon as the giant bell was cast, Ieyasu would use the inscription upon it as his pretext for launching another war. He had already begun plotting with advisors a justification for attack. Because the eight-word inscription "The nation at peace; the lords all content" included both the names of Ieyasu and Hideyori within the *kanji,* Ieyasu decided to claim that Hideyori had inserted his name inside this phrase as an insult. A ridiculous assertion, of course, but Ieyasu needed an excuse to attack Osaka. This plot revealed Ieyasu's true nature and how he had earned the nickname "the old fox." Now, at seventy-three, his concerns revolved around his age. Ieyasu had begun to clearly sense his own body weakening and collapsing.

He would certainly win the war. Yet, despite his plots, it would take a year or two to capture the enemy stronghold—Osaka Castle. Would he live long enough to see Osaka Castle in flames? That was uncertain.

His life largely behind him, Ieyasu saw the immense black shadow of Osaka Castle towering above him. And in that same direction, he saw another shadow—a menacing shadow cast by an enormous, nightmarish cloud . . .

What would become of the Tokugawa lineage? Who should he make next in line after Hidetada to become shogun? The elder brother Takechiyo or the younger brother Kunichiyo?

If Ieyasu selected his older grandson, it would confirm the rule that inheritance passes through the eldest boy. Yet, looking at his eleven- and nine-year-old grandchildren, he felt conflicted. He loved the child, but he knew that the eldest boy, Takechiyo, stuttered and was unable to speak clearly in public. Sometimes Takechiyo seemed dazed and vacant. On the other hand, he could choose the lovable and talented younger boy, Kunichiyo. The idiot elder brother or the wise younger brother?

As he agonized over the decision between his grandchildren, he naturally remembered the fate of his own sons. Thirty-five years earlier, Ieyasu lost his eldest son, Nobuyasu. At that time, Ieyasu had been allied with the more powerful general Oda Nobunaga. Oda Nobunaga told Ieyasu that his son was secretly communicating with enemies. For the sake of the Tokugawa family, Ieyasu choked back his own tears and ordered that his own son be put to death. The leader of the Iga region, Hattori Hanzou, had acted as Ieyasu's messenger of death. Hattori Hanzou forced Ieyasu's son to commit suicide.

Later on, Ieyasu would often remember with disgust and regret the way he had caused his son Nobuyasu to die. After Ieyasu won a crucial victory at the Battle of Sekigahara, he told himself: "I have struggled for so long. If my eldest son were still alive, things wouldn't have been so difficult." He now thought of his dead eldest son, who had been a child genius, and sighed. If his son were still alive, he would not have had such troubles.

His second son was Yuki Hideyasu, his third son Hidetada. Ieyasu had chosen to make the third son—so reliable and trustworthy—his chosen successor, an act that made his second son insanely jealous for the rest of his life.

Ieyasu ached from personal knowledge of the difficulties of royal succession. It wasn't just a problem for the Tokugawa family. In the Oda family as well, the powerful general Oda Nobunaga had spent the first half of his life defeating his younger brother's revolt.

Just thinking about the situation frustrated Ieyasu. His son—the shogun Hidetada—and his son's consort preferred their second son, Kunichiyo, rather than their elder son, Takechiyo. For a long time, Ieyasu had ignored the issue of which of his grandsons would be the future shogun. But now he saw that the entire Tokugawa family was splitting into factions, one side supporting the elder son and the other side supporting the younger son. Ieyasu knew he needed to end the jealousy and conflict.

Ieyasu knew that his son Hidetada was struggling just to maintain peace between his consort, Eyo, and Ofuku, who had breast-fed and raised Takechiyo. Eyo and Ofuku had a natural hatred for each other. Eyo's mother was the younger sister of General Oda Nobunaga. Ofuku's father had been an important official to the man who killed Nobunaga. Naturally, the two women despised each other. Ofuku would later become famous as the Lady Kasuga. In any case, everyone—from concubines to servants to leading officials—had split into camps and quarreled about the succession. Three leading generals were on Takechiyo's side. Two other generals supported Kunichiyo. Even the most clever and coolheaded of his military leaders had picked sides, dividing between the two factions.

Over the winter, someone slipped poison into Ofuku's tea. Not long after, Kunichiyo barely survived an assassination attempt in the middle of the night.

Things must not go on like this!

If the Tokugawa family succession turned into a factional war, then it really would not matter whether or not Osaka was destroyed. If the succession to the throne was a violent mess, then nothing else mattered—because the collapse and destruction of the Tokugawa family would be assured, staring at him like his reflection in the mirror.

But which grandson should he pick? Even the great general Ieyasu became confounded and under stress. Should he strictly follow the policy of having the eldest son inherit the throne? But if his oldest grandson really was an idiot, this decision would destroy his family dynasty. Ieyasu had lived through the age of warring states, and he had watched great families collapse due to incompetent heirs. Should he ignore the traditional order of succession and choose the more reliable grandson?

His inner dilemma grew more painful due to the infighting surrounding him. The difficulty of this issue— follow a set order or pick the most competent successor— can be seen in the fact that Ieyasu would later create laws controlling the family succession—and yet this did not prevent future crises.

Ieyasu alone knew what others did not—namely that the first three generations of shogun would decide the fate of the Tokugawa dynasty for the next thousand years.

And so it was all the more important that the current internal struggle be resolved in a way acceptable to all. As he entered old age, the final years of his life had become entangled with interests, loyalties, resentments, and emotions, so much so that he doubted if he could break through it with a single decisive blow. And yet he had to act soon. With each passing day, his life was running out of time, and the end of the war loomed ahead. He had to resolve the situation immediately. And he had to do it in such a way that his enemies in Osaka did not discover that there was an internal struggle tearing apart his family.

IT WAS a snowy evening in early spring. Ieyasu had invited the Buddhist monk Tenkai to Sunpu Castle. They sat across from each other in his secret chambers. Ieyasu had invited him on the pretext of studying Buddhism, but he actually wanted to discuss a great secret. Tenkai meditated for a while, and then suggested a possible resolution.

"No matter what we do, using logic or compassion will not alleviate the problem, and any bilateral solution would be rejected by one side. So you might as well decide the issue through a duel, with each side sending forth a warrior on its behalf."

Ieyasu lifted his eyes and looked at Tenkai; the monk was basically a member of the Takechiyo faction. Of course, the monk cared even more deeply about the future of the Tokugawa dynasty.

Let the destinies of both sides be decided by their champions on the battlefield! It was a manly solution, fitting for a military family. But it was also too simple.

"One thing . . ." Ieyasu said. "Victory in battle often comes down to the luck of the moment. Furthermore, there are vindictive women tied up in this situation. I doubt that a duel between two warriors would satisfy either side."

"In that case, have three warriors on each side," the monk suggested.

"Just the process of selecting those three warriors would provoke internal battles within each faction."

"Then five warriors each."

Ieyasu remained silent.

"Ten warriors on each side. That allows each side to select its most elite warriors. Nobody will be able to say that luck decided the result. Neither side can be bitter afterward."

At first Ieyasu nodded, but then he shook his head in rejection. "On the one hand, ten fighters on each side would certainly be enough to force each faction to accept the result. But by bringing in ten fighters on each side, we will spread the fighting to all the leading families. I'd be foolish and cruel to force my leading generals to fight each other. And worse, the fighting would spread, turn into blood feuds, and eventually news of the fighting would become public knowledge. My enemies in Osaka would learn about our internal struggles. No. This must remain a secret within the Tokugawa family."

Tenkai closed his eyes halfway and listened to the sound of snow falling. The isolated and quiet depths of the castle keep resembled a hermit's mountain hut. Finally, Tenkai's eyes burst wide open.

"Ninja," he murmured.

"Ninja?"

"Why not use ninja? . . . Just now, the sound of the snow happened to remind me of a snowy night long ago. At the Anyou Temple in the town of Kouji, I spoke with the previous Hattori Hanzou, father to the current Hattori Hanzou. Going as far back as the Genpei War, the Kouga and Iga ninja clans have never been at peace. For a thousand years, the ninja from both sides have been sworn enemies. The Hattori family has acted as mediators, suppressing the hatred between the two sides. But only their agreement with the Hattori family prevents the ninja clans from killing each other. If the Hattori family loosened the reins, the clans would immediately return to their bloody war. Hanzou told me that these two ninja families are extremely difficult to control. They correspond perfectly to the Takechiyo and Kunichiyo factions. So why not tell Hattori Hanzou to let the ninja return to fighting each other?"

An eerie laugh escaped from Tenkai's lips.

"That way," Tenkai said, "your enemies at Osaka would never hear about it, and the two ninja families would kill each other off in a sea of blood. The Tokugawa family samurai would escape unharmed."

For what seemed an eternity, Ieyasu remained sunk in thought. When he finally spoke, he seemed to be speaking to himself.

"Hattori? His father is the man who caused my son

Nobuyasu's death, isn't he? Now I need to bury one of my grandchildren—I suppose it's only fitting to call on that fellow from Iga again . . ."

He laughed bitterly, sending ripples through his wrinkled skin. By putting the plan into practice, he would be placing the fate of the Tokugawa family in the hands of the ninja families. When he issued this order, it would be tinged with a gloomy irony.

3

THE DESTINY OF THE TOKUGAWA FAMILY HAD BECOME strangely intertwined with the ninjas of Kouga and Iga.

But why had the regions of Kouga and Iga given birth to such unrivaled ninja skills? The answer is found in its geography—its combination of mountains and valleys. An endless number of powerful clan leaders appeared, each wielding a small sphere of influence. Because this region is close to the capital, the remnants of the great defeated forces of the Heike leaders Kiso and Yoshitsune could infiltrate this region, and traces of their forces lingered there. Also, during the Northern and Southern Courts period, the impact of the war between the two courts influenced Kouga and Iga.

Throughout history, there are many examples of the Kouga and Iga playing major roles in warfare. During the Jinshin Rebellion, records tell that the instigator of the rebellion used Iga ninja. Much later, legends claimed that a close follower of the great general Yoshitsune had been an Iga ninja. When powerful clans rebelled against the shogun Ashikaga, the Kouga warriors joined the cause and tormented the shogun. "The Kouga bowl of soldiers" became something marveled at throughout the world.

The Iga and Kouga ninja skills grew out of a deep, rich history. Yet one tradition has remained constant—both ninja clans have invariably opposed those ruling Japan. One can sense both their spirit of defiance and their mysterious untamed nature.

In the Warring States period, the "skills of the ninja" were put to use with growing frequency. Spying, scouting, assassination, arson, guerrilla harassment—these became critical talents. Rival chiefs competed to wield the ninja, who were called "Night Bandits," "Crashing Waves," or "Those Who Slip Through." Kouga and Iga displayed their ninja skills in battle and proved to be very valuable. Great families competed to hire Kouga and Iga warriors, until eventually the fifty-three families of Kouga and the two hundred sixty families of Iga became two divisions of ninja skills.

But a difficult age came for those families. As General Oda Nobunaga united most of Japan under his rule, he realized that he needed to master this rebellious region. In part, he worried that Iga and Kouga were too close to the capital. More importantly, Oda Nobunaga—despite having made great use of ninja—had an inherent distaste for the strange powers of the ninja families. Naturally the families opposed him. This uprising became known as the "Iga Rebellion."

During their "national crisis," the Iga and Kouga clan leaders remained united, stubbornly defending every inch of territory. By the end of their resistance, massively outnumbered, they were slaughtered by Nobunaga's troops. Their guerrilla resistance had been incredibly successful, however, repeatedly throwing battalions of Nobunaga's forces into confusion. Their sharpshooters nearly took Nobunaga's own life. During Nobunaga's ruthless mop-up operations, he burned the castles to the ground and demolished the temples and shrines. Nobunaga ordered the slaughter of everyone—clergy and commoners, men and women. The survivors became refugees, scattering and fleeing in all directions, most of them traveling to the Tokugawa lands for protection. They knew that Hattori Hanzou, a member of an Iga clan, had long served the Tokugawa family as a high-ranking minister.

Both Kouga and Iga looked to Tokugawa Ieyasu for protection. Even if he did not care to admit it publicly, these ninja families became a secret pillar of support for the shogun. Tokugawa Ieyasu began to rely on the Kouga and Iga ninjas, and Hattori Hanzou acted as their ambassador.

The Hattori family descended from Heike warriors who had fled to Iga after their defeat centuries earlier. Perhaps the family history extended even further. Some claimed that the Hattori ancestors had once led a branch of the Iga. In any case, Hattori had long ago proven his value to Ieyasu. Hattori had acted as his trusted messenger of death, forcing his son Nobuyasu to commit suicide. After the Iga Rebellion, Ieyasu increasingly relied on Kouga and Iga fighters who had come under his protection. As the leader of the ninja clans, Hattori Hanzou became increasingly prominent.

After the Iga Rebellion, Ieyasu had fought to protect the Kouga and Iga from the clutches of General Nobunaga. As repayment, they saved Ieyasu when his life was in danger by helping him to cross through the backwoods of Iga. General Oda Nobunaga, who had been both an ally and rival to Ieyasu, repeatedly invited Ieyasu to visit him in the Kyoto region. By traveling there, Ieyasu became separated from his home province by three rivers, making communication difficult. Furthermore, because this was a friendly visit, he had few soldiers accompanying him. General Nobunaga betrayed him and Ieyasu became trapped in the region with no escape route. Ieyasu considered suicide. But the Iga and Kouga ninja clans rushed like a hurricane to Hattori Hanzou's call for help. They acted as bodyguards, guiding Ieyasu along a secret route through the mountains to Kouga, and from there to Iga and Ise.

Because of his brilliant maneuvers, Hattori Hanzou received official titles, a palace in the Kouji region of Edo, and became the leader of two hundred individuals from Iga. The present day Hanzou Gate marks the location where Hattori had his palace. Villages in Kanda, Yotsuya, and Azabu all carry the names "Kouga" or "Iga," due to the clans that came to live there. Remarkably, only Ieyasu had been able to win the allegiance of all the Kouga and Iga families.

Despite his importance, Ieyasu did not have an unclouded opinion of Hanzou. As he entered old age, Ieyasu's thoughts turned increasingly dark. Hattori Hanzou reminded Ieyasu of his dead son. Ieyasu's own orders had sealed his son's fate, and so he had nobody upon which to seek revenge. Yet the thought of his son's death became increasingly unbearable. Ieyasu did not dwell upon mistakes made, but his dead son became a source of unending darkness. Hanzou sensed this and took precautions. In Kouji, he constructed a temple dedicated as a memorial to Ieyasu's son. Monks devoted their lives to endlessly reading sutras and praying for his soul in the afterlife.

In the first year of the Keicho period, Hattori Hanzou passed away, and his son took his place. The son also received the name Hattori Hanzou. And now, Ieyasu once again had a tragic yet critical mission, which he would entrust to the second generation of the Hanzou family.

Although both were under the control of Hattori Hanzou, the Kouga and Iga ninja clans despised each other and refused to appear in public together. The two ninja clans buried themselves deep in the mountains.

Because of their debt to the Hattori family, the two clans faithfully followed a vow not to go to war against each other. The clans held back from avenging their ancient blood feuds.

In response to a secret order from Hattori Hanzou, the leaders of the two clans had appeared at Sunpu Castle. The old man was Kouga Danjou, the old woman was Ogen from Iga.

The two leaders had each brought along one of their warriors, who had displayed otherworldly skills. The idea of selecting the third shogun through a battle of the ninja clans stunned the master swordfighter Yagyu Munenori. But not just Munenori. The selection of the third shogun was a huge event that would impact everyone. Many felt resentful and distrustful at the idea of their fate being decided by a mysterious battle between ninja clans. Even Ieyasu felt worried. However, despite thinking about it at great length, he could not come up with any alternative solution.

The sword-fighting master Yagyu Munenori had to accept the strange path of fate, and that the future would be decided through a bloody battle of ninja. Everyone else also agreed to this solution.

Everyone knew that the ninja had amazing skills—disguises, speed, leaping—far surpassing ordinary people. They accomplished this through intense physical and mental training. But there was a limit to what training could accomplish, just as there is a limit to sword-fighting skills. And yet, the godlike skills displayed during the ninja battle had showed that, although they were still human—

or, at least, they were still in the realm of living creatures, doing things that were physically possible—the ninja had completely broken through the limits of human knowledge.

"Danjou," Ieyasu spoke to the old man. "I was impressed by the one called Kazamachi Shougen. But do your other fighters also have his skills?"

The old man glanced at the phlegm-shooting Shougen as if disgusted. The old man spat out his words: "I had to comply with Hattori's orders to bring forth a ninja, but I brought one of the lowest-ranking ones so that our enemies could watch without learning our secrets."

"Shougen is one of your lowest-ranking ninja?" Ieyasu asked, looking at Danjou in shock. Ieyasu then turned toward the old woman. "Ogen, what about you?"

A weird smile appeared on Ogen's face, and she lowered her white head in silence.

"Ten fighters—no, discounting these two, nine more fighters are needed," Ieyasu said.

"Just nine? He he . . ." she laughed.

Why would Ieyasu—the conqueror of all Japan—feel shivers trickle along his spine? He glared at the two. "Are you willing to fight each other to decide the succession to the Tokugawa dynasty?" Ieyasu said curtly.

The old man and old woman responded as one. "It's unnecessary to even speak of fighting for the benefit of the Tokugawa family. As soon as we hear that Hattori

Hanzou has allowed us to fight again, the battle will begin."

"Permission granted! Permission granted!" Unexpectedly, Hattori Hanzou shouted his response and stepped forward. "The clans are hereby released from their vows. Kouga and Iga are hereby granted the power to decide through battle the fate of the shogun succession. Never before has there been such a war between the ninja. Take joy in devoting your lives to this service."

Hattori Hanzou could not forget his father's lifelong regret at carrying out Ieyasu's secret order to kill his son. Hattori Hanzou decided to use this opportunity to dispel the cloud hanging over the Hattori family. However, he was young and did not know that this order might result in even more misery. He also did not know the terrifying truth as to why his father had quarantined the Kouga and Iga ninja clans.

"Well, then, Danjou and Ogen, make a list of your nine warriors," Ieyasu said, motioning toward a servant woman.

The servant woman presented both Kouga Danjou and Ogen with brush, inkstone, and scroll.

Upon opening the scrolls, they discovered them to be blank. The brushes of the old man and woman flickered across the parchment in rapid strokes, and then they exchanged the lists. Finally, they returned the lists to Ieyasu. The scrolls declared:

KOUGA CLAN 10 COMBATANTS

Kouga Danjou	*Udono Jousuke*
Kouga Gennosuke	*Kisaragi Saemon*
Jimushi Juubei	*Muroga Hyouma*
Kazamachi Shougen	*Kagerou*
Kasumi Gyoubu	*Okoi*

IGA CLAN 10 COMBATANTS

Ogen	*Amayo Jingorou*
Oboro	*Chikuma Koshirou*
Yashamaru	*Mino Nenki*
Azuki Rousai	*Hotarubi*
Yakushiji Tenzen	*Akeginu*

Upon the agreement of Hattori Hanzou, the taboo against warfare between the clans has been lifted. The ten warriors of Kouga and the ten warriors of Iga must now fight each other to the death. On the final day of May, the survivors shall bring this scroll back to Sunpu Castle. Whichever side has more survivors shall be the winner, and that clan shall have a thousand years of glory.

Danjou and Ogen each stamped their seals, in blood, beneath the names. After rolling up the scrolls, Ieyasu clutched them both in one hand, and hurled them into the sky. The two scrolls parted in midair, falling to the ground on the left and right.

The scroll that fell near the younger son Kunichiyo had been sealed with the old man Kouga Danjou's blood. The scroll landing near the elder son Takechiyo had been sealed with the old woman Ogen's blood.

Kunichiyo would be represented by Kouga and Takechiyo represented by Iga. The destiny of the third shogun had been put entirely in the hands of these two clans, wielders of astounding ninja powers.

4

KOUGA DANJOU AND OGEN LINGERED BEHIND UNTIL the evening sun had drenched the sky with bright red paint.

They stood outside of Sunpu Castle, close to the Abe River. At that moment, Kazamachi Shougen and Yashamaru were racing toward the west, holding their respective secret scrolls.

"Ogen. Amazing things were said." Danjou sounded as if he were speaking to himself. "For four hundred years, our families—with their unique branches of ninja skills—have fought each other. And now, just when our grandchildren had fallen in love and we finally reached peace with each other—"

"Oboro and Gennosuke might be meeting in the valley of Shigaraki even as we speak."

"Too bad their stars are crossed."

The pair looked away from each other. Oboro was the

granddaughter of the old woman, and Gennosuke was the grandson of the old man.

Suddenly, Danjou spoke in a deep voice.

"We were that way too once. When I was young, I was in love with you, Ogen."

"Do not speak of that." Ogen tossed her white hair. "Our families have hated each other for over four hundred years. The fate that befell us will now befall Oboro and Gennosuke. As long as they weren't yet married, we always knew that something like this could happen. I was afraid of fate, and fate proved me right. Hattori Hanzou ended the ban on warfare between our ninja clans."

"Old woman, shall we fight?"

"We will fight."

The two exchanged looks.

"Old woman, you have no idea of the power of the ten warriors of Kouga Manjidani."

"There are things I know, and things I don't know. He he . . . I don't know the ninja skills used in Kouga. But Danjou, you're the one who doesn't know enough about the ten warriors from Iga Tsubagakure. During the past four hundred years, isolated in the darkness, we have bred the greatest fighters and developed talents that resemble magic. The ten warriors of the Iga clan—"

"Don't you mean the nine warriors?" Danjou asked. He blew something, and it streaked toward her.

Ogen went silent, her eyes glaring at Danjou. As the blazing sunset turned dusky, her white face turned as black as ink, her eyes popping out of her head. Something shone on the sides of her neck, which was covered in wrinkles and looked like the neck of a bird.

Kouga Danjou silently moved four or five steps away. Facing Ogen, he removed a scroll from his kimono. "Ogen, this is the scroll that your ninja Yashamaru should be taking to Iga. Now I have it. Yashamaru is a fool. He hasn't yet noticed the missing scroll. He has raced off to the west without it. Shougen will inform my clan of the war, and only the Kouga clan will know who they are fighting. So the nine warriors you have selected are of no importance—"

He shook the scroll, and it unfurled, revealing the lists of ninja names. At the top, the name Ogen of Iga had been crossed out with a red line.

Ogen made no sound, standing in place like a rock. Tears rolled from Ogen's large eyes, crossing her cheeks. Danjou looked on with a grand smile.

"May heaven look after you!" Something shot out of his mouth. It glinted in the light and stabbed into Ogen, piercing through her neck. A needle. Unlike a needle shot from a dart gun, however, this needle measured a foot in length. Earlier, he had shot a needle through her neck horizontally. Now the two needles had formed a cross through her neck.

Ogen lifted her arms and simultaneously pulled the two needles from her neck. From her mouth burst forth the scream of a strange bird. Danjou did not understand the meaning of that sound. A moment later, Ogen collapsed face-first into the riverbed, from which vapor rose. The needles were coated with deadly venom that caused immediate death upon entering the bloodstream.

"Poor Ogen. This is how ninja warfare goes. Please wait in the underworld; your nine Iga warriors will be greeting you there soon," Danjou murmured as he wrapped up the scroll. Suddenly he placed the scroll on the riverbank. "You were my enemy and I had to kill you; you are also the woman I once loved. I can at least help you to have a water burial." Mumbling these words, he pulled the old woman's corpse by her feet deeper into the river.

Suddenly, a strange beating of wings startled him. Danjou looked back and saw a hawk snatching the scroll from the riverbank and soaring into the air. He realized that Ogen had summoned this hawk with her dying cry. The hawk swooped, its cold, hard talons striking Danjou. He tumbled into the water.

Danjou did not get up. Facing the sky, his body floated. Stabbed through his chest were the needles that Ogen had been clutching in her bluish hands. When the hawk struck him, the needles plunged through his chest. The old woman floated alongside him, facing downward, then climbed atop him. The two bodies floated together downstream.

The hawk turned low circles in the dying light. The scroll that it had snatched had become completely unfurled and blew in the wind, gently brushing against the heads of the floating couple. Below the loosely circling hawk, the pair floated in silence. Ogen's bluish hand moved, tracing over the blood trail on Danjou's chest. Her final movement was to draw a dark red line through the name "Kouga Danjou."

The sun went down.

As the new moon rose, the beautiful bloodred river darkened and turned black. Yashamaru from Iga had rushed back and discovered the dead bodies of Ogen and Danjou, their white hair washed by the water's waves and becoming entangled as they drifted toward the Suruga River and the open sea. The souls of these two old ninja and former lovers were surely floating through the sky toward the sickle-shaped moon, their spirits entangled in an embrace matching the embrace of their physical bodies. No—it was far more likely that the ninja war that never ceased in our world continued, eternally, in the afterlife.

The war between Kouga and Iga had just begun, and the two leaders of the clans had already killed each other and sent each other off to be buried in the waves.

Meanwhile, phlegm-spitting Kazamachi Shougen rushed without pause toward Kouga Manjidani, carrying the deadly secret scroll. But even swifter than he, another scroll was being carried, silently, in the talons of a hawk. It glided through the pitch-black sky toward Iga.

KOUGA ROMEO AND
IGA JULIET

1

THE BORDER BETWEEN KOUGA AND IGA CONSISTED OF mountains sprouting from mountains. Late spring had arrived here on the Toki Pass, and throughout the endless rows of mountains the cries of bush warblers marked the emergence of daylight.

It was just before dawn. The new moon was like a thread, slowly disappearing behind the western mountain range.

Birds and beasts were still asleep. From the valley of Shigaraki to the Toki Pass, two shadows glided like wind.

"Gennosuke?" A high-pitched voice came from the obese trailing shadow, which resembled a huge ball. "Gennosuke, where are we going?"

"We are going to meet Oboro," answered the tall leading shadow.

The trailing figure continued in silence for a while. "I really can't believe it. Even if you two have promised to marry each other, still, I'd be worried about trying to secretly visit a woman under cover of darkness . . . Although it's not a bad idea. I could try it sometime—" He spoke to himself, grinning. "I saw this girl called Akeginu at the Iga camp—beautiful, and as slender as the new moon. I'm a big blubbery guy myself, so I like them skinny. And maybe she likes opposites too, so she might go for a fat guy like me. He he—Gennosuke, you go to Oboro's place, and I will go see Akeginu. The two of us will both visit girls under cover of darkness, like master and servant. Those fellows at Iga will be impressed."

"Idiot," Kouga Gennosuke snapped. He spoke with a serious tone, "Hey, Jousuke—do you know why Grandfather went to Sunpu Castle?"

"Tokugawa Ieyasu summoned the leaders of the ninja clans. According to Hattori Hanzou's letter, Kouga Danjou was supposed to bring a ninja that he had trained from childhood, so that the shogun could view his techniques."

"What do you think of that?"

"You're asking me what I think? Well, probably, Hattori Hanzou heard the gossip that you are going to marry Oboro from Iga. Hattori probably decided that the ninja clans must no longer hate each other. He must have wanted the families to appear in public so that he could officially tell them to accept each other as allies and to go forth in peace. Did Danjou accept it when you told him?"

"If he did, would you be happy?"

The fat one said nothing.

From far away, the wind cried while rustling through the trees. Something resembling snow blew against their faces. Mountain cherry blossoms. Nothing even resembled a path here. They had waded deep into mountain vegetation. The fat man was named Udono Jousuke. His face bobbed in the faint light of the new moon. His comically droopy nose, cheeks, and lips all hung from his face. Now his face crumpled as he twisted around, looking back.

Two large trees stood before him. No more than a foot and a half separated them. Jousuke's flabby, barrellike body was double that size, and yet he smoothly slipped between the trees to the other side.

"To be honest, it doesn't make me happy," Jousuke screeched out in his characteristically high-pitched voice while emerging from the other side of the trees. "But," he continued, "you already know that we're angry about it. And it's not just me. Jimushi Juubei, Kazamachi Shougen, Kasumi Gyoubu, Kisaragi Saemon, Muroga Hyouma . . . everyone is upset. We want to fight with the forces of Ogen of Iga; we desire to shed our blood in battle as ninja. Iga must always be our enemy. I want you to feel in the depths of your stomach that they are the enemy. Hey, don't glare at me about it. You know that I'm no match for your eyes. Anyway, you want to marry Oboro and your grandfather has agreed to it. We are all his subordinates and cannot oppose him. Hey, forget that—if you're happy, I'm not going to protest what you do. As long as you are happy, I will explain your thinking to the others—"

"Great," Gennosuke said gloomily. "That's why I chose you to sneak over here with me." He paused. "I think that you're all idiots. You've learned such incredible skills from Grandfather, and our clan has such monstrous secret talents. I'm sure Ogen's clan is the same way. But I think it's madness that the clans have caused each other to hide away and bury themselves in these mountains. I've felt that way for a long time, and that's what made me first start thinking about marrying Oboro, the granddaughter of Ogen."

Kouga Gennosuke was a graceful young man with an intelligent look about him. In the dark moonlight, his long eyelashes created shadows that expressed gloomy contemplation.

"However," he said, "no matter what clever ideas I come up with, one look at Oboro causes all my thoughts to vanish. Even if I didn't have any special plans about uniting the families, I could never look at that woman and see her as an enemy."

"You're in love with Oboro."

"Completely. She's Ogen's granddaughter, but she doesn't have any ninja skills. The old woman trained her, but it was all for naught. Apparently, the only reason that old woman is willing to give her granddaughter to a Kouga ninja in marriage is because she feels so disheartened that her granddaughter failed her training."

"But," Jousuke said, "whenever I am in front of Oboro, I feel as if my body is being ripped to shreds. It's weird."

"It's because that girl is like the sun," Gennosuke answered. "When the sun rises, the magic powers of the demons of the mountain forests disappear, like mist."

"That's exactly why she's scary. It would be a disaster if she caused our clan to disappear like mist." Udono Jousuke poked his fat face through the tiny gap between another pair of trees and spoke nervously. "Gennosuke, can't you change your mind about all this?"

"Jousuke . . ."

"Huh?" the fat one answered.

"Something feels wrong. Last night, when I was watching the evening sun, I suddenly felt a frightening shadow fly into my chest."

"Uh?"

"It was Grandfather, returning from Sunpu."

"What did Danjou say about his trip there?"

"I don't know. It's because I don't know that I want to go to Iga. Maybe Ogen has returned already and told them something. I want to visit Oboro and ask her."

"Uh?" Jousuke looked up at the night sky. In the tall cedar forest sky, a strange shadow with flapping wings passed overhead. "What was that?"

"A hawk. A strip of white paper is hanging from its talons—" Suspicious, Kouga Gennosuke followed the hawk's movement. Suddenly, he jerked his eyes back to his companion. "Jousuke, get that thing!"

Udono Jousuke bounded off, leaving behind only the echo of his high-pitched voice.

2

HE WASN'T SO MUCH "RUNNING" AS TUMBLING FOR-
ward.

The Kouga ninja Udono Jousuke constantly pointed his
face skyward even as his body rolled, ball-like, upon the
mountain. He differed from a ball, however, in that his
body rolled uphill—

That was not the only thing different. Even as his eyes
faced the sky, his body moved continuously, and so he repeatedly slammed into trees. Or he seemed to slam into
them—but in the next moment, he was moving onward
on the other side without a single scrape. It was like he
was smoke. But that wouldn't be accurate. If one were
somehow able to photograph his movements with high-
speed film, perhaps one could comprehend the strange
phenomenon taking place: he was colliding with physical
objects, but his entire body was hollow, like a ball. He
would bounce back from collisions, but with his face still
pointing toward the sky, and he automatically rebounded
and rushed forward again. He was a ball, but a living ball;
a ball that moved itself.

The hawk flew deeper into the night sky, the long strip
of paper still clutched in its talons. Just maintaining his
eyes on the hawk was exhausting. The hawk's silhouette
dropped lower, skimming the peaks of the cedar trees
overhead. Udono Jousuke drew out his sword and flung it
while rushing forward.

In the moonlight, the sword glittered like a string of light. The hawk loudly beat its wings and propelled itself higher into the sky, escaping miraculously from the sword. But in the process, its talons let go of the paper. It fluttered in the sky, spinning its way down between the cedar trees.

Udono Jousuke caught one end of the unraveled, falling paper. Before he could pick the other end up off the ground, however, he heard a nasal voice behind him like trapped air.

"Hand that over!"

Turning, Jousuke saw an ancient-looking man with a body folded over like a bent nail. His beard swept the blue patches on the ground where sunlight had streamed through the forest branches.

"Oh . . . you are old Azuki Rousai from Iga, aren't you?" Jousuke said, startled. "Uh, long time no see. Actually, uh, I was coming with Gennosuke. We were coming to Iga and, uh—"

The old man was silent.

"It, uh, it wasn't, uh, like we were here to visit any women or anything. It was about that matter in Sunpu. Has Ogen told you anything about it yet? We were worried . . ."

"Hand that over," Azuki Rousai repeated in his nasal voice, skipping introductions. "The hawk you hurled your sword at belongs to Ogen."

"What—uh, what are you talking about? This thing?"

Udono Jousuke glanced at the paper trailing from his hand. It was some kind of scroll. "I guess Ogen sent the hawk back from Sunpu."

"That's none of your business! You're the one who nearly killed that hawk by throwing your sword at it. Now hand it over!"

Jousuke stared silently at Rousai. Hiding his thoughts, Jousuke began rolling up the scroll.

"Ah, so this is what Gennosuke meant!" Jousuke said at last. "Gennosuke said he sensed that there must be news coming from Sunpu. Well, the hawk flew here from Sunpu, carrying a scroll. I think I'd like to take a look at it."

"You—how dare you!" Rousai snarled. "Who do you think you're talking to? I dare you to keep talking like that in front of me. Look at who is standing in front of you— Rousai from Iga! Now, if you dare, go ahead and say what you want."

A strange light flashed in the old man's eyes.

"He he he . . ." Jousuke laughed. "Well, well, Old Rousai. This scroll is yours, and I *should* give it to you, but from the start, you spoke to me in that nasal voice and threatened me. You should watch how you speak!"

"What?"

"Old Rousai, the clans may have hated each other for four hundred years, but Hattori Hanzou has declared a ban on warfare and soon our families will be united in marriage. So we should treat everything as water under the bridge. Good or bad, everything is in the past now. Don't you think so, Old Rousai?" Jousuke giggled uncontrollably. "To put it another way, Old Rousai—your mastery of the ninja arts . . . Well, I don't know what skills you have, but from your reputation, I imagine your ninja skills must be a match for my own. I don't see you as an outsider. You're like my grandfather or a respected elder from my clan. Anyway, let's find out what makes our clans different and which one is more powerful. Obviously, we can't go to war with each other, because Hattori Hanzou has declared a truce. But we can do a little play-fighting with our ninja skills right here. What do you think?"

"Jousuke—play-fighting with ninja powers is equivalent to betting your life on a game of chance."

"If that's how you feel, Rousai, I'm not giving back this scroll. I'll tell you that now."

Old Rousai was so bent over that his waist seemed to crawl on the ground. But suddenly he straightened his back, and it looked like a pole had grown out of the ground. Udono Jousuke's mouth dropped open and he gasped as he stared at his rival.

Azuki Rousai's legs leaped out and kicked full-force into Jousuke's rotund belly.

It was like a sledgehammer pounding a wedge into his body. The kick would have smashed a hole through any normal person. A huge sound reverberated, like a ball being struck, and Jousuke flew and landed ten feet away.

"That's one way to answer, Old Rousai." Pain caused

sweat droplets to appear on Jousuke's balding forehead, and his face warped into a scowl. But with a meaningful gesture, he lifted the scroll back into the air.

"Grah!" A strange roar of fury burst forth from Rousai's lips, and he rushed at Jousuke—

Rousai had a sword tied to his waist, but the old man ignored it. The forest was so thick with cedar trees that he probably could not have used it anyway. Only fireflies had space to move freely.

Was this play-fighting? Rousai had compared ninja play-fighting to a game of chance with one's life. The game that had begun was certainly deadly. Jousuke spun around cedar trees, constantly using new ones as shields between him and Rousai. Rousai's spindly arms and legs chased after him, pursuing Jousuke as if they had eyeballs at their tips. Although the old man's body frequently became separated by rows of cedar trees from his pursuing limbs, those limbs never stopped chasing Jousuke. His fingers and legs curved and wrapped around trees the same as a whip. His attacking limbs were as remarkable as an octopus. It was as if the old man had no bones. Even more stunning, the mere touch of his limbs caused branches to break from trees, as if they had been hacked with a machete. Azuki Rousai had an infinite number of joints throughout his body. This allowed him to twist his head, waist, and limbs in directions and into positions that no ordinary person could.

"You old monster!" Jousuke shrieked. Rousai's face,

body and legs had cornered him and were attacking from three directions at the same time.

Tendrillike, Rousai's arm wrapped around Jousuke's flabby neck. As Rousai squeezed, Jousuke's face crumpled like a rotten pumpkin.

Rousai laughed, his voice shaking. "You fool, haven't you learned the powers of Azuki Rousai?"

His nooselike arm constricted tighter around Jousuke's neck until he was squeezing Jousuke's vertebrae. With his free hand, Rousai grabbed for the scroll hanging from Jousuke's limp arm.

But at that exact moment, his arm slipped on Jousuke's sweat. Instantly, Jousuke bounded three feet away. His body swelled up and he looked like a bag carried in a gust of wind.

"Ah—!" Rousai gasped, dumbfounded.

Jousuke had called him a monster, but Jousuke was the true monster! Jousuke's body—no matter how many times he was struck or choked—always bounced back, uninjured, just like a punching bag. Jousuke and Rousai had different kinds of flexibility: the bones in Rousai's body moved like whips, while Udono Jousuke was a huge ball of flesh.

"It's your age slowing you down, Old Rousai!" Udono Jousuke laughed, sending great waves rippling through his flab and muscles. Azuki Rousai's long white hair and beard had clumped together from sweat.

"This is fun!" Jousuke continued, laughing wildly in a

high-pitched screech. "I'm going to win no matter what you do. And, as I promised, this scroll shall be the trophy for the winner of our contest, and that means I'm going to keep it!"

Udono Jousuke's round shadow went tumbling into the cedar forest. Azuki Rousai, bones stiffening throughout his body, could do no more than watch Jousuke go. More than physically exhausted, he was spiritually defeated. The old man's body was empty.

3

THE MOON WENT DOWN, AND AN ESPECIALLY THICK darkness hung low over the valleys of Kouga and Iga.

In the mountain range separating the two regions, dawn's first rays broke through the darkness. Throughout the mountain range, birds came alive with song, and grass glittered from the morning dew.

The cheerful voice of spring was flowing from the valleys of Shigaraki in Kouga to the Toki Pass in Iga.

"Gennosuke!"

Five figures stood, silhouetted against the turquoise sky.

"Hey, Oboro!"

Like a young deer, one of the silhouettes below broke a branch from a bush and then ran uphill toward him. Her voice sounded happy, but she threw a look back at her companions as she spoke. "My heart has been pounding like crazy all night! I thought I would melt unless I went to see you in Kouga. But it must be that my heart had sensed that you were coming here! Danjou must have brought news. I can tell from your face, Gennosuke, it must be good news—it must be!"

She was wearing a soft pink veil. The night had not yet dissipated—and yet, despite both the night and her veil, her brilliance shone through and reached him. She was Oboro, the granddaughter of Ogen.

In contrast to Oboro's panting voice, the four shadows standing in the darkness behind her remained silent and half-hidden in the night.

Two of them resembled ladies-in-waiting. One was beautiful, with pallid skin and a pale, oval face. The other one was tiny and adorable, but the thing peeking out from atop her head would shock anybody who saw it: a serpent. No mere ornament, it wrapped once around her neck and had slithered up on top of her head. The snake seemed to taste the scent of her hair, spitting out its long, forked tongue in repeated hisses.

"Hey, where is Old Rousai?" Oboro asked.

"He saw something in the sky and ran after it, that's all." The two men looked over Gennosuke as they answered curtly.

It was hard to see them clearly in the lingering darkness. Perhaps the darkness was playing tricks on Gennosuke's eyes. Even so, one of the men seemed to have a bluish, puffy face like a drowned person, and the other one had a horribly shaggy head that far exceeded the normal samurai hairstyle.

"Gennosuke!" Oboro cried.

"Oboro, what's happened?" Kouga Gennosuke approached, his smile vanishing. "I see Akeginu, Hotarubi, Amayo, and Mino have all gathered together. What's going on?"

Oboro laughed. *What's going on?* It was funny that he asked her the very question she wanted to ask him. Her face soon returned to a serious expression. "No, it's just that last night my heart was pounding and I had a sense something happened to Ogen. I wanted to run to Kouga and see if you had received news from your grandfather, Danjou—"

"That's exactly what I came here to ask you about!" Gennosuke responded. "I sensed something was wrong, and I came here as fast as I could—" Gennosuke gazed intently at Oboro, and he recognized the fear in her eyes, despite the veil covering them. He grinned, flashing shiny white teeth. "It's nothing! If anything happens, just remember that Kouga Gennosuke is with you!"

Oboro's big round black eyes sparkled. "Ah, Gennosuke, you're here. All I need is to see you, and my worries melt like snow." Without a glance toward the four gloomy companions behind her, Oboro clung to Gennosuke, as innocently as a child.

No one would have known that these two were the direct heirs of the two mysterious ninja clans entangled for four hundred years in mutual hatred. They looked like a portrait of youth, so full of life, and completely pure and free from troubles. But even if they had won the support of their grandparents, could they unite Kouga and Iga?

They could almost taste the sunlight enveloping them. The sun rose higher.

A shouted voice rebounded upward from the valley, still in shadows.

"He-e-ey! He-e-e-ey!"

Oboro's four companions nodded. "See? That must be Old Rousai."

"No, that's Udono Jousuke's voice. I brought him with me." Gennosuke turned and cocked his head. "That lazy fool—what's he been doing this whole time? Oh, right—a little bit ago, while we were coming here, we saw a hawk flying overhead holding a scroll. Jousuke chased after it."

"A hawk!" shouted the man with the disheveled hair. He was Mino Nenki, a ninja from Iga. "Ogen might have sent that hawk from Sunpu."

"What? Ogen's hawk?" Oboro sucked in her breath.

The blue-faced Amayo Jingorou punched his fist in his hand. "So that's it! That's what Old Rousai was chasing!"

The five exchanged worried looks. Meanwhile, a round pouchlike thing came rolling up the hill.

"Wah!"

Everyone looked at Jousuke as he came to a halt. "So, what's going on?" Jousuke said in his high-pitched voice. "Why is everyone all gathered together?"

"Jousuke, what happened to the hawk?" Gennosuke snapped.

"Oh, it escaped. But the hawk doesn't matter—I've got the scroll it was carrying." Jousuke calmly reached into his tunic and withdrew the scroll. As soon as they saw it, Nenki and Jingorou gasped and stepped forward.

"Now listen up, everyone," Jousuke continued. "You know Ogen sent this from Sunpu, right? Hee hee! I had to work up a sweat playing tag with old Azuki Rousai in order to get this! We were comparing the powers of the Kouga and Iga ninjas. The winner got to keep the scroll."

"Jousuke—"

"What—we were just having fun. That's why I called it a game of tag, see? Listen, you Iga ninjas—you can ask Old Rousai about it. The important thing is, I won the contest between Kouga and Iga ninja, and so I will keep this as proof of my victory—"

Jousuke flourished the scroll, and Gennosuke immediately snatched it away.

"If this came from their leader, then it belongs to Iga," Gennosuke said. "What kind of idiotic prank are you playing? Oboro, please go ahead and read it."

Oboro took the scroll and started to open it.

"Wait!" shouted Amayo Jingorou.

The rays of the morning sun mercilessly illuminated Amayo Jingorou's body. His hideous appearance made others want to vomit. He looked like a drowning victim. Skin crackled from his neck and fingers. Blue mold sprouted on his skin.

"That scroll must not be opened in front of Gennosuke!" Amayo Jingorou demanded.

"What are you talking about, Jingorou?" Oboro said.

"We don't know what happened in Sunpu with Grandmother and Danjou! Anything could have happened. So the contents of Grandmother's scroll—"

"Jingorou," Oboro said, "the problems between the two clans of Iga and Kouga are now a thing of the past."

"I would like that to be true, Oboro. But the two clans are not yet united in marriage. For the moment, the two sides must remain sworn enemies, separated by hatred. . . . To let ninjas from Kouga see Grandmother's secret scroll would be unforgivable and a failure of our duties."

His tone of voice shows that he hasn't accepted being bound to Kouga, Gennosuke thought, smiling wryly. *He's their equivalent of Jousuke.*

"That's reasonable," Gennosuke said. "I'll go over there. Jousuke, come along." He silently turned away.

"What? I'm the one that brought the thing in the first place," Jousuke mumbled, his round face swelling even further. Throwing dark glances back at the others, he followed Gennosuke.

Lightly tossing the scroll at her companions, Oboro walked off, too.

"What's wrong, Oboro—don't you want to see what Grandmother sent to us?"

"The more important thing is apologizing to Gennosuke for the rudeness of my Iga companions," she answered.

When he saw Oboro's upset look, and the single-minded devotion in her choice to follow him, Gennosuke had the overwhelming desire to hug her tightly. He plucked a bundle of Japanese camellias and tucked them into her veil.

"No, no—don't be upset about it," he said. "Our two families have hated each other for four hundred years. There's nothing wrong with what Jingorou said. We can't expect to overcome the situation so easily. Oboro, you and I must become a chain permanently linking Kouga and Iga—a beautiful chain!"

The remaining four—Amayo Jingorou, Mino Nenki, Akeginu, and Hotarubi—spread the scroll open upon the grass. Bringing their heads close, they froze in place for a long time. The sun beat upon their backs, as if upon four crows—augurs of evil fortune.

Oboro looked back and called to them: "Jingorou! What did Grandmother say?"

Jingorou slowly looked in her direction. He spoke in the voice of a drowned man speaking from the bottom of the ocean. "Relax, my dear Oboro. . . . At Sunpu Castle, in the presence of the shogun and Hattori Hanzou, Iga and Kouga completed their reconciliation. Grandmother and Kouga Danjou have agreed to work together. She says that she will spend some time enjoying Edo in the springtime, and then she will return."

4

"SO IT REALLY HAPPENED!"

"What great news!"

Smiling, Oboro and Gennosuke gazed upon each other. The two started to head back, but Amayo Jingorou swiftly rolled up the scroll and approached them instead.

"Gennosuke, please forgive me for my rudeness a moment ago. Unfortunately, ninja are not accustomed to forgiving easily . . ." Amayo Jingorou presented Gennosuke with his best smile. But it was the smile of a drowned man. "All that is in the past now. This is wonderful. Looking at how things are going, one day I suppose that we will be calling you our lord and master. You and Oboro's decision to meet this morning at the Toki Pass has been matched by the will of heaven above, which commands you two to be together. Why not come with us into Iga?"

"Oh, that's a really great idea!" Oboro clapped her hands in happiness. "Gennosuke, please stay in Iga with us. You can really become a member of Iga. When Grandmother returns and sees how much everyone in Iga loves you, she will be so surprised! Grandmother will be so happy . . ."

Gennosuke looked at the cheerful girlish smile on Oboro's face. "Let's stay then," he said, nodding firmly. He looked to his side. "Jousuke, you go back to Kouga. I will accept their offer to stay here in Iga."

"Hold on, Gennosuke," Udono Jousuke said, shaking his head. "You're too impulsive. To just join your enemies and—"

"What are you talking about?" Gennosuke answered. "Weren't we coming here so that I could visit Oboro?"

"But that's different than what's going on now. I'm worried that if you stay here—"

Gennosuke laughed coldly. "Your ninja training has become too ingrained. The members of the Iga clan have just asked for forgiveness, haven't they? And what Oboro says is right—this is a good opportunity to meet all the members of the Iga clan, and try to win them over."

"If you are worried," Jingorou said with a laugh that made his blue mold shake, "you can join us as well. Either I or Nenki will travel to Kouga to inform your clan." He looked Jousuke over carefully.

"That's fine—" Jousuke said.

"Then let's all drink some flower-viewing wine together," Jingorou said.

"—but before that, show me the scroll," Jousuke answered.

"What?"

"If it is true that Kouga and Iga have reconciled, then show me the scroll—if not, I will not set one foot into Iga!" Jousuke screamed.

Behind him, the wild-haired Mino Nenki groaned faintly. Although Jousuke didn't notice, Nenki's head was undergoing a bizarre transformation. His wild samurai hair stood straight up . . .

Oboro nodded and stepped forward. "Jingorou, I want to see it, too. Open the scroll."

"Understood," Jingorou said, and began to open it. Suddenly, his hand froze and he looked up with a smirk. "Hold on for a moment. Jousuke!"

"What?"

"I don't mind showing you the scroll, but first I want to ask a question."

"What?"

"A little bit ago, you said that you won this scroll by defeating Azuki Rousai in a competition of ninja skills."

"It must be very difficult to accept, but that's what happened."

"You're right, it is painful. So, how about testing your ninja skills against one of the four of us right now? If you win, we show you the scroll."

"That's not acceptable," Gennosuke said, confused. "Jousuke played a dirty trick and I yelled at him for it. Forgive what he did. I want us to cease our fights. If you don't want us to see the scroll, that's fine."

"But we just lost a competition of ninja skills," Jingorou

said. "After Kouga and Iga merge, we'll always feel inferior because of Rousai's defeat." Jingorou was intentionally inciting everybody. "In any case, it is just a game. Nobody's going to die."

"Fine, let's begin," Jousuke said. He laughed. "So who will face me?"

Turning, Jingorou saw Akeginu's beautiful face.

"You looked at me first," Akeginu announced, "so I will take you on."

"A woman?" Jousuke spat indignantly, and seemed about to refuse. But soon his face flab bounced in ripples. "So you're Akeginu, right? How interesting. Actually, I've had a crush on you, Akeginu, for quite a while now. Heh heh heh . . . After Gennosuke and Oboro get married, I'd love to make you my bride—"

"If I lose this battle, you can make me your wife."

"Oh, really? How sweet of you! You'd be even more beautiful as my wife. So, even though I hate to even think of fighting with you, hey—things work in mysterious ways! So how shall we decide the winner?" The huge ball of flesh was so overjoyed that he seemed to have forgotten the scroll.

"No weapons," Oboro said. Her eyes sparkled with excitement and worry. Gennosuke remained silent.

"Good idea. Let me borrow this for a moment," Jousuke said, suddenly taking Mino Nenki's oak club, and handing it to Akeginu. "Akeginu, take this and knock my head off. Beat my arms, my head, anything—if you make me bleed, I lose. On the other hand, if I am able to rip your clothes off, I win. How's that?"

Gennosuke could bear it no longer, and started to object, but Akeginu had already agreed.

"Accepted," she said. "So, let us begin—"

"Hah!"

The two suddenly flew apart from each other.

The Toki Pass filled with the dawn's spring sun. The two ninja faced each other in unusual poses: the woman Akeginu holding the club diagonally; the fat Udono Jousuke stretching out his flabby hands. The faint smile on Gennosuke's face vanished as he watched them. He felt an unusually powerful sense of hatred surging from Akeginu.

"E-yah!"

There was a flash of light, as if from a drawn sword, and the oak club swung. The club had rocketed through the air like lightning and executed a sharp reverse slash. There was a sound like a ball being struck, and then Jousuke laughed—even though the club was sunk deep inside his face. Although deep in his face, as soon as it was pulled out, Jousuke's face immediately popped back to its original size. Once more, Jousuke belly-laughed.

"Ah!"

Akeginu leaped backward. With a huge smile, Jousuke chased after her and seized her sash as if to hug her. Like a spinning top, Akeginu spun frantically to escape, striking behind her with the club. Now holding the sash that he had stripped from Akeginu in both hands, Jousuke calmly stuck out his head and allowed it to be struck. Just then—

"We have a victor!" Amayo Jingorou shouted, even as he shot Jousuke a nasty look. Strung across Jousuke's face, which had just been struck by the club, was a thread of fresh blood!

Jousuke put his hand to his face. Waves of shock rippled along his body.

For a moment, Udono Jousuke stood petrified, a foolish expression on his face. Then he touched his face again, and—"This is not my blood!" he screamed. His ridiculous face instantly turned furious with indignation, and he surged at Akeginu just like a wine cask dropping from the sky.

"This is your blood!" he shouted. His hands snatched at her kimono, ripping it and revealing her upper body.

What he saw caused Kouga Gennosuke to immediately scream from deep in his throat. Akeginu's naked body was soaked in red. Her shoulders, her hips, her breasts—everything was covered in fresh bubbling blood.

"No victory—yet," Akeginu shouted. Aiming at Udono Jousuke, who was watching over her with a furious glare, she splattered him with thousands of particles of blood. Every pore on her body was a geyser of blood!

In ancient times, some people had skin that would seem to magically hemorrhage blood. Without the slightest injury, their eyes, head, chest, and limbs would start spilling crimson. Certain bodily reactions caused their blood vessel walls to become more permeable, and their blood cells and blood plasma would leak from their bodies. Akeginu could consciously control this blood hemorrhaging and could make it take place anywhere on her body at will.

Covering his eyes and groping in the air, Jousuke's body was wrapped in a thick red mist. That mist spread outward, until even the rays of the sun were tinged red and became dark. Akeginu's body vanished, somewhere within the mysterious, unearthly red fog. And then, from somewhere deep inside—

"I lo—I lose!" Udono Jousuke's scream could be heard.

THE WORM AND THE SPIDER

"OGEN IS DEAD," SAID THE SOFT-VOICED MAN. HIS was like the voice of a woman.

Fair-skinned with expressionless almond eyes, he had a soft, womanly sense about him. The strangest thing about him was his age. Looking at his dark samurai-style hairdo and his handsome face, one would guess he was thirty. And yet, there was something extremely old about it. The sensation was indefinable. Perhaps it came from his sallow skin or purple lips. In any case, the man radiated a mysterious sensation of endlessly old age.

Only this man could rival Ogen within the Iga clan: Yakushiji Tenzen.

He had known the five fighters crouching around him—including old Azuki Rousai—ever since they were children. Yakushiji Tenzen had looked exactly the same then as now. Despite his young, expressionless face, he had often spoken with Ogen about their memories of the Iga Rebellion forty or fifty years earlier.

As soon as they got their hands on the secret scroll,

Amayo Jingorou and wild-haired Mino Nenki naturally called for his help. Yakushiji Tenzen brought his retainer, Chikuma Koshirou, and hurried over. He opened the scroll, looked at it, and immediately announced that his comrade Ogen was dead.

They were at the Toki Pass, at the border of Iga and Kouga. Fireflies mixed among their bodies. Mountain cherry blossoms danced in the blue sky like windblown snowflakes. The conference of Iga's ninja broke up the mountain vista.

Earlier, Oboro and Akeginu had led Kouga Gennosuke and Udono Jousuke to the village. Jousuke had loudly boasted that he would only go to Iga if Akeginu had made him bleed during their ninja competition—and now he stifled sobs as he trailed his master, Gennosuke, into the Iga valley. Akeginu had covered his entire body in a blood mist and then beaten him to a pulp. Apparently, his talent of turning his flesh into a ball had malfunctioned, because bruises, lumps, and blood covered him.

"So, Kouga Danjou must also be dead," Yakushiji Tenzen murmured in a bitingly cold voice as he looked at the scroll. The names Ogen and Kouga Danjou were crossed out in blood.

Their ninja training held them back from bursting into screams and wails upon learning that their leader—the woman they considered to be a mother to the clan—had died. Although no sound or movement left the ninja group, none could bear to look at the others, and ripe energy surged between them.

"I saw that, too," agreed Amayo Jingorou, the blue mold shaking on his face as he looked up.

"So, we've tricked Gennosuke into thinking that Kouga and Iga are at peace, and that Grandmother and Danjou are currently enjoying the beauty of Edo."

"Why bother with luring Gennosuke and Jousuke to our village?" Mino Nenki asked, grinding his teeth. His samurai-cut hair stood up straight, like a snake. "Those two are already ensnared, like rats caught in a trap." He laughed.

"Not exactly," said Tenzen, shaking his head. "Forget Jousuke for a moment—it won't be easy to defeat Gennosuke. His eyes have a strange power. He's a powerful enemy. Worse, Oboro is in love with him. Everything's a mess."

"Oboro is Grandmother's successor," Chikuma Koshirou said. "Do you think that she would be convinced if we showed her the scroll?"

"Convince her that Gennosuke is her enemy? Even if we could persuade her, it would require a lot of time and effort. She'd waver back and forth and moan about it. Gennosuke would figure out that something was wrong."

"Well then, what should we do?"

"Say nothing to Oboro. For the time being, let Oboro and Gennosuke remain caught up in their lovers' talk."

Tenzen laughed softly. His eyes blazed with a bone-chilling combination of jealousy and hate. He had a dominating personality, and continued speaking coldly. "We're lucky we got our hands on this scroll so quickly. So—other than Danjou, Gennosuke, and Jousuke—there are seven members of the Kouga clan left for us to eliminate. I'd love to cut off their arms and legs and feed them to Gennosuke as he's sitting down for a meal. That would be a great way for him to learn that his Kouga clan has been annihilated!"

"Great!" Chikuma Koshirou said, laughing cheerfully. "I'm so glad that the Hattori family has ended the ban! We'll see what kind of pathetic ninja skills Kouga has!" Chikuma Koshirou was a country youth, about twenty, and he carried a fearsome scythe tucked into his waist.

Everyone in the group felt overjoyed as they realized the ban on ninja warfare had finally been lifted—everyone except one woman. Hotarubi looked around with worried eyes. "But, Tenzen, what about Yashamaru?" Yashamaru, her handsome lover, had traveled to Sunpu Castle with Ogen.

"Hmm. I don't know. There's no line through Yashamaru's name—" He touched it with his finger. "If he's still alive . . . Well, the hawk arrived before dawn, so it must have flown from Sunpu yesterday evening—if Yashamaru left Sunpu at the same time as the hawk, he'll get here late tonight or by dawn tomorrow." Tenzen thought for a moment and then looked up again. "There's someone else we need to worry about. Kazamachi Shougen went to Sunpu with Danjou, right?" His eyes opened wide. "Danjou might have entrusted his copy of the scroll to Kazamachi Shougen to bring back to Kouga. We've got to stop him—we can't let Kouga get their hands on the scroll."

"Right!"

"No matter what, we need to ambush Shougen on his way home. Then we must snatch away his scroll!"

"Good. I'll go!"

"No, I'll go!"

Wild-haired Nenki and Koshirou both leaped to their feet, fighting to be the first to go to battle.

"Amayo Jingorou," Tenzen said, "you go back to Iga alone."

"Why?"

"We're in a hurry. As an assassin, it's better if you stay here in case you're needed. If Gennosuke and his follower—no, more importantly, if Oboro senses that something is wrong, it'll be a disaster. Control them. Watch over them."

"I'd rather just kill Gennosuke."

"Ha ha ha ha. I know you'd love to kill him, but if something went wrong, there'd be a huge commotion and everything would be ruined. Wait until we get back, Amayo Jingorou—don't do anything rash."

"But, then, that means—"

"Mino, Chikuma, Hotarubi, and Old Rousai will go with me. We'll ambush Kazamachi Shougen—he went alone with Danjou to Sunpu. If the five of us attack him together, we'll certainly be able to kill him. Stop laughing, Koshirou! Ninja warfare has nothing to do with rules of war and honorable one-on-one duels. Victory! Killing! Defeating the enemy! That's all there is. Let's go."

"Shall we cross the Shigaraki Valley?"

"No. The enemy would immediately sense it if five Iga ninja entered their territory. Kazamachi Shougen must have departed Sunpu Castle yesterday evening. Even he couldn't cover more than a hundred twenty miles in a day. Even at top speed, he couldn't reach Suzuka Pass, the entrance to Kouga, before nightfall. We don't need to enter Kouga to wait for him. We can leave Iga through Ise, and ambush him between the station and Suzuka Pass. That should do it."

Yakushiji Tenzen looked over the greatest ninja of Iga, all eager to shed blood in battle. He laughed gently. "So everyone's excited. Are you having fun already? Grandmother's death was terrible news, but it is a dream come true to learn that the war with Kouga has begun again. Ready?"

"Let's go!"

Five shadows, like black shooting stars, soared eastward through the mountains separating Iga and Kouga.

The ninja, who had phantasmagorical powers that ordinary humans could not even imagine, were on their way to ambush Kazamachi Shougen—the ninja whose skills had so startled Tokugawa Ieyasu.

2

PASSING THE TOWERING ABURAHI MOUNTAIN, WHICH stood at the point of contact among Iga, Ise, and Kouga, the Iga ninjas soared down upon the Suzuka Pass mountain road like five nocturnal birds. Their eyes did not even absorb the mysterious beauty of Fudesute Mountain, which resembled an ancient Chinese painting. The five rushed down toward Seki station on the Tokaido Road.

"Wait!" Yakushiji Tenzen shouted.

"What?"

"I see someone coming in a mountain palanquin."

And, in fact, a mountain palanquin had just crossed over Suzuka Pass, heading east. It had gone about three hundred feet beyond the pass.

"Wha—"

"That must be Jimushi Juubei, from Kouga," Tenzen announced.

"What are he and the bearers of his palanquin doing on the Tokaido Road? Let's go catch him and find out."

"Jimushi Juubei—his name was on that scroll! Why waste our time asking him questions? We've gotten lucky— let's kill him right here." Mino Nenki looked at the others and licked his lips.

The mountain palanquin came racing forward as fast as an arrow. But as the five figures, standing still, came into view, the bearers of the palanquin slowed down, suspicious.

"Hotarubi, crouch down. Everyone else, go up ahead," Tenzen ordered.

Nenki, Koshirou, and Old Rousai moved on ahead, acting casual, while Hotarubi hunched over, standing along the roadside. Tenzen put a hand on her shoulder. She appeared to be a woman traveler who had injured her leg or was suffering stomach pain.

"Hotarubi, kill only the palanquin bearers."

"Understood."

The wooden carriage attached to a pole was carried by two bearers, one on each side. They ran forward an additional ten paces and then they suddenly froze, the palanquin crashing to the ground. The palanquin bearers clawed at the sky in desperation—twisted around their necks were snakes, appearing from nowhere. Red tongues flickered from triangular heads, drinking blood from the men's necks!

Without a word, the two palanquin bearers twisted and collapsed. Tenzen and Hotarubi walked toward the carriage, while the three others hurried back. Hotarubi extended her arm, and the two pit vipers obediently crawled up. Like babies going to suck their mother's breasts, the snakes moved eagerly into her robes.

"Jimushi Juubei!" screamed Tenzen.

"Yes?" came an absentminded voice. A huge head peered out from the palanquin, looking them over.

He had shockingly dark skin and tiny eyes. Perhaps from laziness, or perhaps because he knew he could not match the five surrounding him, Jimushi Juubei gave no indication of getting out of the palanquin.

"We're Ogen's followers, from Iga."

"Iga? Well, what is it?"

"We need to speak to you. Can you come with us?"

"Well, I'm sorry you've gone to such troubles, but I can't walk. What happened to the bearers of my palanquin? My legs don't work so well. What is it you want?"

"I'm sorry about that," Tenzen said. Nenki and Koshirou will carry the palanquin for you, and we'll bring you to the middle of that mountain over there."

Nenki and Koshirou didn't argue—they wanted to make Jimushi Juubei into their blood sacrifice as soon as possible—but the two Iga ninja sent dark looks at the palanquin. However, now that Ogen had died, Yakushiji Tenzen had become the undisputed leader. They followed his order, shouldering the palanquin and carrying it into the mountain.

"Old Rousai," Tenzen hissed, "if Juubei makes any strange moves, kill him immediately."

"You didn't even need to say it."

After the others had disappeared up the mountain, Tenzen seized the two collapsed palanquin bearers by their necks, and hurled them into a thicket of bushes by the road, as if he were tossing away the corpse of a dead dog. Then he chased after the others.

"Juubei, get out!" Tenzen said after they had departed from the road and entered a thicket of dense bamboo.

"I need feet before I can get out," answered the Kouga ninja.

Like a spring, old Azuki Rousai's leg expanded as it leaped outward, slamming into the palanquin.

Everyone but Yakushiji Tenzen gasped as they saw Jimushi Juubei's body tumble from the palanquin. Juubei was missing both arms. He also had no legs. He looked like a huge worm. None of the Iga ninja, except for Yakushiji Tenzen, knew that Jimushi Juubei looked like this.

A limbless ninja, without the power to move, who could only roll around.

"Juubei, what is the purpose of your trip?" Tenzen asked.

Jimushi Juubei's dark lips smirked. "I could never reveal the reason behind a Kouga trip to ninja from Iga. If you're so eager to hear my purpose, then you tell me what you're doing here first."

Tenzen thought for a while, and then the characteristically feminine smile appeared faintly on his lips.

"Fine. I'll tell you. Actually, we were anxious about Ogen, who had traveled to Sunpu."

"Oh, you, too? My stargazing has foretold that Danjou has encountered ill fortune."

"What stargazing?" Tenzen peered at the oxlike face before him. "Hnnh—so that's your skill?" Even as he spoke, he realized that Juubei—who had been overturned onto the ground earlier—had hidden himself in the shadows. He hadn't needed much time to do it. "So," Tenzen asked, "what sort of fate is awaiting Kazamachi Shougen?"

"Dark stars are pressing in upon him. Four or five very evil stars—"

"Your stargazing is accurate!" Tenzen said, laughing loudly. "Koshirou, Rousai, Nenki, Hotarubi: Leave this fellow to me. It'd be terrible if Kazamachi Shougen came upon us like this. Hurry back to intercept and kill him."

"Are you fine here?"

"Are you talking about this man-worm? Don't be stupid. All he has is a mouth. I'll ask him a few more questions. You guys hurry up!"

"Got it!"

The four turned and raced back to the road. They looked like four stars floating in the evening darkness.

"Juubei." Yakushiji Tenzen spoke. "While we're here, I'm going to ask you about the members of the Kouga clan. I know a lot about most of them, but there are still a few that I'm not so familiar with—including you, now that I mention it. In your group, there is a man called Kisaragi Saemon. I've heard his name. I've also seen him from a distance. But I don't know what he looks like. Describe Saemon's face to me."

Juubei did not respond.

"There's also a blind man named Muroga Hyouma. A blind ninja! What kind of ninja skills could he have?"

Juubei remained silent.

"There's a woman named Kagerou. She's very beautiful. Other than her seductive power, what talents does she have?"

Still no reply.

"So you won't talk?"

"Hee hee hee," Jimushi Juubei laughed.

"So you won't speak. In the end, I guess you're still a ninja of sorts—"

Jimushi Juubei was lying faceup under withered bamboo shoots. A silver line ran the entire distance from his collarbone to his abdomen.

"Jimushi Juubei! Go gaze upon your stars!" Yakushiji Tenzen cried out as he raised a sword overhead. He made a swift calculation and the sword sliced lengthwise through Juubei's clothes—but only through his clothes.

"Will you answer or not? Next time, I will slice exactly the same place—except I will be cutting through your flesh!"

Even within the ninja world, where no mercy is shown in battle, torturing a defenseless opponent was cruel. Jimushi Juubei remained silent. In the twilight, his hazy, wriggling shape resembled a slug. But then Tenzen saw something—

"What the—" Tenzen screamed, staring in shock at Juubei. Something strange glittered from Juubei's chest to his abdomen. Scales! Juubei's skin had changed, and a row of scales had extended outward, just like a snake's!

"Foretell your future!" Juubei laughed. He looked up

at the sky above the bamboo forest. "Your star—it's turned dark!"

At that moment a shot resounded from his oxlike face, and a spear sprang from his mouth. Yakushiji Tenzen leaped to the side, but the spear ripped into his left pectoral muscle, piercing his body and coming halfway out his back.

Without even time to scream, Tenzen tumbled to the ground.

This was no blow-dart. This wormlike man had swallowed a weapon one foot in length, and had held it hidden inside his stomach.

Juubei loosely flipped over onto his belly and began to crawl forward. The huge scales on his belly undulated. Through rippling his intercostals, his ribs could move forward or backward.

Noisily slithering through withered bamboo shoots, he approached Tenzen's dead body, and seized the spear in his teeth. Shaking his head, he yanked out the spear, now coated in blood. With a few gulps of his throat, he swallowed it deep into his belly again, or more accurately in his esophagus. Juubei could shoot the spear from his mouth with terrifying speed just as easily as he could breathe. The muscles along his esophagus had a special vomiting skill.

"If any of my enemies knew of this talent of mine, I'd be doomed. But by the time they learn of my talent, *they're* already doomed." He laughed. Sticking the side of his head against Tenzen's chest, he listened—Tenzen's heart had stopped beating. Juubei watched Tenzen's body turn cold.

"Well, after those Iga fighters attacked me like that, Danjou and Shougen need to be careful," Juubei mumbled to himself, worried. His body undulated in large waves. With unbelievable speed, he beat his way through the brush, returning to the road.

The new moon rose over the bamboo forest. Amidst the flickering stars, one was colored bloodred. Yakushiji Tenzen's evil star.

AN HOUR later, within the bamboo prison of death, darkness, and silence, there was a sound. Bugs? Animals? Wind? No—the sound of a man waking from slumber.

"Ah-h-h—" An unpleasant sound, like a yawn . . .

3

YAKUSHIJI TENZEN'S CALCULATIONS WERE ACCURATE. The four Iga warriors had barely left the thicket when they saw Kazamachi Shougen galloping in from the east. If they had remained in the thicket fighting with Juubei, they would have squandered their time and arrived too late to ambush him.

The phlegm-spitting Kazamachi Shougen traveled at

an amazing speed. He had covered more than one hundred miles from Sunpu to Shono in just over a day. Only a handful of ninja can travel as far as seventy miles in a day. He had been selected by Danjou because Kazamachi Shougen surpassed even that limit. Even more amazing is that he had traveled at this speed while crossing mountains, valleys, marshes, and swamps—he sprinted in a straight line across everything.

Most ninjas move quickly by running on the sides of their feet or on their toes or on their insteps. Shougen, however, did not limit himself to running on his feet. He used his legs and arms together, bounding like a humongous wolf. He had learned to run this way after the sun went down. Whenever he burst past, travelers would gasp and stare after him—*What was that thing?*—unable to identify him as person or beast.

Far off in the darkness, the Iga ninjas watched this bizarre shape dashing toward them and they froze.

"What is that?"

Instantly, the thing had closed the gap by thirty feet—

"It's Shougen!"

"Kazamachi Shougen!"

Kazamachi Shougen, who had been running on all fours, now sprang to his feet and stood tall. The four fighters created a semicircle in the road. Without a word, Chikuma Koshirou ran forward, hacking into Shougen's waist with his huge scythe.

Shougen crumpled, falling on the ground. But suddenly a clump of sticky film spat from the dirt, clinging to Koshirou's face. It instantly turned to glue, blocking Koshirou's nose.

There had been no declaration of war, no acceptance of a challenge. This was how the ninja of Iga and Kouga did battle.

Mino Nenki's club and Azuki Rousai's feet both aimed for the spot on the ground where Kazamachi Shougen lay groaning, but he immediately bounded backward ten feet. He jumped again, leaping into a cedar tree at the side of the road. Hanging upside down, he looked them over with bloodred eyes.

"Iga?" he asked, speaking for the first time in a husky voice.

"Shougen, I know that Danjou gave you the scroll listing the Kouga and Iga ninja!" wild-haired Mino Nenki roared.

"Hand it over!" Old Rousai shouted.

"How do you know that?" Shougen asked, shocked, as he looked down at the two ninjas below. Yashamaru of Iga had left Sunpu at the same time as he had, but Shougen also knew that Danjou had stolen Yashamaru's scroll. It seemed impossible for the Iga to have already received it and know about everything.

Nenki laughed. "Shougen, we are from Ogen's clan. Keep that carved in your heart! Now die." Almost without moving his hands, his club soared upward, aiming at Shougen, crouching on a branch twelve feet overhead.

If he had been on the ground or a stone wall, he could have scampered sideways and escaped. But he was on a tree that shot up directly into the sky. He was trapped; the club struck him in the backbone. A huge crunch sounded as it broke his vertebrae. Even so, he did not tumble to the ground.

"I will admit that you are from Ogen's clan—" he moaned, twisting his head toward them. "But first, I will erase your names from this scroll!"

Along with his words he spat out an uncountable number of threads, which sprayed against Nenki and Old Rousai.

"Uuh!" The two leaped away, but hundreds of sticky strings covered them, adhering to their faces, shoulders, and chests. Panicking, Nenki and Rousai attempted to rip them off their bodies. The threads, however, were extremely sticky. Chikuma Koshirou, whose nostrils had become clogged earlier, had fallen to the ground, still trying to tear those threads out.

Shuu—A strange noise resounded. Kazamachi Shougen continued spitting strings. Opening his mouth, he aimed at the sky. His phlegm arced over the road and attached to the cedar tree on the other side. A long sticky rope stretched across the path.

Shougen climbed from his cedar tree onto the string. With a rustle, he rushed across the strings he had just spat from his mouth, climbing vertically, horizontally, diagonally, like a human spider climbing on an enormous spiderweb.

A stunning geometric design glittered—fluorescent—in the light of the young moon. What gruesome beauty! Having torn the threads out, along with their eyebrows and eyelashes, Azuki Rousai and Mino Nenki gazed upward in frozen horror, watching a nightmare take shape.

"What's wrong, Iga fighters?" A burst of laughter came from the center of the spiderweb.

The Iga fighters snapped back to reality.

"We must put an end to his mocking laughter! Even if we can't kill Shougen, let's at least destroy his web!"

"Don't let him scare you! Don't be intimidated! We're Iga ninja!"

These shouts came from within Shougen's spiderweb. Having peeled off his sticky phlegm, Koshirou, Nenki, and Rousai had raised a furious shout and attacked the web.

But the web was a terrifying thing. Koshirou's scythe, Nenki's club, Rousai's whiplike limbs—each became entangled like moths in the web. The scythe sliced through threads, but became snagged; the club could not even cut the threads. Rousai's limbs became stuck in place, as if doused in glue.

What exactly was this substance that Kazamachi Shougen spat? Saliva. People ordinarily secrete more than one third of a gallon of saliva in a single day. Shougen's salivary glands could secrete many dozen times that amount in a very short span of time. Not only could he produce enormous amounts of saliva, but his saliva was extremely strong and sticky. He had been born with this talent, but had also undergone intense training, learning to use his breath, gums, teeth, and tongue to create clumps of glue to blow upon his enemies, or to turn it into dozens of threads, which he could blow in multiple directions at once.

"Ha ha ha ha!" Shougen roared. "My Iga horseflies. I will cross your names off the list. Your dead bodies will be the souvenir I bring back from my journey!"

Drawing his sword for the first time, Shougen crawled along the threads. Suddenly, Shougen's face warped in agony and he blew on his shoulder. Thick drops of blood trickled onto his chin.

Shougen was bleeding internally from his broken spine, suffered from Nenki's club.

"You slime!" he snarled. But he continued smirking as he turned upside down and crawled into his web.

At that moment, the moonlight disappeared. Kazamachi Shougen looked upward. Had the moon sunk already? Had it become hidden by clouds? But what he saw made Kazamachi Shougen scream in shock.

What was it? A whirlwind covered the entire sky. Yet every tiny segment of the whirlwind glittered and floated on its own, glimmering. It whirled down toward the earth, making an eerie sound. It flung itself upon Shougen's web, sticking to it.

Stunned, Shougen gasped in surprise. He didn't know what it was, but he watched it noisily beating against his web, everywhere. His eyes grew large.

Butterflies. Thousands of nocturnal butterflies flew circles, in front of him, behind him—everywhere. The swirling swarm of butterflies engulfed him in a fog of silver flecks. Peering through the silver mist, Shougen saw her.

Beneath him, one leg kneeling upon the road, her hands clasped before her chest, eyes facing heaven— stood a woman.

4

HOTARUBI.

She had called forth the butterflies. While Kazamachi Shougen was no more than a single spider, Hotarubi's power extended to all the insects and reptiles on the planet. She could manipulate snakes with a flick of her wrists. She far surpassed the limits of ninja talents—even surpassed the limits of human nature. Through concentration, she could radiate her thoughts beyond her own consciousness, rousing the slumbering butterflies, encouraging them to swarm, and directing their movement. Her skills surpassed the limits of the ninja knowledge, bordering on magic.

His eyes strained wide, Kazamachi Shougen remained unmoving.

The whirling butterflies made him dizzy and disoriented. They were also landing on his spiderweb. Although the threads were snagging the butterflies, there were so many butterflies that they soon covered every segment of every thread. The threads had become waves of butterflies. Trembling in the dim moonlight, the spiderweb had transformed into an enormous flower composed of butterflies. The dancing silver flecks—the wings and bodies—covering the strings had robbed them of their stickiness.

Hotarubi seized a mountain sword, approached her entangled companions, and cut them free.

"Shougen—" she shouted, just as Kazamachi Shougen had pursed his lips. He seemed ready to spit out another thread. He spat blood. His night-vision eyes had turned white, and his ugly face had changed color. He had lost the will to live amidst the shock and despair of the battle.

"Hand over the scroll!" Hotarubi exclaimed.

Shougen's head, hanging upside down, moved faintly.

"Uhgh—" he groaned. He lifted the scroll high in the air and flung it as far as he could. As he did so, he fell from the spiderweb with a great thud. He would never move again. The three Iga men examined Shougen's body to confirm that he had died. Then they returned to get the scroll that Shougen had thrown thirty feet away.

But a strange noise came from that location.

"Ah!" the three men shouted.

An unexpected figure made them freeze in place. A long, narrow, sacklike creature was slithering on the ground. By the time they had seen it, the sack had begun undulating, racing away as it made a strange noise. The scroll was gone.

The Iga men realized why Kazamachi Shougen had made that final groan and why he had poured all his dying strength into hurling the scroll.

"That thing!"

Jimushi Juubei.

How could it crawl without arms or legs? And if it was here, what had happened to Yakushiji Tenzen? But in their confusion at seeing that thing escape with the scroll, they forgot their questions and chased after him.

Hotarubi, left behind, carried her mountain sword as she approached Kazamachi Shougen . . .

The three pursuing Iga men could not believe their inability to catch that thing. Although the three were far swifter than ordinary humans, they could not gain any ground on the limbless ninja.

Their pursuit of the otherworldly creature continued over the four miles separating the stations of Shono and Kameyama.

Although the three Iga ninja could see in the dark, they were losing sight of their slithering enemy in the weakening moonlight. They panted in despair—

"Uggh!" In the distance in front of them, there was the sound of an extraordinary groan. Although the three could not see it, a shadow had suddenly appeared before Jimushi Juubei. The groan came from Jimushi Juubei, shocked at what he saw.

"Juubei—spit out the scroll you've got in your mouth," the shadow said. The voice was gentle and tinged with laughter. "If you don't spit out the scroll, you won't be able to fire your spear."

While still holding the scroll in his mouth, Juubei's eyes bulged. The enemy was correct. His only weapon was blocked—and he had blocked it himself. But if he spat out the scroll, it would be a warning that he was about to shoot the spear. This enemy already knew his secret!

Behind him, the three Iga men rushed closer.

Juubei's oxlike face twisted in despair. He spat out the scroll. Instantly, a streak of light shot through the sky.

It vanished into the distance like a shooting star. His eyes watched it go. He had aimed at the crouching shadow, which had been poised and awaiting Juubei's attack. The shadow had leaped over the spear, and had landed behind him. The shadow's drawn blade had sliced through Juubei's back, releasing bubbles of blood that dripped to the ground. Jimushi Juubei became a corpse.

"Tenzen!" shouted Koshirou.

In the faint light of the moon, they saw the smooth, expressionless face of Yakushiji Tenzen.

He should have died in the bushes just a short time ago, when Jimushi Juubei's spear pierced his chest and came out his back.

But none of the others had been in the thicket, and none could ask Tenzen what had happened. Tenzen stared at Jimushi Juubei's corpse. "You were a difficult opponent," he mumbled. "Too bad nobody could give you a hand."

He picked up the scroll that had been in Juubei's mouth and compared it to the scroll he carried in his kimono. "So—they're exactly the same. Well, no need for two." He took some tinder from his waist and lit the scroll on fire. "This scroll would be trouble if Kouga ever got their hands on it."

The fire spread throughout the scroll. Three Kouga ninja—Kouga Danjou, Kazamachi Shougen, Jimushi Juubei—had expended the limits of their intelligence, secret talents, and energy to bring this scroll to Kouga. But now it vanished in a fiery blaze.

Hotarubi approached.

"What about Shougen?" Tenzen asked her softly.

"I killed him," she answered in a low voice. What she meant was that she had slit his throat in a final coup de grâce.

Yakushiji Tenzen spread wide the surviving scroll. He scooped up blood from the corpse next to him and traced a red line through the names of Kazamachi Shougen and Jimushi Juubei.

Tenzen tossed the other scroll, burning, upon the ground. It continued to flare up in reproachful flames that lit the faces of the five Iga warriors. Strangely, they did not seem pleased.

"Seven remain."

The terrifying powers of the ninja they had defeated served as a lesson—and a harbinger of the battles ahead.

The fire burned out. Like a gust of wind, the five ninjas quickly rode back, crossing the dark mountain river. But were they riding toward Kouga or Iga?

HIDDEN IN THE WATER

1

MUTEISHI, A SECRET DOCUMENT OF THE TOUDOU province, states that "Iga is a secret and precious land. It produces wheat and rice and will never lack for provisions for soldiers. The country is firmly defended. Giving fifty rifles each to seven skilled riflemen would be enough to hold off all enemies. They have everything that they need. They are only lacking in salt, and they must import a surprising amount of it . . ."

Iga is enclosed on the east by the Suzuka Nunobiki mountain range, on the west by the Kasagi mountains, on the south by the Murou volcanic range, and on the north by the Shigaraki highlands. Its interior is creased with basins and rift valleys, creating a hidden world. Heaven has locked it away.

Tsubagakure Valley is in the north of the interior. For generations, outsiders did not even know it existed, and even at this time, few warriors of Toudou province would venture inside with confidence. Entering the region meant going into a hidden universe of blind alleys, confusing forests, and thickets of unfamiliar vegetation. Cut off from the outside, geography and directions became incomprehensibly muddled. But in each blind alley, forest, and thicket, intruders felt the cold sensation of eyes watching their backs.

Kouga Gennosuke now had that feeling.

But if intruders entered Gennosuke's own home—Shigaraki Manjidani—they would experience the same sensation.

From the first time Gennosuke had come to Iga, he had unconsciously admired their ninja stronghold, fortified with so many opportunities for ambush and attack: Its seemingly casual placement of trees, boulders, and homes masked the sudden appearance of a fortress. *Amazing,* he thought.

But things felt different this time.

"It's the same mountain, but everything is different here—even spring feels different, Jousuke."

One by one, Gennosuke searched out and confirmed every pair of eyes watching him, but he disguised his actions, pretending to be conversing cheerfully with his retainer, Udono Jousuke.

Jousuke followed behind him, walking with Akeginu. Akeginu never spoke a word to him, but Jousuke didn't care. He continuously blathered on in a high-pitched voice.

"To tell you the truth, this shouldn't be considered spring, it's much more like summer. In Shigaraki, it's still a little cold at night—"

"It's better to live over here," said Oboro in a bouncy voice. She was walking ahead of them. "Everything's better: the weather, the mountains and rivers, and also the people!" Although speaking to members of their rival clan, Kouga, her voice was innocent and empty of viciousness. She smiled.

"I see. It must be much better here, since such big birds want to live here!" Jousuke raised his eyes toward a bird perched atop a cedar tree alongside the road. Suddenly his right hand darted. At that moment, a flurry of wings sounded on Oboro's shoulder, and Jousuke's dagger dropped to the ground, glittering. By beating its wings and creating a gust of wind, the hawk sitting on Oboro's shoulder had knocked down the dagger that Jousuke had been about to throw.

"Don't be an idiot," Gennosuke snapped at Jousuke, turning around. "Are you still playing these stupid tricks? Your parents would be ashamed of your brainless behavior."

"All right. You're angry. I won't do it again," Jousuke hurriedly apologized, and picked up his dagger. The hawk settled on Oboro's shoulder again. Glaring at it, Jousuke muttered, "I don't mind the people here, but that hawk keeps staring at me like I'm its enemy."

"I wonder what's wrong," Oboro said. "I've told him

that you're not his enemy. This hawk is usually smarter than most people." Oboro looked over at the hawk with a confused expression. She appeared to be on the verge of tears.

This hawk had carried the scroll from Ogen in Sunpu. The previous night, at the Toki Pass, Jousuke had thrown a sword at it, causing it to drop the scroll. Naturally, the hawk considered Jousuke its enemy. Jousuke was playing dumb.

"Gennosuke, my fellow Iga members are so stupid," Oboro said. "Even though they must accept the fact that the people of Manjidani are no longer our enemies, those idiots don't want to accept it—not even my hawk!" Oboro shook her head in frustration, and stared at the sky.

"Sakinta!" she shouted. Overhead, a large flying thing froze in place amid thick cedar branches. In a moment, it shifted into human form, and dropped with a thud to the road.

Landing hard on his rear, the man screamed in a loud voice before scurrying away. He had a huge bulge swelling from his back—a hunchback.

"Don't use your powers on me, Oboro!" the hunchback cried.

Gennosuke laughed bitterly.

There had been many people secretly watching them, so Gennosuke was not surprised by this person who had been flying overhead. What shocked Gennosuke was the ninja skill that Oboro had learned. No—that wasn't accurate. She hadn't "learned" a skill—and it wasn't a skill at all. All she had to do was turn her big round eyes in somebody's direction and that person's ninja talents would be shredded like paper.

For his part, Kouga Gennosuke had basilisk eyes. Long ago, his ninja instinct had made him think of training his eyes upon her—"to see, just one time, if my eyes could overwhelm hers"—but the idea had barely occurred to him when he glanced into Oboro's bright sunny eyes. Her eyes calmed him, like the ocean in spring. He had no interest in fighting with her.

Gennosuke laughed gently and shook his head. "Of course they don't trust me. Oboro, you've led me far into your territory, where hatred of me runs deep—it extends to every corner of Tsubagakure Valley. And you've been so brave, leading me openly through enemy territory."

"This is your land, too."

"I would love to make that come true as soon as possible! But, Oboro, that hunchback just now—not just him, but everyone—all the people we've seen in the valley, those chopping wood or working near the road—and they're the same way in my own home, in Manjidani, too—It's frightening how few normal, healthy people there are!" He sighed gloomily.

And what he said was true. During their walk, everywhere he looked, he saw a nation of deformities. Dwarves, hunchbacks, people with cleft palates, villagers with distorted voices, malformed limbs—at least that much could be found in the outside world. But he also saw a man with his tongue hanging down to his chest, drooling; a woman with purple blood vessels poking out like vines through the skin of her face; a young man whose wrists and ankles protruded immediately from his torso, like a seal; and a young lady with skin and lips and hair all snow white, but who had eyes as red as rubies.

On the other hand, the things that were beautiful here were so beautiful that they didn't seem to be part of this world. The one common thread running through everything was that these were all mysterious ninja who should not be underestimated. Both their talents and their deformities had resulted from four hundred years of inbreeding. Gennosuke shivered. Despite the hatred between the clans, they had inflicted far more damage on themselves through inbreeding than through their wars.

"Kouga and Iga have tried to destroy each other," Gennosuke said. "To do so, both sides have intentionally inbred their best warriors, creating ninja with unbelievable talents. But in the process, they have sacrificed their health and their humanity. Nothing could be more foolish or terrifying!" Kouga Gennosuke had unconsciously raised his voice. "Oboro, promise me that we'll put an end to this! Kouga and Iga need to mix their blood—beginning with you and me!"

"Yes, Gennosuke!"

"And we must eliminate the iron wall of hatred separating Manjidani and Tsubagakure. We must flow freely across the two sides, just like wind and nature!"

But the bloodlines had become as firmly entrenched as iron, and the two sides had turned into prisons for their own people. When Gennosuke proclaimed his desire to smash through the crystallized bloodlines, he invited a deadly and destructive protest. Gennosuke knew he was angering those around him, because his Kouga clan was the same way. But—as if challenging the people of the valley and demanding that they listen—he had unconsciously begun screaming. He had committed an unpardonable act by shouting these things while entering Iga territory.

"Yes, Gennosuke," Oboro answered adoringly.

Countless cursing eyes focused on the group, so much so that it felt like a gust of evil wind. Udono Jousuke could feel the angry eyes like knife wounds, and he sank his neck deep into his chest.

"Hey, Akeginu," he said in a worried voice, "that group that we met back at Toki Pass has disappeared."

"You're right," Oboro said, looking around her in confusion. "Akeginu, where did Tenzen and the others go?"

"Oh, they went hunting in the mountains so that we could serve our guests rabbit or fowl," Akeginu answered.

Oboro's eyes looked worried as she turned away.

"Hey, Jingorou!" she cried, and there was the sound of bustling in front of them.

Amayo Jingorou was at the gate to Ogen's palace. He watched them silently, and released the drawbridge for the moat.

2

NIGHT COVERED THE BEAUTIFUL SPRINGTIME VALLEY of Tsubagakure.

At Oboro's orders, the people of Iga had gathered for a feast at Ogen's mansion. The feast lacked any sense of joy, however. Although the banquet honored Gennosuke, did anybody there really welcome him?

Most of those present remained ignorant of the secret war between Iga and Kouga. If too many people knew, Oboro would also hear about it. And if she learned about it, things would get messy. With overwhelming confidence, Yakushiji Tenzen had declared that his group of five would slaughter the entire list of Kouga fighters, and so others did not need to know. But even if they didn't know about the war, those in the room already hated Kouga: Reality was far different from the supposed truce.

Gennosuke responded to the hostile eyes with a smile. Yet the only person in the room who appreciated his efforts was Oboro.

People left. Akeginu led Udono Jousuke away. Eventually, only the young couple remained behind under the spring torches. What lovers' talk transpired there—what passionate dreams of the future did Gennosuke and Oboro discuss!

At last, Oboro, her eyes filled with rapture, left the parlor room in which Gennosuke sat. The young moon would soon rise over the mountain. At about this same time, on the Tokaido Road, the group of five Iga ninja led by Tenzen had ambushed Kazamachi Shougen and Jimushi Juubei as they were relaying the secret scroll. Their battle was taking place at this very moment.

Oboro didn't know about that. But she did find it suspicious that the group went rabbit-hunting but failed to make it back for the banquet. She asked Akeginu about it, but she only said, "Hmm, I wonder what happened to them." They must have claimed sickness or some other excuse to avoid the banquet, despite Oboro's order that all attend. Tenzen and the others must hate Gennosuke so much that they hid themselves.

But she quickly forgot about the Iga ninjas who had not attended the banquet, and her heart filled with thoughts of Gennosuke.

Oboro had gone casually to the edge of the veranda and was about to turn around when she spotted a dullish gray thing shining in the moonlight. It looked like the remains of dried mucus. Something had left a slimy trail coming from the garden.

That was where the salt storehouse stood. Just as was written within the *Muteishi*, "They are only lacking in salt, and they must import a surprising amount of it . . ." Because their stronghold lacked salt, the clan leaders of Tsu-bagakure had created a salt storehouse behind the palace.

The gooey strip of mucus was about seven inches long, and had traveled from the garden toward the veranda, and from there had crawled up a pillar.

Oboro moved again. She walked ten steps and stood still. Facing the ceiling of the darkened veranda, she shouted, "Jingorou!"

Something was there. But it didn't answer. There was only the sound of pouring water. A waterfall cascaded down a mountain, feeding the deep moat that surrounded the mansion.

After a few minutes, unable to withstand Oboro's gaze, something dropped from the ceiling with a thud. It was the size of an infant, and had a bizarre body.

However you looked at it, that thing was not human. It had no limbs, and its surface was a slimy liquid mass. It could be a fetus or a giant slug—in any case, its shape could only be described as a lump. And yet, in the front of that lump—its mouth carried a short sword.

"Jingorou, what—" Oboro burned with fury, and cast her angry eyes upon him. "What exactly do you think you're going to do?"

The beauty of her furious eyes was something unknown except to those ninja who had seen it. The slug trembled violently, as if in agony. As it trembled, a human form began to float to the surface. A tiny, childlike version of Amayo Jingorou appeared there.

What sort of ninja was this! Upon submerging his body in salt, his skin and flesh melted to pulp. He transformed into a semiliquid substance. The human body is composed of 60 percent water, and so Amayo Jingorou could dissolve into a shrunken version of himself. But as he did, his body became unrecognizable, and his movements became glacially slow. As an assassin, however, this man—creeping silently and leaving behind a long, sticky trail—wielded tremendous ninja powers.

"Are you going to murder Gennosuke?" Oboro's eyes glittered with fury. She stomped over and kicked Jingorou from the veranda to the garden. "Jingorou," she yelled in a dignified voice, "you may be a beloved member of Iga, but if you have the slightest evil thought toward Gennosuke, I will finish you off myself."

But at that moment she raised her head and looked up. Far in the distance, someone had screamed. She tilted her head, then ran in that direction.

Amayo Jingorou was left behind, writhing. Halfway through his ninja technique, Oboro had stopped him with her occult-piercing eyes. He began the agonizing return to his fleshly form.

"Water . . . water . . ." A strange inhuman murmur rose from the ground where he crawled.

3

UDONO JOUSUKE ABRUPTLY SAT UP IN HIS ROOM, LIFT-
ing his massive head.

He got up and reached for the sliding paper door. The
paper felt strange. He tapped at it with his fist, and sure
enough, this was no normal sliding paper door. Instead,
paper had been glued on top of a thick wooden door. It
had been bolted on the outside. On three sides were thick
walls. Opposite the door, a sliding shoji screen covered a
window. When Jousuke opened it, he discovered thick
iron bars imprisoning him.

"I should have known," Jousuke said, nodding. He had
been left to sleep in a prison cell.

He wasn't sure if Akeginu had put him here merely as
a precaution or as part of a larger scheme.

Although Jousuke had laughed and joked with the
dozen or so Iga members at the banquet, he had never relaxed. He thought it suspicious that Azuki Rousai, Mino
Nenki, and others never showed up. Jousuke regretted
not peeking at the scroll after getting it from the hawk flying back from Sunpu.

"And what's more, they think that they can lock up a
Kouga fighter like me in a cage like this!"

Jousuke looked at the iron bars on the window and
grinned. He was the biggest prankster in Manjidani. Gennosuke was always yelling at him, but Jousuke could never

resist causing trouble. And now Iga had put him in this kind of place.

Preparing himself, Jousuke went to the barred window. He pressed his circular, flabby face against the bars.

An arm could barely squeeze between the bars on the window, but not even a child could stick his head through that gap. Jousuke's head was far bigger than any ordinary person's head, and yet, as he pushed it against the bars, his head squashed together like a ripened, soft fruit. He pushed it through, and as his head came out, it swelled back to its original size. Finally, his whole head popped out on the other side. He had successfully gotten his head out. Next, shoulders. Then the waist . . .

White blood cells exit blood vessels by first pushing a tiny part of the blood cell through a microscopic gap in the blood vessel. Then the insides of the blood cell follow through the gap, causing the part on the outside to swell. Eventually, the entire blood cell is outside the blood vessel. Right then, Udono Jousuke's body looked like a blood physiology demonstration on a glass slide—but magnified to enormous size.

Jousuke soon stood outside Ogen's mansion, alone in her garden.

"I wonder if Gennosuke is okay?"

Ogen's palace looked like a castle, though it wasn't. It was also distinct from the mansions of other military families of the Edo era, not as wide as a high-ranking military family's mansion, and yet a deep moat protected the outside, and its interior walls soared to dizzying heights. The huge veranda formed a cylinder around a grove of cedar trees. The palace brimmed with wild nature and mystery.

The fortress contained walls, trees, roads—all of which were of heights, sizes, and widths calculated to confuse. They confounded one's sense of distance. Some places made one feel suffocated, as if trapped in a well. But go ten paces, and the space seemed larger than Iga itself.

A work entitled *Ninja Palace* by Kounanchou Ryuu-houshi from Kouga describes the fantastic architecture of ninja buildings. Of course, this work appeared many years after the events narrated here. Even so, it describes houses that appeared to be a single story and that actually concealed three stories, stairs in which secret entrances were hidden, noisemakers scattered everywhere, ropes that allowed ninja to swiftly slide from the third floor to the ground, iron bars disguised as wooden bars, Chinese paper that actually concealed wooden walls an inch thick and capable of stopping swords, spears, and even bullets from a matchlock gun. Moreover, the walls of the storehouses were stuffed with three inches of earth and sand, the ceilings were made with snug-fitting iron planks, and the windows came in three kinds: netting, metal bars, and wooden bars. In some places, two separate doors could be opened at the same time—in fact, they had to be opened at the same time or neither would open and the intruder couldn't escape. Ninja castles were traps for the unwary.

Moreover, this palace had been used for ninja gatherings. During the bloody Iga Rebellion, this had been the headquarters for the leader of the Iga troops. This was Ogen's palace.

Kouga Gennosuke wished to make Oboro his wife, and so he had often visited the palace. But this was Udono Jousuke's first visit.

"So . . . hmm . . . well, that's how they did it . . ." Fascinated, Jousuke nodded his head as his huge body tumbled around the ninja mansion in the middle of the night.

At one point he arrived at Gennosuke's room, but he overheard Oboro's giggling. Making a face that looked like a sneezing Pekingese dog, he waddled away. "Well, Gennosuke seems busy with something else!"

Jousuke returned to the garden and spotted Akeginu standing outside the window from which he had escaped.

Jousuke slowly crept up behind Akeginu—

Akeginu had panicked, trying to ascertain if Jousuke was still there or not.

Perhaps it would be impossible to kill Gennosuke tonight. But Jousuke, at least, must die!

Amayo Jingorou had said so. Yakushiji Tenzen had ordered them to wait until he returned, but they were ninja, and those words only made them want to fight even more.

The iron bars on the window prevented anything other than that human slug from sliding through. The terrible human slug would crawl through the opening in the metal grate and make the room into the final resting place for its occupant. Amayo Jingorou entered the salt storehouse and dissolved his body. Then he had gone to check on Gennosuke and Oboro. While he did that, Akeginu had come back here to keep an eye out. Her spine tingled as she realized that Udono Jousuke had vanished.

"Could it be possible?" she whispered.

Akeginu knew that Jousuke could manipulate his huge ball of flesh, but she had never imagined he could squeeze through the three-inch gap between the iron bars.

Suddenly, her eyes were covered by oily flesh—somebody's hand!

Akeginu screamed.

Far away, Oboro heard this scream.

In a panic, Akeginu shook free from the man's grasp.

"Boo!" Standing beneath the crescent moon was the wise-guy Udono Jousuke with a grinning and arrogant expression. "Please excuse me for having just missed you, Akeginu," he said. "We need to stop walking right past each other." Jousuke stroked his chin. "At Toki Pass, you gave me a terrible time, but I can't stop having feelings for you. It's a seductive spring night . . . we can hear Gennosuke and Oboro talking sweet lovers' words . . . neither of us wants to sleep alone in this prisonlike place.

I couldn't bear it any longer, and so I went out to walk around, and what do you know? You had the same thoughts, and you had slipped over here to visit me . . ."

"Why—" Akeginu gasped for air as she spoke. "Why did you break out of this room?"

"I was thinking of love." Jousuke brazenly groped toward her with his plump fingers spread wide, but Akeginu leaped ten feet away. She pulled a short sword from her kimono. It sparkled in the moonlight like the scales of a fish.

"Huh? We're fighting again? This is really a waste." Jousuke rolled his eyes at her, and his body tensed like a balloon swollen with air. He was ready for Akeginu's talent of spraying blood from her skin. "Well, then, shall we go at it one more time?" Below his droopy eyelids, eyes flashed. "Once again, I will strip you naked, Akeginu. If you don't rip off your sash right away, I will do it for you."

In their rematch, Akeginu had a disadvantage. As Jousuke implied in his taunts, now that he knew her ninja skills, he'd give her no opportunity to reveal her skin. Akeginu stared at Jousuke. A black dot oozed out of her candlewax-white forehead. Near her temples, several more spots appeared, trickling down in long threads. Sweat. Her sweat was blood!

But would she direct those trickles into sprays of blood targeted at his eyes? No—instead she transformed her pale, gorgeous face, until it became crisscrossed with dark stitches of color. Jousuke was too afraid to advance, and so the two of them stood, facing each other like statues.

"Akeginu!" Oboro called as she ran toward them.

Upon seeing Oboro's eyes, Akeginu was like a bowstring being released. She immediately turned limp and collapsed to the ground.

"What are you doing?" Oboro snapped. After discovering Amayo Jingorou trying to slip into Gennosuke's room, Oboro had decided to check on Jousuke as well. Oboro suspected Akeginu was up to no good, but Jousuke didn't know that.

"Oh come on," Jousuke said, grinning. "I'm madly in love with Akeginu, just like I confessed to everyone back at Toki Pass. Just now, I tugged her sleeve to get her attention, and she exploded at me. As you see, we happened upon each other here by accident. Oboro, don't you think that this is fate—symbolic of the reconciliation between Kouga and Iga? I want reconciliation, so why does Akeginu treat me heartlessly? What do you think, Oboro?"

Oboro looked at Jousuke as if giving up on the situation. "Well, then," she mumbled, "in that case, after Grandmother returns, ask her for permission to marry."

Oboro quickly hugged Akeginu. "Akeginu, good night. You can come sleep with me, if you want."

Akeginu climbed to her feet and staggered along. Oboro held onto her, supporting her as they left.

Oboro had not realized that Amayo Jingorou was on his way to kill Udono Jousuke. Rather, she had thought that

Amayo hated Gennosuke and had been clinging to the underside of the ceiling in order to spy on their conversation.

That was unforgivably rude, so she abandoned him outside. He had dissolved his body in salt before she halted his transformation, and she knew this condition made him ache for water—the agony of having no water felt worse than death.

"Water . . . wa . . . water . . ." Jingorou was squirming through the garden. The night was cold, but the ground burned him like hot sand. He was in dehydration hell.

A shadow fell upon the strange slug-man. Someone stood over him, peering down.

"Hmmm . . . what's this thing . . ." A fat hand pinched him tight by his neck and lifted him up. Udono Jousuke.

4

JOUSUKE, ALTHOUGH ALSO ABLE TO SWELL OUT AND constrict himself, stared at the strange creature for a long time before recognizing it. "Amayo," he finally grumbled.

The sluglike beast that Oboro had caused to fall from the ceiling was still a drenched, melted mixture of flesh and skin, covered in a sticky substance. Neither hands nor legs were visible, much less a face. Jousuke could barely recognize it as Amayo Jingorou's body. Earlier, Amayo had looked like a drowned man with skin that was both swollen and shriveled and covered in wrinkles. But now Amayo was the size of an infant.

"What—what happened to you?" Jousuke had barely asked the question when he froze and stared at Gennosuke's nearby room.

"Hey, Amayo! Did you adopt this shape to go to Gennosuke . . ."

"Wa . . . water . . . please . . ." Jingorou moaned in a voice as faint as the murmur of an insect.

"Did you intend to kill Gennosuke, Jingorou?"

"Water . . . ?"

"I understand your hatred of an opposing clan. But why strike now—Kouga and Iga are finally at peace! Why now?" Jousuke shook Jingorou in his hand. "Another thing: Azuki Rousai, Mino Nenki, Hotarubi, and especially Yakushiji Tenzen—who should definitely have been at the banquet last night—where did they all go?"

"Wa . . ."

"Answer me and I will give you water," Jousuke insisted. "Now speak!"

"They went to Tokaido Road . . . to kill Kazamachi Shougen . . ."

"What?" Udono Jousuke was stunned. He did not even know that Shougen was returning on the Tokaido Road. "What happened? Hunh, so that hawk carrying the scroll back from Sunpu—it must have been something important. What did that scroll say?"

Jingorou's lips resembled wilted leaves. They fluttered, but no sound emerged. He wanted to speak. His desire for water made him ready to do anything—the pain he suffered was hundreds of times worse than the agony of a burn victim lacking anesthetic.

Tucking Jingorou's body under his arm like an empty sack, Jousuke stood.

He looked over at Gennosuke's room. He thought about running to Gennosuke and telling him about Amayo Jingorou's confession. But Jousuke remembered that when he had gotten his hands on the scroll, Gennosuke ordered him to hand it over to Iga and didn't even let him look at it. *So I'm not going to tell him yet*, Jousuke decided in a fit of pique. Rather than immediately informing Gennosuke, he would first pry more information from this creature—and shock Gennosuke with it. A reasonable plan, he thought.

"You want water?" Jousuke asked.

The thing nodded. Jousuke walked with it toward the high-pitched sound of rushing water.

A black-painted wall ringed with spikes surrounded Ogen's mansion on three sides. On the side facing the mountain, the earthen wall had been replaced with boulders. But it would be impossible to slip through this area. A waterfall came rushing down from the sky fifteen feet overhead. It had scooped a crater out of the rocks below— a tremendous waterfall pool.

"There's water right there," Jousuke shouted, hurling Amayo Jingorou onto a boulder. "Tell me about the scroll."

Amayo Jingorou was dying of thirst. Jousuke's intention was to torture him into answering questions by letting him hear rushing water. Amayo Jingorou's arms, which had not previously moved, twisted and fluttered in the direction of the waterfall.

"The scroll . . ." Amayo gasped, ". . . announces that Hattori Hanzou's ban on warfare . . . has been ended. The shogun has ordered . . . that ten ninjas be selected from both Iga and Kouga . . . and that there shall be a battle between these two sides."

Udono Jousuke trembled violently, partly because of Jingorou's words, but also because the misty spray from the waterfall affected him.

"Who—who are those ten people?" Jousuke asked sternly.

"On the Kouga side: Kouga Danjou, Kouga Gennosuke, Jimushi Juubei, Kasumi Gyoubu . . . Udono Jousuke . . ."

"I knew it! Forget Kouga, tell me about Iga!" Jousuke's voice swelled with menace. "Tell me the names of the ten Iga fighters!"

"Water, water, please . . ."

Amayo Jingorou was also trembling. But Jousuke did not realize that Jingorou's shudders were not from fear— rather, they were the delighted tremors that withered plants make upon receiving droplets of rain. Jousuke also did not see Jingorou's skin reacting to the water spray. A thin blue mold had begun spreading on the surface of his body.

"Tell me the names of the Iga fighters," Jousuke yelled, "and I will give you all the water you want!"

"Ogen, Oboro, Yashamaru, Azuki Rousai, Yakushiji Tenzen . . ."

"And?" demanded Jousuke.

"Amayo."

Without listening to him finish, Udono Jousuke kicked at the creature. Like a leech, Jingorou grabbed his ankle and clung to it. Jousuke shouted as he slipped from the boulder, not from fear of falling, but with surprise that Jingorou had regained his strength.

The two of them, entangled together, tumbled into the waterfall pool. "I knew it!" Jousuke's shriek echoed in the air even after both of them were submerged.

Struggling against the spinning current, Jousuke's hand still gripped his sword.

Although Jousuke had shrieked in panic, he had complete confidence when it came to hand-to-hand underwater combat. Jousuke had always won every water competition in Kouga. His ball-like shape allowed him to float. Meanwhile, his opponent, Amayo Jingorou, was the size of a child and didn't even have a weapon.

In the swirling darkness of the whirlpool, the two figures turned circles. Jousuke clutched Jingorou in one hand and swung his sword with the other. At that moment, his opponent shifted his shape.

Amayo Jingorou's entire body swelled in size. Reflexively, Jousuke let go. When Jousuke tried to grab him again, Amayo's wet body slipped through his fingers. The whirlpool swung Jousuke around in another circle, and in the midst of the twisting and turning, he lost the sword. Amayo disappeared.

Like an angry blowfish, Jousuke expanded in size and bobbed upward. But as he rose toward the surface, he saw something terrifying. Overhead—his back tucked into a hollow spot in a boulder—a man watched him with inflamed eyes and the swollen discolored skin of a drowning victim. That decomposing skin emitted a haunting phosphorescent glow. The creature nonchalantly curled back its lips, revealing a sword it held in its mouth. Amayo Jingorou had returned for the kill.

It was the last thing Udono Jousuke saw in his life. When the whirlpool sent his body around the third time, and his rotund belly bobbed to the surface, Jousuke had already been sliced open from end to end with a sword.

"Amayo Jingorou did this to me—" Jousuke's groan was swallowed in the roar of the waterfall. Amayo's laughter reverberated off the stone walls.

On this spring night, Kouga Gennosuke slept in the heart of the Iga palace, dreaming. A secret ninja war had begun and four Kouga fighters were already dead. Only six remained.

A DEATH MASK OF MUD

1

THE SKY IN THE KOUGA SHIGARAKI VALLEY BEGAN TO lighten. It resembled light filtering through water. The valley containing the village of Manjidani remained deep in slumber.

In the depths of Kouga Danjou's palace, however, a single torch flickered. Ten or more shadowed figures sat, arms folded on their chests.

Among them was an old man. Another was well built and had a face full of whiskers. A youth was there. A woman, too. These were the leading members of Kouga, all awaiting the return of Danjou from Sunpu.

"I'm worried," one of them murmured in a low voice. Pale-faced, and with samurai hair that fell to his shoulders, he had the air of a scholar. Yet his eyes were closed. He was blind. "Remember Jimushi Juubei's fortune-telling . . ."

"Where did Juubei disappear to?" responded a man, his head bald in the style of Buddhist monks. But his head was not shaved: He had always lacked hair follicles. His baldness was not from age—he also lacked eyebrows and any trace of stubble. His skin was a half-transparent, gelatinlike color.

"Considering the speed at which his snake-belly travels, Juubei should have reached Sunpu by now," the blind ninja answered. "That is, assuming nothing happened to him. His stargazing is infallible."

"Hyouma, he told us that an evil star had appeared above Danjou. Does that mean something happened to Danjou in Sunpu?"

"I don't know, but it doesn't feel right. Worse, Gennosuke has—" The blind ninja Muroga Hyouma trailed off in a disgusted voice.

All of those present knew what he wanted to say and they felt the same way. The entire Kouga Manjidani clan maintained an icy hatred for Ogen's Iga clan. This hatred would never thaw, nor would they ever look happily upon Gennosuke's love for the granddaughter of Ogen.

Gennosuke and Udono Jousuke had been gone since the morning of the previous day. At first, the Kouga ninja had assumed they'd gone hunting, but a servant boy from the Tsubagakure Valley in Iga announced that Gennosuke would be staying with Oboro in Iga for several days and that they should not worry. The message added that Ogen had sent word from Sunpu that Kouga and Iga were now at peace. She and Danjou would travel in Edo together before returning. They shouldn't worry about that, either. The serving boy finished his announcement in a distinctly uncomfortable tone.

Some of them wanted to forget about Gennosuke's trip; others snorted at him. All at least could understand that he was visiting a woman. But they were ninja, and something in their guts felt wrong. Although nodding in response to the servant boy, an eerie premonition—like a dark cloud—had crept over them. Was the message true? Was Gennosuke safe? With four hundred years of hatred to consider, they had decided it best to gather for a meeting in Danjou's palace. The ninjas had spent a sleepless night discussing the situation.

"So it's true—Gennosuke is completely in love with Oboro," said the woman sadly. "I guess it's only a matter of time until he marries her." She sighed. This woman, with beauty resembling a tree peony, was of Kouga Danjou's lineage. Her name was Kagerou.

The hairless monk, sitting near Kagerou, spoke: "How about I travel to Iga and make sure everything is okay?"

"I already sent my younger sister to look around," another man interjected. This man was the only one in the group who did not show fear or concern on his face. He was Kisaragi Saemon, with a round, commonplace face— so incredibly average that people would meet him several times and still not remember what he looked like. He disappeared from their memory the moment he walked out

of sight. Even more amazing, not even his fellow Manjidani ninja could say for certain whether this was actually
Kisaragi Saemon's real face.

"Your sister Okoi has already gone to Iga?" asked the
hairless monk in surprise.

"I think they'd be more respectful toward a woman,"
Kisaragi Saemon answered. "And Gennosuke wouldn't
yell at her for coming after him."

"Well, then, let's wait for Okoi to return."

All sat silently, with folded arms. It was the silence
of the gods of the underworld. Finally, the blind ninja
Muroga Hyouma raised his head. "Interesting . . ."

"What is it, Hyouma?"

"Somebody is trying to slip into Manjidani . . ."

Everyone strained their ears, but the others heard
nothing. One old man placed a ninja listening device, a
kikigane, to his ear, but still could not make out any noise.

"Hyouma, which direction are the intruders approaching from?"

"North. Ninja footsteps."

North—that was the opposite direction from Iga. Naturally, it is extremely difficult to hear ninja footsteps, but the
blind ninja Hyouma could hear them from two miles away.

"It must be Danjou coming back. Or Shougen—"

"No. Those feet do not belong to Kouga ninja." Muroga Hyouma remained frozen, his ear cocked to the side.
"Five are coming. Bloodlust is in their movements."

"Understood. Servant girl—hurry to the village and tell everyone. Until we give the signal, nobody should go out on the street or make a sound."

The hairless monk stood up. His name was Kasumi Gyoubu. "I'm going to spy on them first." Like wind, he silently swept from the room.

2

FIVE SHADOWS SCAMPERED THROUGH THE DAWN MIST toward Manjidani. By placing a paper door on the surface of the water, the ninja crossed streams and moats. They had learned to walk across the paper door without breaking through its surface. Naturally, they made no sounds. None of the spring frogs around them even paused in their croaking.

The ninja were the ones who had murdered Kazamachi Shougen and Jimushi Juubei on the Tokaido Road: Yakushiji Tenzen, old Azuki Rousai, Chikuma Koshirou, the wild-haired Mino Nenki, and Hotarubi.

No different than the valley containing the village of Tsubagakure, the village here was booby-trapped with dead-end alleys. They had been to Kouga before when they served as ambassadors responding to the engagement of Gennosuke and Oboro. However, at that time, Kouga guards had watched over them and guided them through the valley. Now they were trying to enter on their own, and nothing seemed familiar. Moreover, this time they came as enemies, the opening salvo of a ninja war. Their skin crawled from worry.

"It seems like everyone is still asleep," Mino Nenki murmured.

"No," old Azuki Rousai said, looking around uncomfortably.

"Don't worry," Yakushiji Tenzen said, shaking his head. "It's impossible for anyone to have noticed us."

Only Yakushiji Tenzen could guide the group; he seemed as familiar with Manjidani as he was with Tsubagakure.

"Even if they do notice us," Yakushiji Tenzen continued, "I've got a good explanation prepared. We tell them that Gennosuke has ordered Kasumi Gyoubu, Kisaragi Saemon, Muroga Hyouma, Kagerou, and Okoi to come to Iga."

"So we lure them into a trap."

"Those five would probably not be fooled by such a story. I doubt it'd work. But we can use that as an excuse if we're caught. Hopefully, we'll be able to rush down upon each of them, one by one, slaughtering them all. First, we go to Muroga Hyouma's home—"

This conversation was not spoken. Rather, they communicated by silently mouthing the words as they breathed.

Tenzen looked at the sky and smiled. "Amazing—that zelkova tree has really grown since my last visit. When I was a child, it was the same height as I was—"

The zelkova tree must have been 170 or 180 years old. Towering above them, its branches reached into the cloudy dawn sky. But as the ninja passed by the ancient tree with its heavy, drooping branches, they had the sensation that it was reaching out to grab them as its enemies.

Tenzen scanned the area and saw no sign of lookouts. He turned back toward the others. "Don't think this will be easy! Remember how difficult it was to defeat Kazamachi Shougen, and he was just one person." As soon as he said the words, Tenzen's feet froze and his eyes darted around. "Something . . ."

"Tenzen, what is it?"

"Someone or something is very close."

They were in a narrow road, sandwiched on either side by old earthen walls. The morning fog crawled along the ground, but there were no signs of people.

Chikuma Koshirou and Mino Nenki swiftly scaled the earthen walls. They lay flat and slid smoothly along the tiles, peering over to the other side. "There's nobody there."

Tenzen nodded and shrugged his shoulders. "Strange. Well, let's go."

He continued moving forward. Following him, in a murderous mass, were the other four: Nenki, Hotarubi, Chikuma Koshirou, and finally old Azuki Rousai.

Ten steps later, they realized that Azuki Rousai had disappeared.

"What happened?"

Swiftly returning, they discovered Rousai in a strange posture, his back against the earthen wall.

Rousai's legs seemed to have been swallowed into the ground. The upper half of his body was like a shrimp, curled over so that his head was at his ankles. Struggling, Rousai tried to escape from the wall, but he couldn't even move. Behind him, some kind of shadow had grabbed him and held him down.

Escaping suddenly, Rousai pitched forward toward the dirt. As he fell, Azuki Rousai swung his foot backward, slamming like a hammer into the earthen wall and smashing a hole through it. Rousai had incredibly powerful legs. The wall emitted a groan. Something seemed to be stirring within the wall, but the Iga ninja couldn't see anybody there.

"The wall stole my sword!" Azuki Rousai leaped to his feet, his face dusted with dirt. "It spoke into my ear, saying: *Iga fighters, don't you know that the walls of Manjidani have ears!*"

At that moment, a short distance away, an eerie smile seemed to form on the wall.

"Big trouble . . ." Yakushiji Tenzen murmured.

Laughter raced along the wall, vanishing into the morning mist: "Come out!" it shouted, its scratchy voice echoing in the valley. "Fiends from Iga have entered Manjidani!"

Suddenly, shouts roared from both ends of the street.

Petrified, the five Iga ninja realized that they had stumbled into an ambush. Intending to slip into Manjidani undetected, they had instead walked into a trap. Even worse, their secret conversation had been overheard by a "wall with ears."

"No—no, you've misunderstood!" Yakushiji Tenzen waved his hand in panic. "We're not attacking! We've come as messengers from Tsubagakure! We have important news from Gennosuke!"

"Don't tell us lies—why would Iga messengers come from the north?" ridiculed the voice. "I've heard you talking and I know your plots! Catch them!"

The morning mist was dispelled under a swarm of onrushing feet.

"We've come this far—" Yakushiji Tenzen cried to his companions, his face turning pale. "Before we retreat, let's show them what we can do! Ready?"

"What do you have that can match our Kouga fighters?" yelled a voice from the onrushing crowd of Kouga warriors.

Swoosh. In answer, one of the Iga ninja drew a scythe from his waist! Chikuma Koshirou stepped forward, holding his weapon.

The charging swarm of Kouga warriors, blades drawn, bore down upon Chikuma Koshirou. But when they saw him so calmly and fearlessly awaiting their onslaught, the Kouga warriors were so shocked that they froze for a moment. Only a moment. A second later, they were charging furiously again. But that second was all the time that Koshirou needed to strike.

He pursed his lips. *Shuu*. A sound whistled in the empty air.

Immediately, the closest two or three Kouga warriors— about ten feet away—warped in agony, their faces bending, split open, like ripened pomegranates.

"*Uhghh*—"

Dying moans and gasps of horror.

Most of the surrounding Kouga fighters couldn't see what had happened. A few more surged forward, past their fallen comrades. Immediately, their faces ripped apart, and they collapsed to the ground. Those surrounding them fell back, running like an avalanche.

"Let's get out of here!" Tenzen shouted. The group of five Iga fighters sliced through the crowd of confusion.

Mino Nenki's club groaned. Azuki Rousai's four limbs struck madly, becoming a whirlwind. The ground was muddied with blood.

Dead bodies piled up—broken shinbones on bodies killed by Nenki's club and smashed ribs on bodies killed by Rousai's feet. But the most horrifying corpses belonged to the victims of Chikuma Koshirou. It looked like fireworks had exploded inside their heads. Eyeballs burst from their sockets. Noses and mouths split away from their faces.

Coming from the other side of the street, another swarm of attackers rushed upon the Iga ninja. Fighting through a heap of blood and bones, Chikuma Koshirou clasped his giant scythe and again pursed his mouth. As air rustled across his lips, people's heads ripped apart as if a spike had been driven through them.

Was anything capable of defending against Chikuma Koshirou's powers? He did not blow air, nor did anything shoot from his mouth. He did not spit any weapons. Rather, he was sucking air with such violent power that he caused tiny whirlwinds to appear. A vacuum formed within the center of each whirlwind, which ripped apart victims' flesh, the same as if they'd been torn open by his scythe.

Chikuma Koshirou hadn't been able to use this technique during the battle with Kazamachi Shougen because Shougen's phlegm had clogged his nostrils.

As the Kouga attack turned into mob panic, the mysterious voice sounded again. "Why are you quivering? What are you afraid of? If you are worthy of being called Kouga warriors, don't let them escape!"

The Kouga samurai gritted their teeth and charged into battle again. Even Chikuma Koshirou's vacuum whirlwinds would not be able to stop such a huge crowd of onrushing warriors. But—just before the renewed Kouga charge reached the Iga ninja—a huge, cloudlike substance engulfed the Kouga samurai.

Butterflies! Thousands upon thousands of butterflies. An infinity of butterflies swarmed, blocking the vision of the Kouga samurai—blocking them from even breathing! The butterflies rose up in a huge tornadolike mass and flew over the wall.

When the Kouga fighters looked around, they realized that the five Iga ninjas had vanished.

"Over there!"

"They're fleeing that way!"

The Kouga samurai chased after the tornado of butterflies.

Meanwhile, going the opposite direction, Yakushiji Tenzen chuckled.

"Kouga will be full of confusion and gossip tonight! Now they can ponder the ninja talents of Iga."

As the Iga ninja fled toward home, the tornado of butterflies continued leading the pursuing Kouga fighters in the wrong direction.

Meanwhile, four Kouga ninja—Kasumi Gyoubu, Kisaragi Saemon, Muroga Hyouma, and Kagerou—gathered together.

"So this is how Iga's emissaries greet us? Well, now we understand each other. They better expect the blood to flow at Tsubagakure Valley as well! Let's send them some more Kouga guests and repay their pleasantries!"

When they spoke about sending "more" Kouga guests, they were thinking of Kouga Gennosuke, trapped in the enemy palace.

Far away, the Iga ninja laughter faded into the forest.

3

THE FIVE IGA NINJA TRAVELING BACK TO TOKI PASS were dyed red from head to foot with blood. It did not come solely from their enemies. Nenki's club was broken, Rousai had wrenched his foot on a broken chain, and Yakushiji Tenzen had a deep knife wound in the side of his cheek.

They couldn't claim victory. Their attack had not killed any of the Kouga ninja on the list. Worse, they had revealed that a ninja war had begun.

"Well, since the secret is out now, we should kill Gennosuke as soon as possible," Nenki growled.

Tenzen remained silent while the others gritted their teeth and nodded their heads. Tenzen's silence signified that killing Gennosuke would be no easy task.

Tenzen halted, and looked up into the awe-inspiring beauty of the mountain pass. "Hey—look at that," he said, pointing.

"That's the girl Okoi from Kouga."

Tenzen's eyes darted around. "All right," he ordered. "She's coming this way. Everyone hide. We're going to capture her and take her to Tsubagakure Valley."

Like five hunting dogs, they hid in the thick vegetation. The woman approached.

She had a voluptuous, gorgeous, fleshy body. Her large eyes shone brightly, and even from a distance, one could smell her scent of flowers. Her legs and arms seemed especially white and ample in the dark shadows cast by the cloudy sky. Mino Nenki whistled and she froze. Okoi was Kisaragi Saemon's sister.

Okoi dropped into the fighting posture of a female panther, ready to spring. She watched as Yakushiji Tenzen, Mino Nenki, and Hotarubi appeared before her. Taking a few steps back, she suddenly discovered Azuki Rousai and Chikuma Koshirou blocking her escape.

"So here you are—Okoi from Manjidani," Tenzen said with a gentle laugh. "As you can see, we are from Iga, but don't be afraid. Perhaps you already know that Kouga and Iga are no longer enemies. In fact, Kouga Gennosuke is staying in the valley of Tsubagakure right now."

She knew that, but she didn't trust five Iga ninja soaked in blood. Her black eyes widened.

"Oh, this . . ." Tenzen said, following her gaze to his blood-drenched clothing. "Gennosuke sent us to Manjidani just now to meet with Muroga Hyouma, Kasumi, and the others, but they misunderstood and things got a little out of control. That's all."

Standing tall and triumphant, Okoi grinned at the thought of Kouga fighters forcing them to flee her village.

"But if we return without bringing anyone from Kouga, we'll look like fools in front of Gennosuke and Oboro. You, at least, come with us."

"Is Gennosuke okay?" Okoi spoke at last.

"Is he okay?" Tenzen snapped. "If he's not okay, then

what is he? What kind of a stupid question is that? Even if we did want to hurt him, Gennosuke can protect himself."

Okoi laughed again. She had the innocent prideful laugh of a little girl. "That's true," she said.

"Anyway, if you're worried that something might have happened to him, come along with us to Iga and see for yourself."

"Tenzen!" Chikuma Koshirou screamed, stomping his feet. Although he didn't want to chase this woman if she started to run, he'd rather not waste his time on this nonsense. Chikuma Koshirou glared at Tenzen—*Okoi is just another name that we'll need to cross off this list!*

Recognizing the menace within Koshirou's eyes, Okoi slid away. She looked cautiously at Tenzen's smiling face.

"So shall we go?" Tenzen asked.

"No. I need to go talk to everyone at Manjidani first." Okoi kicked the ground and immediately launched into the air, her voluptuous body soaring overhead like a bird. She had vaulted lightly over the heads of the three ninja blocking her path, and landed beyond them.

"Hey!" Mino Nenki screamed. He snarled at his companions, "Leave her to me!" and raced after Okoi. Nenki's long hair curled in the wind.

Okoi shot a look behind her as she fled. As soon as she saw Nenki, several streaks of light raced from her toward him. In a movement too quick for the eye to comprehend, she had hurled four or five knives at her pursuer.

"Raaugh!" Nenki roared—but not in agony. He was screaming so that Okoi would look back at him.

She looked. The four or five knives she had thrown had all been caught by Nenki's hair! His hair had twisted around the knives in midflight. His hair stood up, resembling vines creeping skyward. The knives were a twirling, magical crown on his head.

Mino Nenki's hair was alive. Autonomous from the rest of his body, his hair had its own nervous system. Nenki could use his hair to cling to trees, pillars, or rafters, and to sneak into enemy territory. Mino Nenki was not limited to four limbs—he had tens of thousands of arms and legs crawling on his head.

Terrified, Okoi appeared to have tripped, but it was Nenki who had hurled his broken club between her legs, knocking her down.

She pitched forward toward a scattering of white camellias. Nenki leaped forward and caught her. As he pressed against her, his skin musty with sweat, he laughed in violent waves of insane sexual desire.

"Wait, don't kill her, Nenki!" Yakushiji Tenzen yelled, chasing after them. "There are things I want to ask that girl."

"What?"

"We can use her to lure Gennosuke and kill him," Tenzen murmured to Nenki as he gazed on her, sobbing in the dirt. "We can cross her name off the list later."

Rain fell, whining like a wounded animal as it beat against the pine trees.

4

THE GLOOMY SKY RELEASED A TORRENT OF DREARY wind and rain. The rainwater ran red on the roads of Manjidani.

Within the Kouga clan, those bloodied in battle ached to don their armor and go forth to fight. But what had happened? It could hardly be called a surprise attack, because they had known the whole time that the Iga warriors were coming. Yet, in moments, more than a dozen Kouga fighters had been slaughtered—and the entire attacking force was able to escape!

At the time of the Iga Rebellion, Kouga and Iga had made vows, sealed in blood and confirmed through sacrificial offerings to the protective gods of their village shrines. Most important, the vows stated: "Agreed: If one side discovers an invading force approaching from another region, it shall inform the other side so that both can fight together against the invaders."

"Agreed: If anyone invades the opposing region, all shall fight against the invader, even if that means fighting one's own kinsmen, children, or siblings."

Similar vows appeared in other sections, too. The vows had been signed by the leading figures from Kouga and Iga. And yet, Iga had launched a surprise attack, insulting the gods of the covenant and of the region.

Kouga warriors bellowed with rage, insisting on invading Iga.

"Wait!" cried the blind ninja, Muroga Hyouma.

Countless eyes glared at the blind man's face. But those furious glares turned to horror as Hyouma spoke.

"We must not act rashly," Hyouma said. "Gennosuke is in the valley of Tsubagakure."

His words were like chains restraining the village warriors.

Hurriedly, the leading Kouga ninja held a council.

First—why had they been attacked? What had happened between Kouga and Iga?

And what had happened to Gennosuke in Iga?

Rain splashed on the leaves. Pallid light filtered into the conference room. Old veterans of Kouga ninja warfare breathed tensely.

Only one person remained calm: the blind ninja, Muroga Hyouma.

"Just now," he said, "we fought off their attack. I know you are angry that they escaped. But if we immediately counterattacked against Tsubagakure, we would be like mice running into a trap. If we do attack, we must expect that few of us would escape alive."

"I'm only worried that Gennosuke will be killed!" shouted an old man, his white beard trembling.

Hyouma thought for a moment, and then turned his face toward the voice, smiling faintly. "I trust Gennosuke. I don't think Iga can kill him so easily. And, anyway, Jousuke is with him."

"But—"

"Think about it. Do you really imagine that they could kill Gennosuke? It's impossible. We must think carefully. We need to think things over before striking. The question we must answer is this: The two clans will soon unite in peace. Why would Iga attack us now?"

"There must be a faction in Iga opposed to any friendship between the clans. After all, many Kouga fighters would love to attack Iga, if only Hattori Hanzou ended the ban on warfare."

"Well . . . perhaps Hattori Hanzou *has* lifted the ban on warfare," the blind ninja said.

"What?"

"Jimushi Juubei's stargazing has worried me. I fear something happened to Danjou while he was at Sunpu. Hey, Gyoubu—"

"Uh?" answered the hairless monk with the gelatinlike skin.

"A little while ago, when you had hidden yourself in the wall, you overheard some of Yakushiji Tenzen's conversation."

"Oh . . ." The hairless monk repeated what he had heard: "'Don't think this will be easy! Remember how difficult it was to defeat Kazamachi Shougen, and he was just one person.'"

"So . . ." said the blind ninja. "Now that I think of it, Shougen was returning from Sunpu. Those fiends also came from the north. In fact, they came from Tokaido Road. Hmm . . . I think . . ."

"Hyouma, what is it?"

"Shougen must have been coming back with an urgent message. I suspect that those Iga ninja killed Shougen somewhere along the Tokaido Road. That must be the secret behind Iga's morning surprise attack!"

The hairless monk Kasumi Gyoubu leaped to his feet. "I'll go to Tokaido and scout around."

Kisaragi Saemon stuffed his ninja blade into his waistband. "Gyoubu, I will go with you."

5

YASHAMARU FROM IGA RACED ALONG THE RAINY TO-kaido Road.

He was a full day behind Kazamachi Shougen. He'd already gone halfway to Iga on the Tokaido Road when he realized the scroll was missing. In shock, he had run back to Sunpu, but he could not find the scroll anywhere. Finally, he gave up and raced back toward Iga again. Fear and frustration had turned his handsome cheeks gaunt and faded. Now he looked like a white-faced Asura—a frenzied Buddhist creature of the underworld.

Yashamaru realized that the ninja scroll must have been stolen from him by either Danjou or Shougen. He also knew that while he had been searching in vain for the scroll, Shougen had probably already reached Kouga. Once they saw the list, the ninja of Manjidani would invade Iga.

Yashamaru had seen his lover's name—Hotarubi—listed among the Iga ninja. The thought of her in danger sent tremors through his body. And when he thought of what had probably happened to Oboro, he felt like he'd been hit by a heart attack.

Overwhelmed with fear and anger, Yashamaru shot forward like a fired bullet. He had just passed a station on the Tokaido Road when he heard a shout: *"Heyyyy!"*

He ignored it, but then it came again: *"Heyyyyyyy, Yashamaru!"*

Yashamaru froze.

Only the day before, a fierce battle between Yakushiji Tenzen and Jimushi Juubei had taken place in a thicket nearby, but Yashamaru knew nothing about that. All he knew was that this voice sounded familiar.

"Is that you, Tenzen?" he shouted, and looked around.

But he saw no one. An old temple's earthen wall stood on one side. On the opposite side was a stone wall. Sandwiched by walls, Yashamaru saw only diagonal sheets of silvery rain smacking the ground. For a while, silence answered him.

"Yes, it's me, Yakushiji Tenzen," came the gloomy response. It was definitely Tenzen's voice.

"Tenzen, where are you?" Yashamaru asked.

"Well, you can't see me right now, Yashamaru. But what happened in Sunpu?"

"I've got important news—" he panted. Yashamaru halted in midsentence. He didn't know how to start telling Tenzen about losing the scroll. "Anyway, Tenzen, why can't you show your body?" he asked in a low voice. "Is it because you were murdered?"

What a strange question! But Yashamaru asked it naturally. He stood in the middle of the rain, asking questions of a dead man.

"Was it Kazamachi Shougen from Kouga who killed you?" Yashamaru continued.

"Uh . . ." The voice groaned vaguely, and then continued: "Yes, I was killed by Kazamachi Shougen."

"Oh, I see. I'm sorry for that. I also had a ninja scroll, but Danjou stole it from me. It's good that only one of us was killed. Is everyone else on the list okay?"

Tenzen's voice sounded surprised. "Yashamaru, what is this ninja scroll you're talking about?"

"Tenzen, when we were in Sunpu, the shogun informed us that the Hattori family had ended its ban on warfare!"

"*What?* The ban is over?" The voice changed. Yashamaru leaped back.

"You're not Tenzen! Who are you?"

Yashamaru spotted a shadow moving on the other side of the earthen wall. The shadow dashed away from him like a gust of wind, leaving behind tiles still creaking from where its feet had been. Yashamaru swiveled, following the shadow's movements. Like a flash of dark lightning, his rope snapped out—and, thirty feet away, it snagged the fleeing shadow. The figure screamed in agony and collapsed on the road.

"So you were trying to trick me, huh?" Yashamaru leaped upon the man, pinning him down. Yashamaru's entire body convulsed with fury. This person—and his amazing vocal cords—had fooled him into revealing Iga's secrets. "Are you from Kouga?" Yashamaru demanded.

The rope tightened around his enemy's body. Despite excruciating agony, the man said nothing.

"Tell me your name! Speak!" Unlike Tenzen, Yashamaru didn't know the ninja from Manjidani. The man twisted his head around, but it was a face that Yashamaru didn't recognize. The rope constricted further, tearing through the prisoner's skin.

"Ki—Ki—Kisaragi . . . Saemon . . ." the man gasped.

Unconsciously, a smile flittered across Yashamaru's beautiful face. Kisaragi Saemon—he had seen that name on the scroll! So perhaps his trip to Sunpu wasn't such a failure after all! He could bring the Iga clan a souvenir from his travels—news of this ninja's death! With this victory, he could show his face again at Iga! Yashamaru smoothly pulled out a mountain sword, his hand trembling with joy. "Saemon—this rope will continue torturing you in hell!"

Yashamaru raised his sword to cleave off Kisaragi Saemon's head. But a huge fist seized his arm. Something had suddenly appeared behind him.

As an expert ninja, Yashamaru's talents went far beyond his rope fighting. His eyes, ears, even his skin—all of his senses should have recognized this attacker's presence behind him! Yashamaru hadn't seen anyone else on the street during his fight with Saemon. But someone had somehow appeared behind him and grabbed his arm.

Before he could even look back, the attacker's other hand closed around his neck. As Yashamaru's eyes bulged from his head, he saw the hand choking him. It was the same color as the earthen wall. As Yashamaru went dizzy, his brain told him that the hand had reached out of the wall itself. But was that possible? Or was it the lack of oxygen . . .

He never had the chance to make a sound. Yashamaru of Iga was strangled to death.

Yashamaru's body crumpled on top of Kisaragi Saemon, the two of them becoming a heap on the road. Silver rain pelted Yashamaru's back. No sound, no movement. Only rain.

No—that wasn't true. The wall from which the two arms had grown began to squirm. Something huge and transparent, like a flattened jellyfish, expanded outward from the wall. Bursting out—a naked person . . . a hairless monk with gelatin skin.

Kasumi Gyoubu laughed softly as he stood over Yashamaru's dead body. Gyoubu had already separated himself from the wall. He had also used his occult camouflage technique to terrify Azuki Rousai at Manjidani.

Gyoubu dragged Yashamaru away from Kisaragi Saemon's body. He then took the mountain sword from Yashamaru's fist and used it to slice his throat. Warm blood spread from Yashamaru's body and awakened Saemon from his blackout.

"That was close," Saemon said, laughing bitterly. "I was so stunned by what he was saying that I forgot to continue imitating Yakushiji Tenzen's voice."

Gyoubu returned to where he had stashed his clothes, a short distance from the wall, and put them back on. Staring at Yashamaru's terrifying rope, Kisaragi Saemon sighed.

"I didn't want to kill him," Kasumi Gyoubu said, returning. "I just wanted to bring him close to death, but once I started I couldn't help myself." The two of them had traveled eastward looking for Kazamachi Shougen when they unexpectedly spotted Yashamaru running toward them. They decided to try to trick Yashamaru into revealing information, but they killed him before they had learned much. "Anyway, I doubt he would say much even if we tortured him," Gyoubu said.

"Even so, he revealed some amazing information. Tokugawa Ieyasu has ended the ban on warfare between the clans."

"So Muroga Hyouma was right! But what was Yashamaru saying about a list of names on a scroll?"

The two of them looked at Yashamaru's dead body with frustration and regret.

They remembered something else that Yashamaru had said—but they didn't understand what it meant. Yashamaru had asked Tenzen: *Is it because you were murdered?*

If only they had understood those words, Kisaragi Saemon would have been able to avoid his dark fate—a line of red blood through his name.

At that moment, however, Gyoubu and Saemon were gazing toward the western mountain range.

"We must go to Tsubagakure."

"We need to make sure that Gennosuke is safe!"

Kisaragi Saemon crouched down. He extended his hands toward the ground, which was muddy from rain. He heaped up dirt and mud, carefully leveling the top. Then he took Yashamaru's face and softly pressed it into the tiny mud plateau.

After a while, he cast aside the dead body. The imprint of Yashamaru's face remained in the mud. The imprint was so exquisite that it matched even the tiny lines of Yashamaru's eyelashes. Kisaragi Saemon knelt before it, and pressed his own face into that mud death mask.

Minutes passed. During that time, the hairless monk Kasumi Gyoubu stripped Yashamaru's body of his clothes, and then carried the naked corpse away.

When Gyoubu returned, Saemon was still facedown in the mud. His position resembled the praying position of Indian religious ascetics.

Another few minutes passed. Kisaragi Saemon slowly lifted his face. But it was the face of Yashamaru!

"Looks good," Gyoubu said, grinning. Although he already knew about Saemon's special ability, his eyes still shone with admiration.

"We don't have time to go back and warn Kouga," Kisaragi Saemon said as he put on Yashamaru's clothing. He laughed. "But no one in Kouga is better suited for sneaking into Tsubagakure and rescuing Gennosuke than you and I!"

Kisaragi Saemon stuffed the black rope in his waistband and rose to his feet. He had a handsome figure, with cherry blossom cheeks, shiny black eyes, and a rapid, powerful laugh. He had become Yashamaru of Iga.

HELL OF HUMAN FLESH

1

THE HEAVY EARTHEN DOOR CREAKED OPEN.

Through the slight opening, flashes emanated from the outside world. It was not yet dawn, but the steadily pounding rain reflected light.

A person entered, holding a pine tar torch. His other hand closed the door, enclosing him in the dark storehouse. His white hair floated in the air. He was old Azuki Rousai.

"Girl——" he called in a hoarse voice.

Okoi, who was stretched out on the floor, lifted her head. She had become disheveled during her attempt to escape from the attackers the day before. Her clothes had torn, revealing voluptuous flesh. Nothing about her appearance had changed from when they kidnapped her at the Toki Pass.

Rousai walked over and stuffed his torch between the rows of sacks heaped in this storage room. Then he sat down on one of the sacks, which was made of woven straw. These did not contain rice. The straw sacks had suffered gashes and rips in many places, and white flecks leaked out. This was the salt storehouse. In the torchlight, the old man's sunken eyeballs shone bright red. Those fierce eyes stared at the loose flesh of his prisoner, who looked younger than twenty years old.

"Now, if you answer my questions," Azuki Rousai said, "you might be able to get out of here alive. So if you care about life, answer truthfully." He pulled the ninja scroll from his kimono. "First of all, what are the special ninja skills of that blind man Muroga Hyouma?"

Silence.

"What about the woman named Kagerou? What skills does she have?" Rousai asked, staring at the scroll.

Earlier, Tenzen had asked Jimushi Juubei these same questions and had received no answer. No secret was more precious to the ninja clans than their secret ninja techniques. Knowledge of opponents' techniques was the key to killing them. In ninja battles, a single mistake or missed opportunity could lead to death.

"Tell me what Kisaragi Saemon looks like. Is he young? Old? Dark-skinned? Light-skinned?"

Okoi's lips twisted into a slight grin. Kisaragi Saemon was her older brother.

"Answer!"

"Do you think that I would tell you?" Okoi answered, without breaking her smile.

To reveal a ninja technique is equivalent to filming mystical secrets: When touched by the light of day, they lose their powers. Ninja uphold a solemn rule of secrecy to prevent the revelation of their secrets. Not only do they not speak about their skills to outsiders, they cannot even instruct their own parents, children, or siblings without permission. Hattori Hanzou noted this in his *Discussion of Ninja Secrets*: "These are great secrets that must be hidden from even the closest confidantes." A member of Kouga would never reveal the clan's ninja secrets to Iga, not even if the sky and earth ripped open.

But Rousai continued his interrogation. "And tell me about your own techniques," he commanded coldly. "Girl, don't think you can refuse to answer me. Watch—"

Still sitting on the sacks, he wound one arm back and casually punched a sack. He did not punch particularly quickly and he was not holding any weapons, yet mere contact with the sack caused it to explode open, like it had been chopped by a battle-axe. Salt poured down to the floor. Okoi's eyes swelled wide open. This old man's fist was far more powerful than any sword.

"So, then . . ." Rousai snarled. "Shall I cut off your ear first? What's next—an arm? Or your breasts?"

Okoi shut her eyes, clasping herself tight. Her pure white shoulders trembled. Smiling faintly, Rousai stood up and grabbed her shoulder.

He grabbed her shoulder as a warm-up to striking her. He started to threaten her again, but the words froze—

His face twisted in shock. He could not pull away the hand that had touched her shoulder!

Azuki Rousai dropped the scroll from his other hand. Panicking, he reflexively grabbed Okoi's other shoulder with that hand. But when he tried to pull back his arms, he could not get them free. They were glued to the girl's shoulders.

"Ughh, you little—!" Screaming, Rousai bent the lower half of his body, warping into the shape of a bow. His legs wound up to kick her—but at that same moment, Okoi's legs attacked him. Her legs coiled around Rousai's waist. The two of them collapsed in a heap. Rousai struggled but could not rip his hands from her shoulders.

Beneath him, Okoi's breath came hot and fiery on Rousai's chin. "As you wished, I'll show you my ninja technique," she said. Her lips attached to his neck and sucked.

Rousai tilted his head back, shaking his white hair. His head looked like the dance of the lions from kabuki theater. But the woman's lips did not separate from his windpipe. The old man's eyes bulged. His skin shriveled like a withering leaf. His face became the discolored white of paper.

Several minutes passed before Okoi lifted her head. She twisted her shoulders in a strange way and pulled free of Rousai's stiff, clutching hands. She stood up silently. The old man had been transformed into a mummy, hardened and frozen on the floor.

Nobody could have expected that this old ninja—so terrifying during the assault on Manjidani—could be swiftly killed by a young weaponless girl.

Two red handprints remained on Okoi's revealed shoulders. She smiled and wiped them with her ripped sleeve. This only turned the handprints purple. She walked to the side of the sacks and stooped over. A fat string of blood slowly drizzled out of her mouth.

She continued regurgitating blood until it turned the entire sack of salt red. This was not her blood—it belonged to Azuki Rousai. This gorgeous woman, so full of wild beauty, was a vampire. No wonder Azuki Rousai could not escape her grasp!

Her skills were not limited to sucking blood. A slight wriggle of her body could transform her skin from seductive soft flesh into something with the power of octopus suckers. She had used this technique to glue Azuki Rousai's hands to her skin.

Okoi picked up the fallen scroll.

Before she had a chance to read it, however, she sensed someone approaching from outside. She hurriedly shoved the rolled-up scroll between two sacks, and she dumped salt over Azuki Rousai's corpse. Then she flopped back into her original position.

The earthen door opened and a man came inside.

2

HE HAD A DROWNED MAN'S FACE, CRAWLING WITH BLUE mold—Amayo Jingorou.

Jingorou had only intended to peek inside, but the

sight of the woman lying on the floor under a blazing torch caused him to enter and close the door behind him. He leered at her.

"Hey!" he barked. "Azuki Rousai must have just come in here. An old man with white hair."

Okoi was trembling and crying.

"I can tell that he came in here," Jingorou said, "because his torch is still burning. So did he finish his interrogations and leave?"

"Unfortunately . . ." Okoi moaned.

"Ha ha ha ha. So you admit it. Even if you are a Kouga ninja, you're still a woman, and there was no way that you could withstand him. It must have been very painful."

"Kill me . . . After the torture he put me through, I don't want to live . . . I want to die. But first . . . let me feel what it's like to be a woman once before I die . . ."

"What?"

"I don't want to die without knowing what it's like to be a woman," she repeated.

He snatched Okoi's black hair and jerked her head back. Her lips began trembling, and tears ran down her cheeks. Her tears resembled camellia petals. Thick and soft, they moistened her lips.

She seemed completely defenseless.

Jingorou bit her lips. The girl tried to twist her face away, but Jingorou just grinned. "Rousai, he might have been healthy for an old man, but I'm the lucky one who will enjoy your beauty."

His breath came out like flames, and he swiftly stripped off his clothes. Okoi was already close to nakedness. This woman was like a female panther, and she was a member of the archenemy Kouga clan. Rather than take any chances, they planned to kill her the next morning after interrogating her all night. But, overwhelmed with lust, Jingorou forgot the danger.

Jingorou's body, crawling with blue mold, leaned over Okoi.

One minute—two minutes—indescribable groans burst forth from Jingorou's lips, and his entire body jerked in agony. Excruciating pain covered his body, as if thousands of leeches were sucking his blood. Jingorou arced backward, his body writhing, but Okoi remained glued to his body. Her beautiful lips fastened upon Jingorou's windpipe. The two of them twisted into a bizarre formation, rolling upon the ground.

In another minute, Jingorou would be dead. But they rolled onto the salt that had been spilled across the floor.

"Ah—"

Okoi cried out in confusion. She had been sucking on her opponent's flesh, but now he smoothly slid out of her grasp. Upon being coated in salt, Jingorou's body rapidly turned gooey, slimy, and wet. He dissolved into a shrunken pool of goo.

Okoi gasped and bounced to her feet. The embryo-like creature beneath her feet was wriggling. Like a night-marish vision, the shrunken beast—neither human nor anything else—fled into the gap between the salt bags, leaving only a sticky trail of slime.

Paralyzed with fear, Okoi watched it escape without reacting. But then she saw the sword he had left on top of his discarded clothes. She smoothly picked up the sheath, slid out the blade, and approached the rows of salt sacks.

Just then, the door opened for the third time. Okoi looked back, and her face changed as soon as she saw him. Mino Nenki.

Without a word, Okoi sliced her sword at him diagonally. He leaped away, but her blade sliced his kimono open from shoulder to waist. She struck again, slicing through his club. The end of the club went flying away, but Mino Nenki ignored it and charged her, snatching her in his grasp.

"What are you—?" he shouted. Most of her clothes had been ripped away and hung limply from her body.

But Okoi wanted it that way. She knew she could not beat Nenki in a swordfight. But she also knew that she couldn't use the same trick as she had with Amayo Jingorou, luring him in with seductive words.

Okoi flung her naked body at Nenki, pressing her flesh against his. This was the only way she could kill him.

She was a young virgin girl. She was beautiful, but she also had a fierce determination. As a member of Kouga, she was well trained in ninja techniques. Death did not frighten her. She had summoned her strength to kill Azuki Rousai. Although she was ashamed of touching Amayo

Jingorou, she had repelled him. She needed to read that scroll! What did it say? She wanted to steal it and take it to Kouga after making sure that Gennosuke was safe. With these goals in mind, she hung tight against Nenki, coiling her burning-hot arms around his body. She pressed her breasts against him, even as disgust sent shudders rippling through her.

Mino Nenki snatched Okoi's hair in one hand and twisted her face to one side. The girl's mouth hung open, panting. Her tongue trembled. He stared deep into her throat as if desiring to lick every inch. Her rear molars looked like a line of pearls and her throat resembled red silk stretched taut.

"What happened to Rousai and Jingorou?" he demanded, his voice scratchy. Even as he asked the question, Nenki became insane with lust. His breathing became thick and bestial desire overwhelmed him as he sniffed the scent of mountain flowers on Okoi's breath. He tumbled to the ground with her.

"Nenki—she's dangerous—" A tiny voice as soft as an insect cried out from behind the sacks of salt.

Nenki did not hear it. She was indeed dangerous: He was the third man lured into this vampire's sensual trap.

When Okoi pulled tight into an embrace with Nenki, she had shuddered in disgust at the thick mass of black fur that covered his chest, arms, back—every place that his clothes had covered!

There is a handful of people—sometimes called

"wolfmen"—who are born with their entire bodies covered in fur. Their hairiness originates from a mutation that causes everything, including their entire face, to be covered in thick fur. Not just their cheeks and chins—fur covers their foreheads and noses as well. They barely resemble humans.

Everything hidden by Nenki's clothes was actually covered in thick hair. For Okoi, it was as horrible as if she were tightly embracing a bear or a monkey. Nenki pressed down upon her, creating an image like some ghastly painting of a woman being attacked by a wild beast.

"Muuh . . ." A groan sounded, but from whose lips?

"She's dangerous, Nenki—" Once again, the weird voice chirped. Amayo's voice.

Did he hear it or not? Nenki's face changed color and his hair stood on end.

The one writhing in agony was Okoi. Their bodies were glued together, but fresh blood began to well in between them. Nenki's body hair had not merely stood on end—it had become porcupinelike spikes. This wasn't hair—these were needles!

Okoi tried to scream, but Nenki bit her lips and did not let go. Countless needles pierced her chest and belly and thighs. Squeezing tight against the writhing woman, Nenki's eyes turned bloodred, and he convulsed with pleasure.

It was a pool of blood, a hell of needles.

Tremors of death and ecstasy rocked their bodies.

Nenki did not notice the man and woman who had entered the storehouse behind him.

3

"NENKI!" THE WOMAN SHOUTED.

He lifted his head at the woman's voice, but it was the man who made Nenki's eyes grow wide. "Yashamaru!" he cried.

Standing before him were Yashamaru of Iga and Hotarubi.

"Yashamaru, when did you come back?"

"Now," Yashamaru answered curtly. He did not look at Nenki or the dead woman. He stared at the dark, oily smoke rising from the flame of the pine torch.

"What happened when you were at Sunpu with Grandmother?"

"Grandmother? . . . Well, before I can tell you, I need to meet with Oboro."

"So you haven't met with Oboro yet?"

"I heard that she was busy discussing something important with Tenzen, so I came to see you first."

"I see," Nenki said. "Well, it won't be easy for Tenzen to convince Oboro to fight with us. The ninja war between Iga and Kouga has already begun, and Tenzen won't tell Oboro. He thinks Oboro is too much in love with Gennosuke."

"So Gennosuke is alive?"

"That's right. Tenzen is too afraid of him! I doubt his basilisk eyes are that powerful. Hmmph. Of the ten Kouga ninjas on the list, we killed Kazamachi Shougen and Jimushi Juubei on the Tokaido Road. We killed Udono Jousuke last night in the palace. Just a few moments ago, I killed Okoi. What are you shrinking back for?" Mino Nenki snickered. He stood up, revealing the millions of shining droplets of blood hanging from his body hair.

For the first time, Yashamaru looked at the dead woman. Okoi's naked body had been painted red with blood. He dry-heaved in horror, and felt his body become weak.

Okoi. My Kouga girl—you died here a prisoner, in such a horrible way. You were all alone in this hellish storeroom, demonic beasts coming and going, torturing you to death. Your ghost will be tortured by bitterness for eternity. But at least you fought back bravely and sent one of your attackers to his death.

Yashamaru mumbled his sad words.

"What? What did you say, Yashamaru?"

"Nothing. Nothing at all. I said that you did a great job."

"Great job—don't be an idiot. She was just a lone girl. Actually, I didn't intend to kill her, but she used an unusual technique to attack me. I couldn't help but kill her. Anyway, that girl was on the ninja scroll list, so her days were already numbered."

"The ninja scroll list?"

"Yashamaru, don't you know about the ninja scroll?" Nenki looked back at him suspiciously.

Yashamaru looked down, and then sat down on a sack of salt. "I'm tired . . ." His words were a mumble. He reached out and took Okoi's listlessly stretched-out hand. With a start, he realized that her soul had not yet departed—she was breathing her last breaths at that moment.

"It's natural for you to be exhausted, Yashamaru," Hotarubi said, looking at Yashamaru anxiously. "You ran all the way back here from Sunpu."

Hotarubi looked at Yashamaru with the eyes of a lover. She and Yashamaru were engaged. When he returned safely, she went insane with joy.

"Ugh . . . I need a nap," Yashamaru said, yawning slightly. His finger touched the tip of Okoi's finger.

"Well, then, Yashamaru, hurry over to see Oboro so you can get some rest," Hotarubi said. Her voice was gentle and yet concerned.

Mino Nenki snorted at them. "Anyway, Old Rousai and Amayo should be here," he said with a bitter smile. "Where are they? Especially Old Rousai. He had the ninja scroll. I'm worried about him." Nenki looked around.

As he did so, Yashamaru took Okoi's hand in his and watched over her as she finally passed away. A faint smile appeared on her cheeks as her spirit departed. Her brother had come.

In the midst of the heaps of salt that had spilled to the floor, they found the shriveled corpse of Old Rousai. Soon after, they discovered the weak cries of Amayo Jingorou, who was also amidst the sacks of salt.

"Oh! Rousai!"

While Hotarubi ran to Rousai's side and Nenki pulled Jingorou free, Yashamaru discovered the ninja scroll among the sacks of salt.

"Hey . . . give him water!" Nenki carried Jingorou to the door and threw him into the rain-spattered garden. Immediately, Jingorou responded to the rain by swelling up and returning to his original size.

Just then, Yakushiji Tenzen led Oboro to the storehouse. Chikuma Koshirou and Akeginu followed them.

"What? You've kidnapped a girl from Manjidani and brought her here? What were you thinking?" Oboro looked around her in outrage and disbelief.

Hotarubi approached her. "Oboro, Yashamaru has returned from Sunpu."

"Huh? Yashamaru? When?"

"Just a moment ago. You were discussing something important with Tenzen, and so he waited for you here. Yashamaru, hurry and greet Oboro—"

Yashamaru stood up. Oboro looked at him with her big, round eyes. Her eyes stayed on his . . .

Suddenly, Yashamaru's handsome face began to warp. More than warp—it crumbled. And not just his face—his entire body rapidly transformed into something or someone else.

A bloodcurdling scream burst forth from Hotarubi.

They had never before seen the man standing before them, holding the secret ninja scroll in one hand. Oboro's occult-piercing eyes had broken through the shape-shifting powers of Kisaragi Saemon.

"He's from Kouga!" Mino Nenki screamed. Kisaragi Saemon immediately hurled the scroll through the open door of the storehouse.

Everyone turned. Out of nowhere, a man appeared in the middle of the rain.

He was a naked monk with pallid, gelatinous skin. He caught the scroll in one hand, and then turned and ran.

"Get him! Catch him!" Yakushiji Tenzen screamed. Everyone raced from the storehouse after him.

The monk ran until he reached the walls of the palace. He looked back and laughed. Pressing his gelatinous body against a gray wall, he looked just like a jellyfish that had been flattened and spread against it. In moments, he turned completely transparent—and disappeared.

It had been raining since the previous day, and the entire garden was mud.

They followed holes in the mud that led from the storehouse to the wall of the building. They didn't know what they'd seen, but the holes seemed to be footsteps—it must be some kind of creature from Kouga. Petrified with terror—trapped in a nightmare—they discovered that the footsteps led to the outside of Kouga Gennosuke's room.

They scattered countless spiked traps on the ground,

and stabbed the walls. But nothing cried out in pain, and eventually even the footsteps melted in the rain.

They also discovered that the man who had taken on Yashamaru's shape had disappeared.

It was clear that at least two Kouga ninja had infiltrated the Iga palace, undetected, as if by magic.

A LETTER OF CHALLENGE
FOR A NINJA WAR

1

THE VALLEY OF TSUBAGAKURE IN IGA WAS READY FOR war. Iga had prepared for an incursion by the Kouga Manjidani clan.

The preparations were not limited to Ogen's palace. The mountain folds, the valley hollows, the trees, the homes—everywhere, eyes burned with threatening glares, and they concealed weapons ranging from swords and spears to bows, axes, ropes, nets, and sickles with attached chains.

But no matter how much effort he had spent on building these defensive preparations, Yakushiji Tenzen spent far more energy hiding them from Oboro. If she sensed what was happening, she would immediately inform Gennosuke. Tenzen could not stop worrying about how Oboro would react to knowledge of the war—and it turned out that he had understood her perfectly.

If Gennosuke learned about the war, everything would become very difficult. Already, for two days and three nights, they had successfully kept Gennosuke cooped up inside Ogen's palace. Tenzen wouldn't hesitate to kill Gennosuke and was not afraid to do it; he was a man of action. He did worry about how to kill Gennosuke. But his main reason for waiting was that he wanted to kill all the other Kouga ninjas first. Tenzen's evil plan was to kill Gennosuke after first informing him that all his friends had been killed.

Fortunately, Oboro was so innocent and so deeply in love that she did not notice the changes in her surroundings. And as long as her innocent eyes remained deceived, Gennosuke would look into them and remain at peace.

One thing had broken through Gennosuke's daily nonchalance.

His retainer, Udono Jousuke, vanished.

"What happened to Jousuke?" Gennosuke asked the morning after Jousuke had disappeared. It was a natural question to ask.

Akeginu blushed and described how Jousuke had grabbed at her that night, and how she had refused his advances. Oboro had been there, and she confirmed Akeginu's story. Oboro's eyes told Gennosuke that this was the truth, and who could doubt her eyes?

"That sounds just like Jousuke," Gennosuke said with a bitter laugh. "He tried to make a move on you, got rejected, and went running back to Kouga with his tail between his legs. That must be what happened."

And so Gennosuke never realized what was taking place around him.

The Iga clan spent the first night after their assault on Manjidani expecting a Kouga counterattack. But no attack came. It seemed that, as long as Iga kept Gennosuke locked inside their palace, Kouga would be too afraid to attack them.

Finally, Tenzen decided to tell Oboro the truth. He could not keep ignoring Gennosuke's presence, and he couldn't deceive Oboro forever. But there was another, more important, reason why he needed to talk to her . . .

Only Oboro could kill Kouga Gennosuke!

Tenzen knew that only Oboro could survive Gennosuke's basilisk eyes. If she turned her eyes on him, his would lose their power. But Tenzen needed to tear the lovers apart—make them hate each other! He looked forward to this with sinister delight.

And so he brought Oboro to the salt storehouse to show her the Kouga girl Okoi. Tenzen had not planned to kill Okoi yet. If necessary, he thought that he could use her as a shield while fighting Gennosuke. But to his surprise, Nenki had already killed Okoi. That little girl had managed to drag Old Rousai with her on her way to the underworld.

Worse, Okoi and her older brother, Kisaragi Saemon, were able to communicate without words. She had told him the location of the secret ninja scroll.

Despite all the guards, lookouts, and military preparations throughout Tsubagakure Valley, the Kouga ninja Kisaragi Saemon and Kasumi Gyoubu had slipped inside.

But there was nothing he could do to stop them—Saemon had taken on the appearance of Yashamaru of Iga, returning from Sunpu. Gyoubu could turn invisible to the eye.

Kasumi Gyoubu's talents were not limited to dissolving into walls. According to his desire, this ninja could disguise himself as easily as a chameleon or a ptarmigan, and he could freely camouflage himself in the color of dirt or grass or leaves.

These ninjas far surpassed ordinary people in their physical and mental powers. How did Kisaragi Saemon feel upon seeing the horrific death of his sister? His heart must have been sobbing when he touched Okoi's hand and pretended to yawn.

With his sister already halfway into the underworld, the older brother had spoken with her through his fingertip. Pushing, pulling back, caressing—in the darkness, the fingers asked questions and answered them. From that, he had been able to find the scroll and give it to Kasumi Gyoubu.

Kasumi Gyoubu had vanished.

In desperation, the Iga samurai raced into Kouga Gennosuke's room. Gennosuke stood there, staring at the unraveled scroll. The hunchback Sakinta, who had been standing guard, was now in a crumpled heap on the veranda. Kasumi Gyoubu, who had thrown on his clothes, was kneeling on one leg, looking up at his master, Gennosuke.

Gennosuke threw a glance toward the Iga samurai standing in the garden in the pouring rain. He nodded sadly. "Gyoubu, let's go back to Manjidani."

2

ALTHOUGH HIS VOICE WAS SAD, HIS FEATURES RE-mained composed. He looked like somebody who had unexpectedly gotten up and decided to leave after playing a board game at a friend's home.

Kouga Gennosuke quietly rolled up the scroll and placed it inside his kimono. His sword drooping from his hand, he went onto the veranda and looked out onto the garden. No—he wasn't looking anywhere. His eyes were half shut, as if he were still asleep.

"Let's kill him!" roared Mino Nenki.

"Wait!" shouted Yakushiji Tenzen at the same moment.

The other Iga warriors could not understand why Tenzen was still holding them back. Gennosuke resembled a gloomy flower in the misty rain. What was so dangerous about him?

Tenzen and Nenki had both shouted at the same time. As if choosing which voice they preferred to hear, six Iga samurai near the front of the veranda charged.

Instantly, a golden light shone back upon the six flashing blades. Gennosuke's eyes!

The rays of light from his eyes looked like streams of

melted gold. The six attacking Iga samurais staggered, twisted, collapsed. They became a whirlwind of blood, their swords slashing, slicing. All of them were dead. Their shoulders and chest and necks had been hacked apart— not by each other, but by their own blades.

"Gyoubu, let's go." Gennosuke stepped into the garden as if nothing had happened. Once again he closed his eyes halfway. His footsteps were inaudible. Kasumi Gyoubu followed him, grinning at the stunned Iga fighters.

The vast crowd of Iga warriors were frozen in place, petrified with fear. Tenzen had often told them about Gennosuke's basilisk eyes. But this was the first time that they had witnessed it. Six had died before their eyes. And Gennosuke had done it without the slightest effort.

What were Gennosuke's basilisk eyes?

Their power consisted of intense hypnotism. Anyone harboring the desire to harm or kill Gennosuke would be destroyed by his eyes. No matter how much they tried to avoid his powers, they were drawn into looking at his eyes and became absorbed in them. Gennosuke's eyes would then release a spark of golden light. That flash of light affected the enemy's nervous system. Instantly, his attackers fell into a trance, attacking their allies and sometimes hacking at themselves with their weapons. No matter what ninja talent an attacker intended to use against Gennosuke, it would rebound against the perpetrator.

Gennosuke hung his head and folded his arms, walking across the garden toward the gate. He seemed deep in meditation. Was he lamenting the renewal of warfare between Kouga and Iga? Or thinking of the Kouga warriors whose names had already been crossed off the list?

Just the act of watching this seemingly defenseless man walk across the garden affected the Iga fighters. They watched him go. They seemed to be bound hand and foot, unable to move to stop him.

"I will kill him." The voice belonged to Chikuma Koshirou.

"Koshirou—" Tenzen began. He turned his bloodshot eyes to the side. "Don't let that one escape! The pride of Iga is on your shoulders—"

Tenzen seemed to be pushing Koshirou forward into a duel to the death.

But Tenzen knew that this was the perfect opportunity. And he was not actually speaking to Koshirou anymore. He was speaking to the Iga samurai at his side—and he was warning them not to let Oboro leave. She was the key to defeating Gennosuke! "No matter what, don't let Oboro get away!"

Oboro was staring vacantly, her jaw hanging open, eyes vacant. She looked like a terrified little girl.

"Gennosuke is leaving," Tenzen said to her.

What was Tenzen thinking as he said those words? The words "Gennosuke is leaving" were a blow to Oboro's heart. *How had things come to be like this? Why had they murdered that young girl from Kouga? Why were those Iga fighters killed?* But more than anything else, Oboro was devastated by the sight of Gennosuke's cold, broken-hearted figure walking away, without a word or a glance in her direction.

"Gennosuke!" Oboro cried and ran toward him.

Gennosuke and Gyoubu had already reached the gate. The Iga samurai had scattered, and these three stood alone at the gate. The drawbridge was being lowered across the moat by Kisaragi Saemon.

"Gennosuke!"

Kouga Gennosuke looked back. The members of Iga had formed a semicircle around him. Chikuma Koshirou stepped forward from that group, alone. His huge scythe hung from one hand, a turquoise light gleaming from the metal. Koshirou radiated bloodlust—it leaped from his body in a bonfire of pale white flames. Gennosuke faced him, perfectly still, as if his feet were nailed into the ground. His eyes watched the lone Iga warrior approaching him.

A distance of twenty paces separated them.

"Oboro . . ." Tenzen whispered. "Oboro . . . Go there. Get between them."

"Of course!" Oboro said in sudden realization. She hurried forward.

"But don't look at Koshirou!" Tenzen cried, snatching her arm. "Look at Gennosuke!"

"Why?" Oboro said.

"Chikuma Koshirou is the only member of Iga who we can count on to kill Gennosuke!"

It was true. Nothing could stop Koshirou's whirling vacuums—those miniature black holes could rip Gennosuke's face to shreds.

Her face as white as candle wax, Oboro whispered, "Why do you want to kill Gennosuke?"

"Just . . . protect Koshirou—it's dangerous—"

Koshirou was coming closer to Gennosuke. Fifteen paces separated them.

Oboro, unable to stand it any longer, ran between them. Trembling violently, she screamed, "Koshirou, stop it!"

"Princess, don't be frightened," Koshirou said, ignoring Oboro. He continued moving forward.

"Gennosuke's eyes are deadly!" Tenzen screamed. "Oboro, look into Gennosuke's eyes! Your own eyes are the only thing that can stop his basilisk eyes!"

"I . . ."

"If you don't, he might kill Koshirou!"

Ten paces.

Chikuma Koshirou halted. Gennosuke had remained as still and meditative as a pool of water. There was no movement between them—only rain, falling in silver threads. Those watching closed their eyes. An overwhelming sense of danger floated in the air, warning them not to watch.

Among the bystanders, Yakushiji Tenzen realized in shock that Oboro had also closed her eyes—

"Oboro!" he shouted. "Open your eyes!"

"Your eyes! Your eyes!" His screams overflowed with pure hate. "Do you want your own ally Koshirou to be killed by Gennosuke's basilisk eyes?"

A strange sound rustled through the empty air. Oboro opened her eyes. But she turned her gaze toward her ally Koshirou!

Tenzen screamed. Chikuma Koshirou staggered backward and fell. His hands pressed against his face, which was spouting thick fresh blood. His face had been ripped open by his own whirling vacuum.

Was it because of Gennosuke's basilisk eyes or Oboro's occult-piercing eyes?

Gennosuke coldly turned and walked across the drawbridge. Kasumi Gyoubu and Kisaragi Saemon grinned and followed. Nobody had the strength to chase them.

"He's left . . . Gennosuke has left . . ." Oboro mumbled. Tears dropped from her eyes, closed once more.

3

THE RAIN HAD STOPPED, AND THE DARKNESS OF DUSK closed in.

Deep within Ogen's palace, a single torch burned in the sitting room. A large group sat in silence.

They were Yakushiji Tenzen, Mino Nenki, Amayo Jingorou, Akeginu, Hotarubi—and, of course, Oboro.

"So our enemies have learned about the war," Tenzen said in a low voice. "A battle to the death between Iga and Kouga has begun." He finally informed Iga that the Hattori family ban on ninja warfare had been cancelled.

On this single day, eleven members of the Iga clan—including Azuki Rousai—had been killed. Chikuma Koshirou's face had burst like a squashed pomegranate. Miraculously, he was still alive. Oboro's occult-piercing eyes had looked into his eyes, causing Koshirou's whirlwind to collapse upon him. He had barely survived. A dark and deadly mood hung over the entire valley of Tsubagakure. It was not caused by the rain clouds alone.

"Of the ten on our side, Azuki Rousai is dead, Koshirou is wounded, and Yashamaru is probably dead as well," Tenzen murmured.

"No, that's not all—Grandmother is dead, too," Jingorou said.

Oboro wept.

Nenki glared at her. "And they stole the ninja scroll! Don't forget—the survivors of the battle to the death must take the scroll to Sunpu Castle. We must get that scroll! This should be a joyous day—we have all been waiting for the chance to fight our archenemies again. But I, for one, cannot celebrate. I'm sure the rest of you feel the same way. I will not rest until I turn all of Kouga into a hell of blood! We must win! We will win—I am certain of it!"

Tenzen seized Oboro's hand. An aura of sparkling light surrounded Oboro's entire body.

"You must be our leader in this bloody war, Oboro,"

Tenzen said, gnashing his teeth. Strangely, he'd suffered a sword wound to the cheek only a day earlier, and yet only a faint threadlike scar remained. "Oboro . . . why did you fail to kill our enemy Kouga Gennosuke? Why did you turn your heartless eyes upon your own ally—Koshirou? If you were not the granddaughter of Ogen, I'd accuse you of betraying your clan—and declare you unworthy of looking upon the skies of Tsubagakure."

"Tenzen, please forgive me," she said.

"If you want to apologize, apologize to Grandmother! And to four hundred years of our Iga ancestors! Or, better yet, devote yourself to this great ninja clan war."

"Ohhh . . ." she moaned.

"Oboro—someday soon, Kouga Gennosuke must be killed by your hand."

In agony, Oboro shook her head no. Five ninja stared at her in disgust. Tenzen's fears had come true.

"What is wrong with you?" he screamed. "War is not a game for children!"

"Kill Gennosuke? I can't—" she said.

"—can't fail!" Tenzen screamed at her, finishing her sentence. He seemed to have forgotten that she was the clan leader. Usually so calm, Yakushiji Tenzen changed color in rage. "The entire Tsubagakure clan—children, mothers, the elderly—whether they live or die all depends on your eyes!"

Quietly, Oboro looked up. She appeared to be dead,

her face as white and cold as carved ivory. But her eyes shone like black suns. The five held their breath.

Without speaking, she stood and went into the rear sitting room.

Startled, they watched her leave—and then return a moment later. She sat down silently. She carried a jar so small that it fit in her palm.

She broke the seal and dipped her finger into the liquid, then dabbed it on her eyelids.

"Wha—what is that?" Even Tenzen had never seen that jar before. None of them had ever seen Oboro do this to herself.

Oboro closed her eyes and spoke in a low voice. "One day," she said, "Grandmother said something to me. 'Oboro, you are the woman who will lead the ninja fighters of Iga, but you are also an incompetent girl, unable to learn ninja skills. Your eyes—you were born with those. That is not a ninja skill. That is not something that I taught you. I am afraid of those eyes. I have the feeling that these eyes of yours will destroy the Tsubagakure clan from within. You will throw everyone into an abyss of death.' That's what she said. Now when I listen to Tenzen, I remember her words."

Silence pervaded the room.

"And she said something else, too. She told me, 'If that day ever comes, if your eyes bring disaster to the clan . . . Oboro, you must put this secret potion, Seven Days of

Blindness, upon your eyelids. Your eyes will be sealed. You will be unable to open them for a week.'"

"Ah—" Yakushiji Tenzen gasped. He snatched the jar out of Oboro's hand.

The other four ninja watched with wide eyes, their breath caught in their throats.

"I too am a woman of Iga. It kills me to listen to Tenzen. What could I possibly say after seeing so many of our villagers killed? . . . But I cannot fight with Gennosuke." Her voice sounded as if she were coughing up blood. "Not only am I unable to fight with Gennosuke . . . I would . . . probably be unable to stop myself from using my eyes to hurt my fellow Iga members. I am scared of my own eyes. So for that reason . . . I have blinded myself."

"Princess!"

"I have blinded myself. Now I can see nothing, nothing in this world . . . and I cannot see my fate anymore, either . . ."

The other five stared at her, stunned. Oboro's eyelids had already closed and glowed a faint white.

Her frightful eyes were gone. At that same moment, the sun vanished from Tsubagakure.

What could anyone say? What could anyone do? What could anyone think?

The sound of hurried footsteps broke through the silence.

"Tenzen! Tenzen!"

"What?" he snapped. Flicking his head around, he saw a young samurai holding a letter case.

"This thing, it was left at the gate—"

"What is it?" He snatched the case away and pulled off the lid. Tenzen's eyes widened. In the middle of the case was the secret scroll that Gennosuke had stolen from them that morning.

Tenzen pulled off the string and opened the scroll. The contents were unchanged—except for the names. Those who had been killed were each crossed out in red.

KOUGA CLAN 10 WARRIORS

~~Kouga Danjou~~	~~Udono Jousuke~~
Kouga Gennosuke	Kisaragi Saemon
~~Jimushi Juubei~~	Muroga Hyouma
~~Kazamachi Shougen~~	Kagerou
Kasumi Gyoubu	~~Okoi~~

IGA CLAN 10 WARRIORS

~~Ogen~~	Amayo Jingorou
Oboro	Chikuma Koshirou
~~Yashamaru~~	Mino Nenki
~~Azuki Rousai~~	Hotarubi
Yakushiji Tenzen	Akeginu

"Hunh . . ." Tenzen groaned.

Chikuma Koshirou's name did not have a line through

it. Somehow they had anticipated that he would live. This made them even more dangerous as enemies. But who had brought this to their gate? Of course, it had to be Kouga Gennosuke. But, then again, either Kisaragi Saemon or Kasumi Gyoubu could have brought it from Manjidani as well. Saemon could adopt the appearance of any of their members; Gyoubu could camouflage himself against anything. Either one of them could easily accomplish this task. But why did they return such a precious scroll?

He found a letter tucked in the bottom of the case. Picking it up, he saw that it had been sealed on the left side—that meant it was a letter of challenge.

> To the Iga Tsubagakura clan,
>
> The Hattori family has lifted the ban on warfare between the two families.
>
> However, I do not like to fight. I also do not know why we are fighting. For that reason, I am going to Sunpu. I intend to ask the shogun and Hattori Hanzou their reasons. That is why I have returned the ninja scroll to you. Also going with me are the four others: Kasumi Gyoubu, Kisaragi Saemon, Muroga Hyouma, and Kagerou.
>
> Thus, even if you come to Manjidani, we will already be on the Tokaido Road. Know that if you kill innocent people, Heaven will destroy Tsubagakure.
>
> Although I do not like to fight, I will not flee from

KANZAKI/IVAN H
Flt 2233
WN/A/DCA/T/1/SSK/S0007
07/23/2023 11:27AM
CONF 2HM7AQ   **CMH**

CLAIM 0526218874
Southwest Airlines

1. Peel This Tab Off

E
IVE.

N THIS
STUB
OR YOUR
RECORDS.

This baggage check is t...
baggage identification...
ticket described by Article...
Convention as amended at T...
All that is stated with lugga...
in the transportation ticket. Bagg...
delivered to whoever presents th...
check without notability to the carrie...

3. Keep this Tab As Your Claim

BAGGAGE CLAIM CHECK

Baggage checked subject to Conditions of Contract or Tariffs, including Limitations of Liability therein contained. See also notices "Advice to International Passengers on Limitation of Liability and Notice of Baggage Liability Limitations".

your pursuit. There are seven of you left. Until we
reach the gates of Sunpu Castle, I expect the five Kouga
and seven Iga will enjoy the journey. If you are not
afraid, whip yourselves into action and come to the
Tokaido Road.

KOUGA GENNOSUKE

THE CAT EYE CURSE

1

FROM SHIGARAKI VALLEY TO THE MINAKUCHI STA-
tion, the Tokaido Road edges dangerously along the side
of the mountains. The average traveler's eyes and ears are
so overwhelmed at the sight of the mountains, the mur-
muring of the rivulets coursing through the gorges of
Daido River, and by the song of the bush warbler, that
they would not notice the five shadows on the deadly
road, flowing northward like the south wind itself.

Their speed alone was astounding, and other travelers
would gasp in amazement as they saw a woman in the
group. But what left them stunned and staring was the realization that one of the men was blind and moving with
his eyes closed.

Five ninja from Kouga were racing toward Sunpu.

The Seimu emperor had a detached palace called the
Shigaraki Palace, which later became Kouga Temple. It
eventually collapsed, and now only foundation stones and
old bricks remain, scattered in this area near the Dairi
fields. In the wild grasslands, a balmy breeze, pregnant

with light, marked the end of spring and beginning of summer.

The blind ninja Muroga Hyouma suddenly stopped and put his ear to the ground.

"There are no pursuers," he murmured.

The hairless monk Kasumi Gyoubu came over. "Even if they are from Iga, they will not cut through Kouga Valley to pursue us," he said with a strange smile as he gazed toward the southern mountains that they had just crossed. "But will they chase us? We'll be in trouble if they don't chase us. I'm worried that they might follow the Ise Road instead. The Tokaido Road to Sunpu is a long route, and if they followed the Ise Road, they could get ahead of us and ambush us along the way—"

Kasumi Gyoubu looked at the silent blind ninja. Gyoubu continued speaking in a whisper. "We can't wait around for the enemy to attack. Some of us must strike them first! They intend to ambush us, so we should ambush them! Our next move should shock them. My idea is to let them see that we've gone ahead on the Tokaido Road, and then secretly circle back and strike the enemy. I'd rather leave the group and go fight Iga alone. I'm worried about our leader—is he really ready to fight?"

Gyoubu could not accept Gennosuke's behavior. Certainly, Gennosuke seemed to be furious with Iga. But the necessary qualifier "seemed" made Gennosuke's followers uncomfortable.

After sending his letter of challenge to Iga Tsubagakure, Gennosuke had begun his journey to Sunpu. This much made sense. But Gyoubu did not understand why Gennosuke had also returned the secret ninja scroll to Iga. Hadn't Tokugawa Ieyasu ordered the survivors to "bring" the secret scroll to Sunpu? So why give it to Iga? And why did Gennosuke want to go to Sunpu and question the shogun as to his reasons for restarting the war between Kouga and Iga? It made no sense. Kouga and Iga had hated and fought each other for four hundred years. Now that they were permitted to fight again, why ask for reasons? If Gennosuke wanted to ask Tokugawa Ieyasu why, first kill all ten Iga ninja and *then* go ask.

That was what Kasumi Gyoubu thought. He doubted Gennosuke's will to fight.

"He is ready to fight," Muroga Hyouma said, nodding. But after a pause, he added, "If the enemy pursues us."

"What if they don't pursue us?"

"The enemy will come. You said so yourself. Gennosuke knew they'd chase us after receiving the letter of challenge. He included the scroll because he knew that Iga would bring it when they chased us. And—if it's necessary—you wouldn't mind stealing it back, would you?"

"*If it's necessary?*" Gyoubu howled, as if in pain. "Is Gennosuke prepared to kill Princess Oboro?"

Hyouma remained silent.

The feet of the five ninja rode on the wind.

Kouga Gennosuke sometimes turned worried glances

at Kisaragi Saemon, walking next to him. Gennosuke looked gloomy. Obviously, he was thinking about Oboro.

Gennosuke did not want to fight against Iga. He knew that the two sides were steeped in four hundred years of mutual hatred. And now, both Manjidani Valley and Tsubagakure Valley overflowed with so much blood that it had probably soaked into every blade of grass and every tree. But if these people could only come to their senses, they would realize that all of this was madness! No matter what kind of gruesome murders took place four hundred years ago, it was madness for these two ninja clans to blindly kill each other. Madness and idiocy!

But it was impossible to avoid fighting with Iga.

Determination and fury boiled in Gennosuke's chest.

Kouga had offered peace, but Iga responded with violence. Starting with his grandfather, Danjou, they had slaughtered five of the ninja on the list—Kazamachi Shougen, Jimushi Juubei, Udono Jousuke, and Okoi. They had also attacked Manjidani, killed ten innocent villagers in a whirlwind of blood, and then run away. What kind of monsters were they? At this point, even if he could somehow control his own fury, he would never be able to control the rest of the Kouga clan.

And yet, his blood yearned for revenge!

Despite his calm and rational nature, he could feel his blood screaming at him to join in the dark and bloody violence. By the time he had even realized that they were at war, half of the ninja had already departed this world.

Pain and fury roared inside his heart. And everything was due to his mistakes—his stupidity!

He saw the phantoms—the heroic Kazamachi Shougen, the carefree Udono Jousuke, the lovely Okoi—their faces, frozen in death, whizzed past him. He had to turn away. He hung his head in shame. *They were dying, and I was dozing, enjoying the spring nights of Tsubagakure.*

I have been a fool!

He gritted his teeth. Like cold water splashed on his face, he had an instant realization. Oboro! Had Oboro been part of the plot from the beginning, luring him to Tsubagakure? Perhaps her innocent face was just another ninja disguise! At this point, it would be impossible to believe she wasn't involved. And yet, his heart and mind were torn.

Could Oboro be a vicious monster in disguise? The thought made him shudder. It couldn't be true! There must be a mistake. Could Oboro really be so evil? But even if everything was a mistake—even if she was a perfect angel—what could be done now?

Gennosuke's gloomy face expressed his twisted soul. His own foolishness . . . his doubts of Oboro . . . He was filled with rage toward Tokugawa Ieyasu and Hattori Hanzou for all the destruction they had caused.

Gennosuke had begun his journey toward Sunpu with the intention of unraveling the riddle of this unneeded war. Gennosuke also wanted to leave Kouga, so that innocent bystanders in Manjidani and Tsubagakure would not be harmed. After all, Ieyasu and Hattori Hanzou had only ordered the ten ninja on each side to fight. If they must fight, let it be limited to them. Gennosuke also had another reason for leaving Kouga.

Would the seven Iga ninja chase them?

Gennosuke believed it.

The Iga ninja were burning with the desire to fight. They knew that they only had to cross off five more Kouga ninjas and they would be victorious. Of course they would chase him! And just to make sure they did, Gennosuke had sent them a direct challenge.

They will come and we will wait.

Gennosuke's eyes shone with a dull golden light as a cold, faint smile crossed his lips. He hoped that Grandfather, Shougen, Juubei, Jousuke, and Okoi were watching from heaven. He would put their souls at rest.

The Iga ninja would come. But would Oboro come with them? And what if she did?

Here Gennosuke's thoughts halted. He burned with fury at her betrayal. But the thought of her lovely, smiling face and her sunlike eyes carried an unstoppable magic power. Those eyes made his fury and fire disappear. *Could I fight Oboro?* Gennosuke ground his teeth.

As if shadowed by passing clouds, Gennosuke's face became alternately bright and dark. Kisaragi Saemon frequently glanced over at him. So did Kagerou.

Kagerou's eyes gazed intently on him. She did not realize that her gaze had become suffused with sexual desire.

A butterfly dancing in the breeze came too close to Kagerou and fell immediately, unmoving, to the grass. If the two ninja behind her, Muroga Hyouma and Kasumi Gyoubu, had noticed this, would they understand what it meant?

Whenever this female ninja felt sexual desire, her breath turned to poison!

But Hyouma was blind and Gyoubu had disappeared.

"Gyoubu—what happened to Gyoubu?" Gennosuke asked Hyouma as they found lodgings at Minakuchi.

"Well, I don't know. Gyoubu easily disappears from the sight of people who can see. I am blind, so I have no idea where he is."

But blindness had never limited Muroga Hyouma before. His confusion now seemed to be a conscious choice.

Shigaraki Road continued a little farther east and then merged with Tokaido Road.

2

IF THE MEN OF KOUGA MANJIDANI WERE ASKED TO pick which of the ninja in that valley was most terrifying, they would think about it for a while, smile strangely, and answer: Kagerou.

Not Jimushi Juubei, who shoots a spear from his mouth; not Kazamachi Shougen, who spits spiderlike threads; not Udono Jousuke, who makes his body swell or shrink like a rubber ball; not Kasumi Gyoubu, who changes into ten thousand shapes and colors; not Kisaragi Saemon, who makes death masks from mud and uses them to adopt the faces of others; not Okoi, who turns her skin into octopus-like suckers; and not even Kouga Gennosuke, whose basilisk eyes force attackers to wield their fighting techniques on themselves.

They would choose the poison-breathing Kagerou.

But it was her great beauty that made the poison deadly. Because even though her poison breath was well-known, and even though Kouga Danjou had strictly controlled the clan, some men could not control themselves before her seductive powers.

It was unsurprising that Yakushiji Tenzen did not know Kagerou's secret power. Her breath did not carry the scent of death. And her power only emerged when she felt sexual desire.

Kagerou's power was also her tragedy. She could never enjoy married life. Among some insect species, the female immediately kills the male after copulating. Kagerou's mother was the same way. As she gasped in ecstasy, her mates sucked in her poison. Three men had died in her arms. Kagerou was born from the last of these men.

Kouga Danjou had ordered these three sacrificial victims to their doom in order to transmit the mother's genes. All of them had been overjoyed to sacrifice themselves in this way for the sake of Kouga Manjidani.

Kagerou had grown up. And, just like her mother, sacrificial men would be provided for her until she gave birth to a girl. Before Danjou had left for Sunpu, he had indicated that it was time to provide Kagerou with a new partner. He had talked about it around the hearth with young Manjidani men.

Drinking from the wedding cup with Kagerou would be equivalent to drinking from the cup of death. It terrified the young men, and yet none of them fled from the possibility. They would obediently follow the orders of Kouga Danjou and the sacred rules of the valley. But even in the absence of Danjou's orders, many of the men would be willing to die in exchange for a night of pleasure with her. They were insects drawn to a Venus flytrap.

But why compare them to the insect kingdom? Human beings are no different. Some women will radiate youth and beauty for a short period of time, and yet all the men in the world are prisoners to their beauty, following them blindly.

Until she had matured into a young woman, Kagerou did not know her own secret. When she discovered that secret, her suffering began.

But her agony did not result solely from her tragic

physical problems. In fact, many ninja had physical characteristics even more shocking than hers. Almost everyone in Manjidani suffered from some kind of physical deformity. Kagerou's unique misery began when she realized that she loved Gennosuke.

For better or worse, her family lineage within Manjidani qualified her to be Kouga Gennosuke's wife. And when she compared herself to other women of similar age and lineage, she felt proud of her own beauty. Her gorgeous appearance matched her personality. In short, she would be a good match. Even as a little girl, she frequently dreamed of becoming Gennosuke's wife.

However, fate had cursed her. She was a woman who, upon reaching sexual ecstasy, would kill her lover!

Destroyed, she abandoned hope of becoming his wife. But she also became obsessed with Gennosuke's selection of a wife.

Gennosuke's selection of Oboro—the granddaughter of Ogen and a member of their archenemy Iga—disappointed the entire village of Manjidani. But none matched the jealousy and anger of Kagerou. *I could accept him choosing a woman who was not from Manjidani. However, to pick the granddaughter of Ogen . . . !* She explained her rage to herself as a reaction to Gennosuke's marriage with the Iga clan. In reality, however, this was merely an excuse for her bitterness.

Since then, Kagerou had been submerged in poisonous

fantasies—fantasies that she would never have imagined could come from her own mind.

She had venomous breath. Gennosuke's basilisk eyes protected him against anyone trying to harm him. His eyes forced attackers to use their ninja powers against themselves. But she did not intend to attack or kill him. She was in love with Gennosuke. If she were to breathe on Gennosuke in the heat of passion, would her breath kill him or her?

If that was the price for one night together, Kagerou would be happy to watch him die. And if it was she who died, she would still have no regrets. Submerged in these thoughts, her breath took on the scent of apricot flowers— the scent of death for her lovers.

But now, Kouga Danjou, the clan leader, had died! Fate had forced Gennosuke to become mortal enemies once again with his beloved Oboro!

Nobody was more ecstatic than Kagerou upon hearing that war had erupted with the Tsubagakure clan. Not because it gave her renewed hope of marrying Gennosuke. She knew that the clan would not allow her to love him. And yet she did love him. Precisely because she knew her love was outlawed, she desired him all the more. And as she thought of him, she became inflamed with passion. The men of Kouga were correct to consider Kagerou the most terrifying of the ninja. Unconsciously, uncontrollably, Kagerou breathed poison. This journey gave her the rare opportunity of walking by his side, sleeping with him under the same roof. But the living things that came close to her breath died.

Traveling east from Minakuchi, the Ise Road merged with the Tokaido Road. Dark clouds once again blocked the sun. Rain beat against the Tokaido Road.

Speed was not their main concern. Crossing the Suzuka Pass at nightfall, they decided to sleep at the Seki station.

This was where, a few days earlier, Kisaragi Saemon and Kasumi Gyoubu had killed Yashamaru of Iga. As they sat in the inn, watching the sky turn dark, the featureless face of Saemon told his companions about that ninja battle. Eventually, however, he and Hyouma went to separate rooms to sleep.

"Kagerou, you go, too," Gennosuke said to her. She had been preparing the bedding and moving the lantern. "You need to sleep. We get up early tomorrow."

Kagerou sat down beside the lantern. "I'll go. But what's the plan for tomorrow? Will we leave by boat from Kuwana City?"

"No. I doubt the boats will sail in this rain. The wind looks like it will get worse, too. I think we will have to take the land route."

Gennosuke suddenly looked up at Kagerou's face. Her dark eyes were constantly staring at his. Without thinking, he became sucked into her eyes, moist with emotion.

But, just then, a moth attracted to the lantern's flame whizzed close to her face and immediately dropped dead.

Gennosuke snapped back to his senses. Kagerou had twisted toward him, her hot flesh heaving. She collapsed upon his knees.

"Kagerou!" he cried.

"I love you, Gennosuke!"

She lifted her face toward him. Like a flower releasing its scent, her lips breathed upon him. Gennosuke became dizzy. Panicking, he tried to push her away, but Kagerou was holding him tight and his strength was fading . . .

"Kagerou—look at my eyes!" he cried.

His eyes shone golden in the light of the lantern. Kagerou saw them. Immediately, her eyelids fluttered and she dropped to the ground. She had become paralyzed from her own poison.

Gennosuke took the teapot from beside the pillow and poured tea into her mouth. Her eyes opened.

Gennosuke's face remained pale. Unable to break free of her grip, he had forced her to look into his eyes, escaping death by a hair's breadth. More shocking to him than that brush with death was the realization that this woman was in love with him.

She preferred to kill the man she loved! Traveling next to Kagerou on this journey meant that he would be swallowing poison throughout the trip.

"Kagerou, do you want to kill me?" Gennosuke asked. His eyes remained on hers. "If you tried to do something so foolish, you would die." He laughed weakly.

"I want to die," she answered. "With you, Gennosuke."

"Don't be stupid. If you want to die, first kill all those Iga ninja on the scroll. Then you can die."

"All the ones on the scroll? Including Oboro?" At last, she had spat out Oboro's name.

Gennosuke held his breath and remained silent.

Kagerou spoke in a voice raspy from hatred. "As a woman, I cannot kill Oboro. Gennosuke, will you kill Oboro?"

The rain pounded louder. The wind roared through the trees.

"I will kill her."

He said the words in a moan. He did not speak the other words: *I am unable to kill her.*

Staring hard at Gennosuke, Kagerou laughed coldly. "In that case, I will give myself to each of the enemy men. Alone, I will kill every man from Iga!"

And then Kagerou left.

LATER THAT night, Kouga Gennosuke jerked awake and sat up, as if awakening from an anesthetic. Even in the midst of sleep, his ninja-trained ears were alert. And in addition to his ears, his sixth sense remained constantly on guard for enemies. Neither Gennosuke's ears nor his sixth sense had detected any person approaching. Nevertheless, something was wrong. He leaped to his feet.

Gennosuke's eyes soon focused on the ceiling. The

candlewick within the lantern had been extinguished, making the room dark and hazy. He shot arrows of gold light from his eyes at the ceiling; any Iga ninja would have immediately screamed and dropped to the ground.

But what Gennosuke saw wasn't human. It was a serpent, staring at him with red eyes and clutching an egg in its fangs.

He shouted and leaped through the air. Metal flashed in his hand and instantly the snake split in two. Snake blood splattered on him—but something else struck his face as well.

Gennosuke had never expected to be attacked by something not human. Even as Gennosuke's blade had bisected the snake, it had also split its egg open, and the contents had splashed on him. It was no ordinary egg.

Sensing something strange, Hyouma, Saemon, and Kagerou rushed inside. Kouga Gennosuke stood like a rod in the middle of the room, his sword hanging low from one hand.

"Gennosuke!" the three shouted.

Gennosuke's hand pressed against his eyes. A soft, frightening groan came from his lips.

"Hyouma," he said, "my eyes have been destroyed."

The three held their breath.

The Iga warriors had come. They were here. But they had used a snake to attack in their stead. And at the first contact with Iga on the Tokaido Road—120 miles from

Sunpu—their young leader, Kouga Gennosuke, lost his most powerful weapon. His eyes had been sealed shut.

3

THE TWO IGA NINJA HAD NOT INFILTRATED THE INN. Instead, they had climbed atop the roof of the inn opposite.

Exposed in the darkness to the pelting rain and wind, Hotarubi leaped to her feet and made a signal to Mino Nenki. He was crouching beside her, staring intently at the inn opposite them.

The sliding shutters to the room where Kouga Gennosuke was staying were open. Nenki's eyes pierced through both the darkness and rain. He spotted Kisaragi Saemon, who looked panicked. He pulled out his sword as he watched the commotion taking place. He clearly heard the bloodcurdling cry of a woman: "Gennosuke can't see! His eyes!"

"It's done," Nenki murmured, grinning. "Everything else will be easy."

He watched through the darkness, calculating.

"The ones with Gennosuke are the blind ninja, the woman, and that one." *That one* referred to Kisaragi Saemon.

The seven Iga fighters had left Tsubagakure and traveled to the intersection of Iga Road and Ise Road together.

But Yakushiji Tenzen decided to give Mino Nenki and Hotarubi a special assignment. The two of them were to hurry ahead to Suzuka Pass and catch up with the Kouga group when they lodged at Seki. But when Nenki and Hotarubi arrived at Seki, they could only recognize Gennosuke, the blind ninja Muroga Hyouma, and Kagerou. A fourth man was wearing hooded robes, and they couldn't tell through the rain whether it was Kisaragi Saemon or Kasumi Gyoubu.

There should be five members of Kouga, but Nenki only counted four. Who was missing?

He pondered the question for a long time. Suddenly, Mino Nenki jerked his head up in surprise.

"What happened to Kasumi Gyoubu?"

Nenki had remembered Gyoubu's particular ninja technique. He could silently disappear into walls and mud. *Where was Gyoubu?*

It must be that, just as he and Hotarubi had separated off to pursue Kouga as a detached force, Gyoubu had also separated from his companions to attack Iga on his own!

"Hotarubi, we need to be careful. The fact that we don't see Gyoubu anywhere means that he must have disguised his appearance and headed off to ambush Iga while his companions rested at the inn. Hurry back and warn the others."

"But what about the ones here?"

"I will watch them. A seeing person watching the blind—it'll be easy." Nenki laughed. As if the idea had suddenly popped into his mind, he added, "Hotarubi, when you leave, release a cloud of butterflies. It will lure out the ones who can see. I want to watch the blind ones groping in confusion."

"It's easy for me to summon the butterflies, Nenki, but it's risky. Tenzen told us to avoid danger."

"I know that."

Yakushiji Tenzen's orders had been: First, catch up to the Kouga group and keep an eye on them. Second, destroy Kouga Gennosuke's eyes.

The second of these tasks had been accomplished with unexpected alacrity. But he also had to complete the first half of the mission. He had destroyed Kouga Gennosuke's eyes! They had used the secret Seven Days of Blindness potion.

Tenzen had said that this would not be an easy task. This meant that Tenzen did not believe Mino Nenki and Hotarubi could do it. *I will have to blind him myself*, Tenzen had implied. But he had to stay back with the main group in order to protect Oboro, who was now blind. So he had ordered Hotarubi and Nenki to catch up to Kouga and to report on their location.

"Hotarubi, you must summon the butterflies," Nenki said.

"Fine, I'll do it." She leaped to her feet and folded her hands together. Immediately, a strange wind whistled through the night sky. From every location, hordes of night rain butterflies appeared. Like a phantasmagorical tornado, they whizzed through the trees, and over the rooftops, finally arriving at the shutters of the inn across the street.

Kisaragi Saemon opened the shutters and scowled as he looked outside with bloodshot eyes. He shouted and ran into the garden with his sword drawn. Kagerou followed after him.

Nenki laughed soundlessly, and looked over. "Good. Now go, Hotarubi."

WHILE THE mass of butterflies flew eastward, Hotarubi ran toward the west. After watching Kisaragi Saemon and Kagerou race down the road in the wrong direction, Nenki lowered himself to the street.

His eyes burned bloodred and his hair stood up straight. Nenki slipped into the garden and approached the window. His feet barely skimmed over the ground. In one hand he held a sword. His hair wrapped like a snake around tree branches, and they swung his body forward through the air.

Mino Nenki had agreed to Tenzen's orders. He knew that Tenzen did not wish for them to attack Gennosuke because they might not survive the attempt.

But this order goaded his ninja pride. It had been unexpectedly easy to blind Gennosuke. This encouraged him. Fear for his life? There were only two blind ninja! Time to attack!

Mino Nenki was the most ferocious and courageous ninja in Iga. He slipped through the window of the inn and entered the tatami room.

The lantern had been snuffed, leaving the room pitch-black. But like all ninja, he could see in the dark. He saw the two seated shadows, waiting in silence.

Kouga Gennosuke and Muroga Hyouma. Both of them had their eyes shut.

"You're from Iga," Gennosuke said softly.

Nenki froze with terror. But upon seeing that Gennosuke could not open his eyes, Nenki snickered. "Can you see me, Kouga Gennosuke?"

"No, I can't." Gennosuke grinned. "I will not be able to see your dead body either."

"What?"

"Hyouma—look at him!"

Gennosuke had ordered the blind ninja, Muroga Hyouma, to look at Nenki. Hyouma slowly opened his eyes. His eyeballs were gold.

"AHH!"

Instantly, Mino Nenki leaped back as if his brain had been pierced by a streak of light.

Gennosuke was not the only one who had mastered basilisk eyes!

Nenki's hair, which had been standing straight up, transformed into a tangled, seaweedlike mess of confusion. Two clumps of hair braided together and then stabbed into his own eyeballs. Fountains of blood gushed onto his cheeks.

With his last strength, Nenki lifted his sword overhead and charged at Hyouma. But before he could reach the blind ninja, his hand twisted the handle and sliced the sword through his own belly.

Nenki's body tumbled out the open window, landing in the garden, faceup. Soon it ceased moving. Rain pelted on the large-handled ninja sword sticking out from his chest.

Muroga Hyouma once again closed his eyes.

Hyouma had been Kouga Gennosuke's teacher in the art of basilisk eyes. But Hyouma was blind and could only open his eyes and release his golden death rays at night. The student had surpassed the master. Muroga Hyouma could only substitute for Gennosuke at night, but the Iga ninja did not know that. In fact, Yakushiji Tenzen had occasionally doubted whether Muroga Hyouma had any ninja talents at all. This was exactly why Tenzen had tried to find out Hyouma's ninja skills from Jimushi Juubei.

"Saemon! Kagerou!" Gennosuke shouted.

Having lost the trail of the butterflies, Kisaragi Saemon and Kagerou returned.

"We have killed one of the Iga ninja. Based on his voice, I think it was the man named Mino Nenki."

"Wha—?" In shock, they noticed the dead body on the ground.

"So he was the one who created the butterflies?"

"No. A woman called Hotarubi is able to control insects. Saemon, where did the butterflies go?"

"To the east."

"Then Hotarubi must have gone to the west."

4

HOTARUBI RAN THROUGH THE RAIN.

She headed west from Seki along the Tokaido Road and through the Suzuka Pass. There, Hotarubi left the Tokaido Road and hurried along a road to Iga.

On her right side, small rivulets swept close to the edge of the road. On her left side, she also heard the sound of water. She crossed endless rivers. From ancient times, this area had been called the Eighty Rapids. This road also went through Iga, but unlike the Tokaido Road, it was not heavily traveled. This made it even more perilous. Thirty-two years earlier, when Tokugawa Ieyasu had fled for his life, Hattori Hanzou had led him along this road, protected by three hundred ninja from Kouga and Iga. That escape to the east on this road had constituted the only great threat to Tokugawa Ieyasu's life. The danger of the road remained unchanged.

Less speedy than the other leading ninja, Hotarubi progressed slowly along the fast-flowing rapids.

She had hoped to come across Oboro's group on this road. With the rain pelting so hard, however, they had probably changed their plan and rested for the night in a mountain lodge. But if they had, their lives were in danger. That ninja with transparent, gelatinous skin and the ability to vanish at will—Kasumi Gyoubu—had targeted them.

"Heeeeey!" From far behind her, she heard a voice. She froze.

"Heeey, Hotarubi!"

It was Mino Nenki's voice. In the midst of the rain, Hotarubi's eyes opened wide.

"Nenki—I'm here!" she cried.

Although she had left him at Seki just a short while ago, the unmistakable Mino Nenki was splashing through the water and approaching her now.

"Ah, so you're still here. I've got good news, Hotarubi—"

"Huh? What happened to Kouga Gennosuke and Muroga Hyouma?"

"I killed them. Killing those two blind men was easier than chopping radishes." Nenki grinned, showing his teeth. "Not only that, I also killed that girl Kagerou when she came back, still confused from those butterflies."

"Really! What about Kisaragi Saemon?"

"Unfortunately, he got away. As she was dying, Kagerou told me that Saemon was the one who had killed Yashamaru of Iga."

Hotarubi squeezed Nenki's hand tight. Yashamaru had been her lover. After discovering that Kisaragi Saemon had taken on Yashamaru's appearance, she had assumed he must be dead. Even so, hearing it now made her ache from anguish. She seized Nenki and shook him.

"How could you let Saemon escape, Nenki? I don't give a damn about the rest of them—I just want to kill Kisaragi Saemon!"

Only a short time earlier, she had warned him against taking risks, but now she had forgotten her warning and went into a rage. She gnashed her teeth. "But," she said, calming down, "maybe fate has chosen me to kill him . . ."

"Do you think you can kill him, Hotarubi?" he asked. "That man can change into anything. He can steal other men's faces."

"If Saemon is Yashamaru's killer, then no matter what face he puts on, I would see through his disguise . . ."

Suddenly, Hotarubi's hands stiffened on Nenki's arms. Shudders raced up her spine. She had suddenly realized that this man did not have Nenki's hairy arms.

She leaped backward. The man pursued her.

"Will you be able to see through Kisaragi Saemon's disguise, Hotarubi?"

Hotarubi leaned away from him, quickly clasping her arms before her chest. But a silver blade flashed and her white arms were instantly amputated. The blade had sliced through them horizontally, and the amputated arms flew through the sky like a falling pinecone.

"Kisaragi Saemon!" Her frightened scream was the last word she spoke.

"Your name and Nenki's name have been crossed off the list," Saemon answered.

His voice did not reach Hotarubi's ears. He had reversed the sword's direction and plunged it deep into her chest.

Only the white droplets of rain brightened the darkness. Kisaragi Saemon rested one foot on a boulder and watched Hotarubi fall from his sword, plunging toward the valley stream below.

"I never wanted to kill a woman . . ." he said, in a miserable voice that echoed in the valleys. "But this body—Nenki's body—killed my sister, Okoi. Hotarubi, ninja wars are a blood-soaked hell."

A single white butterfly floated up from the depths of the valley. Then another. A third . . . Weakly, like flowers from the underworld, the butterflies hovered in that place for the longest time.

BLOODSTAINED KASUMI

1

THE RAIN CLEARED, BUT THE OCEAN BORDERING KU-wana City remained gray. The waters were a little rough.

In that age, most people hated traveling by boat. Few customers waited at the port. The five figures sitting in the shade of the teahouse's reed screen drew numerous eyes: three men and two women. One of the men had covered his face with a white handkerchief. Only his mouth was visible. There was also a woman whose beauty outshone the lamp. She was blind.

These were the remaining members of Iga Tsubagakure: Yakushiji Tenzen, Amayo Jingorou, Chikuma Koshirou with his entire face bandaged due to severe injuries, Akeginu, and the blind Oboro. They all wore gloomy expressions.

"Do we need to cut across fourteen miles of ocean?" mumbled Amayo Jingorou, gazing across the water to the other side.

There were few customers, but lots of baggage. Many people refused to ride the boats but would ship their bag-

gage across to Miya (now called Atsuta). Heaps of luggage
of all sizes rode on the endless sampans that made the
ocean crossing. Chests, palanquins—even horses were
brought aboard. A large boat capable of carrying dozens
of people waited for them offshore.

"The waves are still fierce," Jingorou muttered glumly.
"It would be better to go around the long way, on land."
He was referring to the Sayamawari route. But that re-
quired crossing a major river, and it was much longer.
Crossing fourteen miles of ocean was far quicker than
traveling the loop by land.

Amayo Jingorou did not fear the ship—he feared the
ocean. That was because of his physical composition.

Why do slugs dissolve when they come into contact
with salt? The salt's penetrating effect causes the slug to
lose the water in its body. Most organisms—and all higher
animals—have cell membranes that limit this phenomenon. But if a normal person is submerged in salt for a long
time, a lot of the water from that person's body would be
absorbed into the salt. Furthermore, within the body, liquids are under an atmospheric pressure of eight. In the
ocean, however, the atmospheric pressure is twenty-eight,
which is extremely high. Amayo Jingorou, who shrinks
when in contact with salt, would become extremely permeable in the ocean's salt water. Like many ninja, his
unique weapon was also his Achilles' heel.

"Stop being such a selfish whiner," Tenzen said, looking disgusted. "We're not swimming through the ocean.

We're crossing on a boat. Anyway, the Kouga group seems to have taken the land route. If we chase them by land, we'll never catch them. Two members of our group are now blind."

The rainstorm had held them back for a day in the mountains, just after they crossed Kabuta in Iga. Traveling on mountain roads during a rainstorm would normally be an easy task for ninja, but neither Oboro nor Chikuma had become accustomed to their blindness.

How far ahead was the Kouga group? They had asked around earlier, but found no signs that Gennosuke's group had come through the port. They must be traveling by land—and so Tenzen would catch them by boat. But ripping at Tenzen's heart was the knowledge that Mino Nenki and Hotarubi had vanished, just like the Kouga group.

Perhaps they had been killed by Kouga!

For now, that was the only explanation. Nenki and Hotarubi must have checked on where the Kouga group was staying, only to be attacked and killed by them.

Idiots!

Tenzen gnashed his teeth in fury. If Nenki and Hotarubi had been killed, then only five remained on his side—the same as his enemies. And two of his ninja were blind. Worse, Chikuma Koshirou was wounded and useless—he only traveled with them out of a desire for revenge. And as far as Oboro, who knew whether or not she would fight Kouga Gennosuke?

A hawk, Ogen's messenger, perched on Oboro's shoulder, but Oboro just sat with her head drooping, thinking.

Oboro thought about Kouga Gennosuke.

The realization that fate had destined her to be archenemies with Gennosuke devastated her. She had no idea what this trip was for. All she knew was that Tenzen had pulled and dragged her through the mountains as if she were a marionette. Why had things become like this? Why had Tokugawa Ieyasu and Hattori Hanzou suddenly ended the ban on ninja warfare?

Despite all of fate's blows, she had only plunged into complete emotional darkness when she heard the words in Gennosuke's letter. "There are seven of you left. Until we reach the gates of Sunpu Castle, I expect the five Kouga and seven Iga will enjoy the journey." Gennosuke had clearly counted her as one of his enemies.

Also, she thought, *when he left Tsubagakure, he didn't even cast a glance at me. I remember how he coldly turned his back to me. Naturally, Gennosuke should be angry. While he was talking of love with me, the ninja of Tsubagakure were killing off the members of Kouga one by one. I didn't know that. But why would he believe me? Gennosuke must think I was planning to entrap him from the beginning. And it wouldn't be unreasonable if he did believe that. Back at Toki Pass, my companions had gotten that scroll and then they refused to let Gennosuke see it. Jingorou had lied, saying, "Iga and Kouga completed their reconciliation." And then, not realizing what was going on, I escorted Gennosuke into Tsubagakure and kept him entertained there. Why would he believe me anymore?*

I am a horrible, despicable woman. That must be how Gennosuke sees me. I only wish that Gennosuke learns I'm not the monster he thinks I am.

The only reason I came on this journey was to prove that to him. But—

Even if I could convince Gennosuke of the truth, it's already too late. Our lives have become filled with daily murders. It would be impossible for us to be together again. But in another realm—yes, in another realm, I will wait for Gennosuke. And to prove my regret, I will let him kill me with his sword.

Oboro had become obsessed with the idea of letting Gennosuke use her blood to wipe her name off the list. For the first time, a faint smile appeared on her pale cheeks.

Yakushiji Tenzen directed a suspicious sideways glance at her faint smile.

"He-e-e-ey, the boat is leaving! Passengers, hurry up and get onboard!" a voice cried out from the waters. Everyone stirred and got to their feet.

2

AS THEY BOARDED THE BOAT, YAKUSHIJI TENZEN HAD a sudden idea. "Akeginu," he whispered, "you and Amayo stay in the stern of the boat. I'm going to take Oboro into the ship's hold. And also talk to Chikuma. Tell him to sit outside the door to the hold and not to let any other passengers come inside. No matter what happens or what anyone says, he must remain seated right there. Tell him not to let anyone come inside."

"But why?"

"I expect that we'll come across the Kouga group soon after we reach Miya. But I worry about Oboro—just look at her face. Before we finish crossing the ocean, I will find out what she's thinking and make sure that she'll fight on our side."

Akeginu nodded. They needed to convince Oboro to fight on their side. But she still didn't understand why Tenzen wanted the rest of them to stay so far away.

In any case, the water was choppy, and so she and Jingorou preferred to sit in the stern. Twenty people were traveling on the boat: five women, three children, two old men, and the rest were men from the village. In contrast, the heaps of luggage made movement difficult. Chikuma Koshirou sat down in the narrow passageway that led to the hold.

Whenever anyone spoke to him, he answered huskily, "You cannot come here."

Only his mouth was visible. The rest of his face had been wrapped in a smooth, flat white handkerchief. As Tenzen led Oboro into the hold, he grinned, knowing that anyone who saw Koshirou would gulp and hurriedly head in the opposite direction.

On Tenzen's face, only a speck of a scar remained from the sword wound.

The crew winched up the sail and the boat set off.

Oboro could hear no sign of people, only the fluttering of the sail in the wind, the creaking of the mast, and the echo of pounding waves. Sitting quietly in the hold, Oboro suspiciously asked Tenzen: "Where are Akeginu, Jingorou, and Koshirou?"

Yakushiji Tenzen remained silent. Sitting directly across from Oboro, he leered at her as if he wanted to run his tongue over her face. He had always controlled his desires around Oboro due to his position as a high-ranking supporter of the clan leader. He had also been intimidated by the dazzling power of her eyes. But now Ogen was dead, and her occult-piercing eyes were closed.

Those eyelashes that cast such long shadows, that adorable nose, those soft, rose-colored lips—until now he had seen her as an angel or a princess. But now, for the first time, he gazed upon her with the sexual desires of a man. Her luscious femininity incited him with a hunger to taste her flesh.

A dark shadow crossed her beautiful face.

"Tenzen—"

"Akeginu and the others are in the stern of the boat," Tenzen said in a hoarse voice.

"Why aren't they here?"

"Because I have something that I need to discuss with you."

"What?"

"Oboro, you told me that you would not fight Kouga Gennosuke. Do you still feel that way?"

"Tenzen, even if I wanted to fight him, I'm blind."

"Your eyes will eventually open. You smeared your eyes with Seven Days of Blindness. Two nights have already passed. After five more—"

Oboro's head drooped. "During those five days, I hope to be killed by Gennosuke," she said in a tiny voice.

Yakushiji Tenzen glared at Oboro, his eyes burning with hatred. *I hope to be killed*—she wasn't making a terrified prediction. She was confessing her desire.

"I expected you'd say something like that. You won't change."

Oboro raised her blind eyes toward Tenzen. His voice sounded strange and disturbing, like he had decided to act forcefully.

"Tenzen, are you going to kill me?"

"I will not kill you. You will live. And you will be filled with life—young Iga life!"

"What do you mean, young Iga life?"

Tenzen clawed his fingers into the wooden floor, propelling himself toward Oboro without getting up. "Oboro, be my wife."

"Get off me!"

She tried to shake free from his grasping hands, but Tenzen's arms twined around her waist like snakes. Every part of him pressed against her. Even his voice glued against her ear: "This is the only way to make you forget Kouga Gennosuke. You'll never learn to see him as your enemy . . ."

"Let me go, Tenzen! Grandmother is watching over us!"

Tenzen's body reflexively stiffened. Ogen had been the only person who could control him. During this era, only the ninja clans had established ethical duties around the hierarchies of master and servant. The rest of Japanese society had not yet created a moral duty of giving and following orders. The ninja clans, on the other hand, had established ironclad rules of discipline. But Tenzen only paused for a moment.

"Unfortunately," he sneered, "Grandmother is dead! And if she were alive, she'd certainly tell you the same thing! 'Why must you marry someone from Kouga,' she'd say. Grandmother's bloodline must be preserved. You must pass on her genes. So who shall be your husband? Ogen selected six Iga men for her ninja list. You must choose one of them. Three are already dead. Jingorou, Koshirou, and I remain. Who do you choose?"

"None of you! Tenzen, just kill me!"

"I will not kill you. I need you to remain alive to serve as a symbol of Iga's victory throughout the world. From the very beginning, your engagement to Gennosuke has been an act of sheer madness. You have so infuriated our

Tsubagakure ancestors that their spirits will turn their backs on us during the next bloody ninja war with Manji-dani. You and I must be united—"

Tenzen wrapped his arm around Oboro's shoulders like a chain. Without hesitation, he stuffed his other hand into her kimono. His hand squeezed her scented pearl-like breasts. His eyes transformed from those of a servant to the eyes of a wild beast.

"Akeginu! Koshirou!" Oboro screamed. Beneath her sealed eyelids, she became dizzy with anger and fear. What kind of advisor behaved like this? Was he even human? Tenzen's actions—even Gennosuke had never dared to treat her like this.

"Akeginu and Koshirou are in the stern," Tenzen said. "Oh, you've turned hot, haven't you, my lady? I suppose there never has been a ninja skill powerful enough to steal a woman's heart—"

Tenzen pressed Oboro against the wainscoting, which stank of ocean waves. He pushed his mouth toward her lips.

"Koshirou!" she screamed.

"Shut up! Everybody already knows what I'm doing to you!"

Neither Amayo Jingorou nor Akeginu could hear her screams over the sound of the sail and the pounding of the waves. But Chikuma Koshirou, seated near the entrance to the hold, heard. Even though his entire head was wrapped in thick cloth, her screams pierced his eardrums.

What was happening?

In shock, he moved to stand, but then sat back down. Tenzen was doing something terrible, but he could do nothing about it. And Tenzen had raised him from childhood as his personal servant. Koshirou could not fight his master—but even if he wanted to, the only uninjured part of him remaining was his mouth.

And yet, below the cloth, his mouth twisted unconsciously into a pointed shape.

This is Oboro!

Oboro was also his master. She ruled all of Tsubagakure. Even if Tenzen wanted her to be his wife, he had no right to treat her so cruelly, so violently!

Koshirou's fists shook. His pursed lips made a sound. *Shuu.* That terrifying ripping sound reverberated in the air. Immediately, the swollen sail overhead was shredded.

"Koshirou!"

He leaped in the air in response to her scream of agony. "Tenzen, stop it!" he shouted. He would protect Oboro at all costs—even if it meant his own death. Young Koshirou saw Oboro as a sacred princess, not to be defiled, even by Tenzen. "Oboro!" he screamed again and rushed, trancelike and staggering from blindness, into the hold.

But at that moment, all noises coming from the hold

suddenly ceased. Koshirou became paralyzed with a terrible thought: He was too late.

What had happened?

After wrestling Oboro to the floor, Yakushiji Tenzen suddenly froze. His breathing ceased. His face turned black and purple.

An arm had twisted around Tenzen's neck. It was a thick arm, the same brown color as the ship's wainscoting.

Long strands of clotted blood hung from Tenzen's nose. His eyes became perfectly white. The hand felt Tenzen's carotid artery, verified it had no pulse, and then released him. Koshirou ran inside just as that mysterious hand vanished silently into the wainscoting. But no shadows remained on the floorboards, and there was no other sign it had been there. It was as if the hand had sunk beneath the ocean waves, swallowed without a trace.

"Oboro!"

"Koshirou!"

The two of them called out to each other. One of them was blind; white cotton covered the other one's face. Neither was able to witness the magical hand's attack.

Oboro sensed Tenzen's body becoming heavy and motionless on top of her, his skin turning cold. She screamed and sat up, forgetting her disheveled appearance.

"Did Tenzen die?" she asked.

"Tenzen?" he repeated.

"Koshirou . . . did you save me?"

"Has Tenzen died?" he asked. Hurrying toward Oboro, Koshirou tripped over Tenzen's body. He landed on the body and clung to it. "Did you do this, Oboro?" Koshirou asked, lifting his head in her direction.

Oboro remained sitting, vacant and confused. At that moment, a brown arm surfaced behind her neck and bare shoulders, leisurely bending toward her. She didn't know it was there, and it was impossible for Chikuma Koshirou to see it.

3

EVENING FOG SETTLED OVER ISE BAY. THE SINKING sun shone like a bright red bowl upon the waters. The passengers watched this beautiful image, enraptured.

Partway through the fourteen-mile trip across the ocean, the high waves calmed and the passengers who had so reluctantly boarded the ship became thankful that they could enjoy the beauty of ocean and sky.

Only one thing disturbed them: a hawk.

The bird of prey perched on the gorgeous woman's fist as she sat in the stern of the boat. Although hunting with a hawk was not unusual, it was remarkable to see a young woman bring a hawk on a sea journey. A stranger spoke to her, using an upper-class and overfamiliar tone, but the woman ignored him. And upon a closer look, the woman's appearance—her skin was as white as candle wax—made other passengers uncomfortable. Her companion was equally bizarre: Blue mold grew from his moist skin. He looked like a drowning victim. Everyone avoided eye contact and stayed away from them. In any case, the beauty of the ocean absorbed their attention. But that hawk—it kept beating its wings, flying up into the air, turning circles, and returning. It made the passengers nervous.

The two strange passengers were Akeginu and Amayo Jingorou. As they boarded the boat, Tenzen had asked that Oboro give Akeginu the hawk.

"Jingorou, it's upset about something," Akeginu said. "Something must have happened." She gestured with her chin in the direction of the hold. Heaps of luggage blocked her view, so that she couldn't see the entrance to the hold. She couldn't even see Chikuma Koshirou.

"What happened?" Jingorou said absentmindedly, looking around.

"Jingorou, I think something's wrong."

"Nineteen people . . . " Jingorou mumbled.

"Nineteen people?"

"There are only nineteen people here . . ."

"Huh?"

Amayo Jingorou snapped to his senses. "Akeginu, other than us, there were twenty passengers, right?"

"Now that you say it, I don't see the man who was wearing the bamboo hat," Akeginu cried, looking around.

When they had first gotten on the boat, there had been a man wearing a low-hanging bamboo hat. From the rim of the hat hung cotton fabric netting that looked like mosquito curtains. Beggars frequently wore this style of hat. The man who had been wearing the hat had a huge bump on his back—apparently, he was a hunchback. When they first saw him, they assumed that he wore this hat with its hanging cotton netting because he was ashamed of being a hunchback and he wanted to cover his face. But now both hunchback and bamboo hat had suddenly disappeared.

Jingorou stood up and nervously looked over at the luggage. Suddenly—

"Hey!" he shouted. "There's the hat—he left it behind!"

The man had left the bamboo hat in the shadows of the luggage. The man's clothes had been left behind as well, heaped up in a pile of rags. But the man had vanished. After stripping naked, where could he go? Into the ocean?

The hold!

Jingorou screamed, his face blanching. He ran into the hold, Akeginu following close behind.

They raced inside just as the strange arm wrapped around Oboro's neck. In the time it took their eyes to adjust to the darkness inside the hold, the arm disappeared. They didn't see it.

"Tenzen!"

"Tenzen, what happened?"

Oboro and Koshirou struggled to explain. Only moments earlier, they had discovered that Yakushiji Tenzen was dead. They didn't know how it happened.

"It must have been him!" Jingorou said. *The invisible Kasumi Gyoubu.*

Akeginu clung to Tenzen's body. Jingorou whipped out his sword and began searching the room like a madman. But he found no suspicious shadows. His face full of fear and worry, Jingorou slashed his sword against the walls and the floorboards. Nothing happened.

Jingorou left the hold.

Faint laughter sounded from the shadows of a chest near the edge of the boat. Jingorou shuffled toward it. Suddenly, his sword-holding hand was seized. Another hand grabbed his neck. From the side of the black chest sprang two dark hands.

"Ah—Akeginu!"

That scream was the final sound to escape from Jingorou's throat. There was the sound of running footsteps, and then the arms hurled Jingorou over the side of the boat.

Jingorou was still screaming as he plunged into the ocean.

Akeginu had run to his voice, and, terrified, she looked over the edge of the boat. The crew of the boat also came running. They didn't yet understand what had happened. One of them had grabbed the rail of the boat, ready to jump into the sea, when he saw something that made him scream.

"What is that?" cried a sailor, who also saw it.

"That guy, he's—"

When Jingorou had screamed, it was not in reaction to the hands throwing him or the distance he fell. He screamed out of fear of the ocean.

As he convulsed in the blue water, a sticky, gooey substance leaked from his collar and sleeves, spreading on the water's surface. His body shriveled in mere seconds.

Those on the boat were watching a human being dissolve into a strange, slimy liquid.

Akeginu immediately tore off her sash and stripped out of her kimono. She had no time to worry about who saw her body. She revealed her breasts to the setting sun and aimed her naked body for the ocean . . .

But before she could dive, she heard a bloodcurdling scream behind her.

The scream had come from the chest. But not from inside it. It came from the surface of the chest. Strange wrinkles rippled along the black paint.

The ship's crew nearly fainted as they watched a naked monk bubble up from the surface of the chest.

"Kasumi Gyoubu!" Akeginu shouted, jumping back.

But Gyoubu was not looking at Akeginu. Instead, he was staring transfixed at the door to the ship's hold.

Standing in the doorway was Yakushiji Tenzen.

The shock of seeing Tenzen had broken Gyoubu's concentration and he lost his camouflage.

Earlier, Gyoubu had strangled Tenzen to death. Blood had trickled from Tenzen's nose, and Gyoubu had confirmed that his heart had stopped beating.

"So it's you, Gyoubu," Tenzen said, his purple lips lifted in a complacent smile. He smoothly drew his sword and rushed toward Gyoubu like a gust of wind.

Kasumi Gyoubu's face showed fear for only a moment. Then he smiled. His gelatinous, transparent body once again began sinking mysteriously into the chest's paint.

"The god of war will not help you escape this time, Gyoubu!" Akeginu shouted.

As she shouted, a geyser of red mist erupted from her nipples, solar plexus, and belly. Millions of blood droplets sprayed forth from every pore of her skin.

A moment later, the blood mist had cleared. Nothing moved on the surface of the chest, which was now painted red.

But seven or eight feet away, a red figure stood out against the wall of the boat like a giant red spider. Tenzen leaped through the air, and plunged his sword through its chest.

There was no cry. But the red figure convulsed, and then turned limp and ceased moving. When Tenzen pulled his sword out of the wall, the resulting hole in the wood plank gushed forth a waterfall of blood.

Once Kasumi Gyoubu had been covered with the blood mist, it was impossible for him to vanish.

Yakushiji Tenzen and Akeginu looked back at the ship's wake. Ripples from the wake shone in the moonlight, but the rest of the ocean remained vast and dark. The western horizon still had traces of red light, but there was no longer any sign of Amayo Jingorou.

Yakushiji Tenzen removed the ninja scroll from his kimono. He moistened a finger in the blood that had spilled from the wooden planks. He drew a thick red line through the name of the Kouga warrior Kasumi Gyoubu.

After thinking for a while, he gloomily drew lines through the names of the Iga ninja Amayo Jingorou, Mino Nenki, and Hotarubi.

"Both sides are even. Four against four," he grunted.

Even after we arrive at Miya, it will still be eighty-eight miles to Sunpu, Yakushiji Tenzen thought. As he calculated, a cold smile fluttered across his face. If he divided the eighty-eight miles in two for the two sides of Iga and Kouga, the result was forty-four. Forty-four—four lives remaining on each side. He calculated further. Who would survive? On his side, two of his remaining ninja had recently been blinded. He continued to consider his options in this deadly game of ninja chess, but his confidence and his laughter were gone.

THE SEDUCTIVE KILLER
KAGEROU

1

THREE MILES TO THE EAST OF MIYA WAS NARUMI. ANother four miles away was Chiriyuu. In between them was the bridge called Sakai. Sakai Bridge marks where the Tokaido Road crosses the border between Ohari and Mikawa.

Something horrible had been planted at the foot of the Sakai Bridge. Travelers would stop in front of it, twisting their necks as they stared, and then shudder at the image and run away.

It was a large plank of wood. Although old and chewed on by insects, it was a sturdy plank. A reddish-black mark stained its surface. "What is that?" people would ask, stopping to look. But soon they would recognize the smell of blood and see the shape of a human figure. Without speaking another word, they would flee from that gruesome object.

The spring sun had begun sinking when four passing travelers froze and stared at the wooden plank. Three of them were warriors. One was a woman. And among the three warriors, one wore a hooded cloak.

Unlike the other travelers, they remained at that spot, silent, for what seemed an eternity.

At last, they took down the board. A warrior with handsome features placed the board on his back and carried it from the road. He walked along the river. The woman crouched and plucked flowers.

They placed the board on the surface of the water and the woman placed flowers on top. The river carried the board away in silence.

In ancient times, this region had the tradition of sending off the spirits of the dead with floating lanterns. This eerie tradition was called *tourou nagashi*.

"Gyoubu was killed by the enemy. May his soul rest in peace," the man in the hooded cloak murmured sadly.

"But the fact that that thing was placed here means . . ." the woman mumbled as her eyes followed the board floating away, ". . . that board came from a ship. Gyoubu was killed onboard a ship. These are dangerous enemies."

"And our enemies left it here as a challenge," the hooded man said, grinding his teeth.

A second hooded man spoke up. "I sense that the Iga ninja are watching us right now."

The young warrior looked up and scanned his surroundings. He was Gennosuke. Miraculously, his eyes were shining brilliantly. The Seven Days of Blindness had forced his eyes shut, but they were open again after only three days.

KOUGA GENNOSUKE'S basilisk eyes sliced through vegetation as he searched the area. Nearby, two figures flattened themselves behind an embankment. They had barely escaped Gennosuke's basilisk eyes, but they could feel his gaze pass overhead and the hairs on their bodies stood on end.

The two spies watched the four travelers return to the road.

"So we meet at last," Yakushiji Tenzen mumbled.

"Tenzen, what do we do now?" Akeginu asked, raising her head. "There are four of them. We also have four members, but the other two are blind—"

"There are still eighty miles to Sunpu. We can wait for the right opportunity. And remember that they have a blind member, too—Muroga Hyouma."

They didn't know that, back at Seki, Hotarubi had temporarily blinded Gennosuke. Even if they had known, it didn't matter. His eyes were open now.

"So what about that hooded one?"

"Hmm. I think he must be Kisaragi Saemon. For the time being, let's start by killing the blind ninja—Hyouma. Let's see where they stay tonight. They might stay at Chiriyuu, but more likely, they will keep going until they reach Okasaki. In any case, we kill Hyouma tonight. As for Oboro . . ."

The blinded Oboro and Chikuma Koshirou were staying in an inn at Chiriyuu while Tenzen and Akeginu went scouting for the Kouga band.

"She will just be a burden—physically and mentally. Keep it a secret that we've found Gennosuke and the others. Tonight, while you keep Oboro company, pretend you don't know about Kouga."

"What about you?" she asked.

"I'll take Koshirou with me and we'll go after them. Koshirou seems to have recovered a lot. The two of us will attack the Kouga group."

"I hope everything goes well," she said.

Yakushiji Tenzen stared at Akeginu. She had a feminine smile.

"Are you concerned about me?" he asked.

"No, I'm concerned about Koshirou," Akeginu answered. Her pale cheeks flushed. Throughout their journey from Iga, she had sympathized with the injured Koshirou. Feelings for him had begun to bud in her heart.

"Akeginu, this is not a round-trip journey," Tenzen said harshly. "Either we kill them or we are killed. We should each expect to lose our life. Don't be stupid."

"I understand!"

"What I want to say is that the men and women in our group have developed feelings for one another on this journey." He grinned. "Akeginu—if we succeed in killing all the Kouga ninja, perhaps we can hold two weddings."

2

AS TENZEN PREDICTED, THE KOUGA NINJA PASSED through Chiriyuu without stopping. Apparently, they intended to reach Okasaki. But the sun was already setting.

To the east of Chiriyuu there was a place called Komaba. In ancient times, a river split in eight directions, like the shape of a spider. Because there were eight bridges, the region became known as the Eight Bridges. At a place called Kakitsubata, the poet Narihira used the five syllables of the word "Kakitsubata" to begin each of the five lines of his famous poem: "The Chinese robe that I have become so accustomed to wearing—picking up its hem, I think of the long journey that I have taken and I think of the wife that I am used to." He was describing this place. But the river had long ago dried up, replaced with vast plains.

Every year from April 25 to May 5, a famous horse market is held at this spot. Horse dealers, merchants, and four or five hundred horses—the fields are filled with the sounds of neighing, shouted deals, and kicked-up dust. As the Kouga ninja arrived at this field, the horse market had just ended. On either side of the road, one saw unending waves of grass, and in the distance the moon rising like a thread in the sky.

The four Kouga ninja traveled the road like a gust of wind: Kouga Gennosuke, Kagerou, and two men wearing hoods.

Overhead, they heard a strange flapping noise. They looked up.

"Ah—that's it!" Kouga Gennosuke shouted automatically.

A hawk. This was not the hawk that had flown over the Toki Pass clutching the proclamation announcing a war to the death between the Kouga and Iga. But just like that hawk, this one clutched an unfurled scroll in its talons!

"What is that?" asked Muroga Hyouma, inside his woven-hemp hood. He was blind and could not see it.

"It's a hawk, carrying that scroll—"

Faster than words, two of them chased eastward after the hawk. Gennosuke raced out ahead. Kagerou ran behind. The fluttering scroll skimmed the grass as it sped farther and farther away. Without realizing it, they had been lured from the others.

"Wait!" Hyouma yelled, but his voice did not reach them. The other hooded figure silently sat on a rock. Both of the hooded Kouga men hung behind.

A figure rose like fog from the grass and soundlessly approached. He had a smooth, expressionless face: Yakushiji Tenzen. Perhaps from fear, perhaps from caution, he stopped and stared at the two hooded figures.

He had used the hawk as bait to draw away the three Kouga members with eyesight. He had expected to be left alone with Hyouma. The fact that two Kouga members had remained behind meant that his plan had gone awry. But the dangerous one, Kouga Gennosuke, was gone. The remaining ones were just Muroga Hyouma and Kisaragi Saemon. From hearing his shout, Tenzen recognized that Hyouma was the one standing. Then the seated man must be Kisaragi Saemon. Even so, he sensed something was wrong.

The seated man lifted his hooded head and spoke. "Yakushiji Tenzen?"

That voice startled Tenzen. The faint moonlight shone on the face of the man in the hood—

"Kouga Gennosuke, you're blind!" he shouted.

In a flash, Tenzen realized what had happened. When he saw Kouga Gennosuke chase the hawk earlier, it had actually been Kisaragi Saemon. Tenzen knew that Saemon could imitate the voices and appearances of all the Iga ninja. But Tenzen hadn't expected him to adopt the appearance of his own ally Gennosuke. Saemon must have done that to trick the Iga ninja into believing that Gennosuke was not blind. Back at the bridge, when Tenzen had seen Gennosuke with his eyes open—that wasn't Gennosuke at all, it was Kisaragi Saemon pretending to be Gennosuke! Gennosuke was still blind and hiding beneath a hood. *Hotarubi and Mino Nenki must have succeeded in that part of their attack. The Seven Days of Blindness potion must have closed his eyes.*

"Ha ha ha ha ha!"

Tenzen couldn't help but roar with laughter. He laughed not only because Gennosuke's eyes had been destroyed, but he was also laughing at himself for being so worried the past few days. "So, we have two blind men?" Tenzen said. "Too bad you weren't able to enjoy the sight I left for you at Sakai Bridge. And I had gone to so much trouble!"

"I saw Kasumi Gyoubu in my heart," Muroga Hyouma answered. "I appreciate it that you showed him to me. Thank you."

"Can you also see this in your heart?" Tenzen screamed. Metal flashed. His blade ripped through Muroga Hyouma's hood. Muroga Hyouma took several steps back, just as if he could see his attacker's location. His hood had been torn in half vertically, revealing his intelligent face. His eyes were closed. He carried no weapon and he seemed to have no way to defend himself.

Tenzen confidently turned toward Gennosuke. But he felt an uncomfortable cold sensation behind him, coming from Hyouma.

"Kouga Gennosuke!" Tenzen cried in an unintentionally shrill voice. "I wanted to leave you to die last. I had intended to exterminate the entire Kouga clan first, and then make you watch me marry Oboro before I killed you. However, fate has brought you here. You will die by my hand first."

"Too bad . . ." said Gennosuke. Sitting on a rock, the blinded, grinning Gennosuke laughed. "I won't be able to see you wed Oboro. Because you are about to die!"

"What?"

"Your death is the only thing I will be able to see. Me— and Hyouma!"

Tenzen swung his sword at Gennosuke, but in the process he glanced at Muroga Hyouma.

From between the two shreds of his torn hood, Muroga Hyouma was looking at Tenzen. His eyes were open wide, and a golden ray of light shot out.

"Hyouma, you—!"

Tenzen intended to execute a reverse-cut with his sword, but his arm began to twist in an awkward movement. Not only did his arm twist—Tenzen's feminine face became a mass of twitching flesh and muscles. His sword cut into his own shoulder and chopped down diagonally. Blood spurted. He took five or six steps to the side, and then tumbled into the grass.

Hyouma once again closed his eyes. Gennosuke remained sitting on the stone.

Not long after, Kagerou and Kouga Gennosuke returned, pushing through the high grass. Not the real Gennosuke, of course—it was Kisaragi Saemon. He and Kagerou looked flustered.

"Ah, you're safe!" Kagerou said, releasing a huge gasp of air. Saemon was panting so hard that his shoulders heaved.

"The hawk was mocking us," Saemon said. "We were tricked into running in circles in the fields. When we finally realized what it was doing, we hurried back. I'm glad that nothing happened while we were gone . . ." He paused in the middle of his sentence as he noticed something splattered like an oil stain on the road. He swallowed.

Hyouma smiled faintly. "Yakushiji Tenzen showed up."

"Uh—what happened?"

"I killed him. I think his dead body fell in a clump of grass over there."

Kisaragi Saemon climbed through a thicket of grass that had been battered down and smeared with streaks of blood. Kagerou started to follow him, but Gennosuke called to her.

"Kagerou, did you catch the hawk?"

"Well, the thing about the hawk is—something seemed to be hiding in the grass, controlling its movements—"

"I asked if you caught the hawk."

Kagerou stared at Gennosuke's displeased face. She sensed his heart was focused on Oboro. Even now, Gennosuke was thinking about Oboro. He was wondering whether it had been she guiding the hawk. He was wondering what had happened to her. He looked concerned.

"The hawk escaped," Kagerou said.

Was it her imagination? Gennosuke seemed somewhat happy at the news.

She scowled. "Saemon threw his knife at it, and the

hawk dropped the scroll. By the time we picked up the scroll, the hawk had disappeared. But one thing's for certain: The Iga ninja are all here, somewhere, hiding in the high grass."

Kagerou had the beauty of a tree peony—but now her beauty was outlined with a glowing air of fury. Gennosuke didn't see that. He coughed and continued.

"So, you were able to get the ninja scroll. Let me see it." He stopped and corrected himself. "I mean, read it to me." He stood up.

Kagerou opened the ninja scroll. She held it up against the thin moon to read it.

"Gyoubu's name has been crossed off," she said.

"Hmmph."

"On the Iga side, ahh—Mino Nenki, Hotarubi, and Amayo Jingorou—"

"What, Amayo Jingorou as well? Gyoubu must have killed him."

"There are four Kouga and four Iga left."

"No, only three Iga," Kisaragi Saemon said. He sliced his knife all the way across the neck of Yakushiji Tenzen, who had already ceased breathing.

"Gennosuke, how do we win this war against Tsubagakure?"

"I don't know yet," he said. Gloom flickered across his face.

"Anyway," Saemon said, "Yakushiji Tenzen was the worst of them. His ninja skills weren't what made him so frightening—it was his infinite selfishness. Two of the remaining three are women. Even if Chikuma Koshirou is traveling with them, he's probably still unable to see. Gennosuke ripped his face apart during their duel at Ogen's palace." For some reason, Saemon picked up Tenzen's bloody body. "Kagerou, you go with Gennosuke and Hyouma to Okasaki."

"What about you, Saemon?" she asked.

"I have some use for this dead man." He grinned. "So, those three are our only remaining opponents. Even if they try to attack us, we're ready for them. Oboro's eyes are powerful, but we have Hyouma's eyes on our side. And Hyouma cannot see Oboro's eyes! That makes Hyouma a much more powerful opponent for Oboro than Gennosuke! So all we need to worry about is Akeginu's blood mist."

Kagerou also grinned. She tugged the distressed-looking Kouga Gennosuke by his sleeve.

"Let's go then, Gennosuke."

Kagerou, unlike Gennosuke, looked overjoyed.

The three figures faded into the moonlight as they headed eastward. Kisaragi Saemon turned and dragged Yakushiji Tenzen's body into the grass.

Traces of the water current that had once earned this place the name Eight Bridges still appeared here and there in the Komaba fields. A little while earlier, Kisaragi Saemon had heard the faint sound of a stream. He searched for it now.

Saemon found a thin stream of water and laid the corpse lengthwise alongside it. He meticulously kneaded the water and mud. Kisaragi Saemon had begun the mystical ritual for adopting another person's face.

3

FROM THE DARK MOONLIGHT AT THE EDGE OF THE field came a distant shout. Kagerou, Gennosuke, and Hyouma, who were walking along the path, froze in place.

"It's a man's voice."

The speaker burst through the grass, approaching them.

"He-e-e-e-y, Tenzen!"

A silhouette appeared, standing unsteadily at the end of the road.

It was a very strange-looking silhouette. A hawk perched upon the man's shoulder. A scythe with a three-foot-long blade hung from one hand. Also, its entire head above the neck—excluding the nose and mouth—was wrapped in white cloth.

Chikuma Koshirou. He had been hiding in the high grass, and he had directed the hawk through his movements. Tenzen would kill Muroga Hyouma, he believed, while Koshirou distracted the other Kouga fighters. Koshirou had complete faith in Tenzen. Tenzen had raised him from childhood.

As for me, Koshirou thought, *I have already made*

peace with death. But I also am confident that, if the chance arises, I will be able to kill at least one of my enemies.

However, the Kouga ninja did not discover him directing the hawk. When the hawk returned to his shoulder without the scroll in its talons, he concluded that the enemy had been satisfied with merely obtaining the scroll and had given up the chase. But what happened to Tenzen?

Driven by worry, Koshirou finally left the thicket where he'd been hiding. He was fully aware that the Kouga group might still be in Komaba. Regardless of whether Tenzen had killed Hyouma, or whether Tenzen had been killed by him, Koshirou's sense of duty and desire for revenge drove him to try to kill the entire Kouga group by himself. His lust for battle pushed him to act in an uncontrolled, unplanned frenzy.

"Where are you, Tenzen—" he pleaded in a heartrending voice.

When his hawk suddenly circled up from his shoulder, the three prepared Kouga fighters were at a distance of thirty feet. Kagerou had snapped a branch from a cherry tree and was tossing it out of the way—

"You're from Kouga!" Koshirou shouted, and he pursed his lips.

Kouga Gennosuke's hood ripped open, the rags scattering. "Watch out!" he screamed. The cherry branch that Kagerou had tossed ahead of them was ripped apart in the whirlwind, shreds flying in all directions. Kagerou, Hyouma, and Gennosuke dived to the side of the road and crouched in the grass.

Chikuma Koshirou's powerful sucking could create whirling vacuums in the air. Despite his injury, he had never lost this power. It was a terrifying weapon. During the Iga surprise attack on Manjidani, they had witnessed his black holes ripping apart the faces of numerous Kouga fighters—their heads looked like ripe pomegranates bursting open.

Kagerou scampered through the grass, circling around to the side. Koshirou lifted his scythe high over his head and swung it across the empty road. Those watching immediately recognized that this man whose entire face was covered in white cloth was blind.

Kagerou's knife glinted in the moonlight, and the hawk immediately swooped between the two of them.

"Come on!" With a yell, Koshirou's scythe cut like a comet, making a huge loop. Kagerou leaped out of the way, her back hitting the ground hard. Overhead, the droopy heads of Japanese pampas grass immediately burst apart from the violent pull of a vacuum.

The hawk circled over the heads of the three warriors, its beating wings making a tremendous noise. Koshirou accurately aimed his strikes—ripping the air with black holes—by relying on that sound. The three Kouga ninja tumbled through the grass in a desperate retreat. It was a remarkable sight—a single blind, wounded ninja ferociously chasing three opponents.

"Kagerou, protect Gennosuke!"

Kagerou heard Muroga Hyouma's voice even as she threw herself over Gennosuke's crouching body. Glancing up, she saw Hyouma run out onto the road, waving one hand at them. He was telling them to run. His other hand carried a sword.

Kagerou shielded Gennosuke as they raced back down the road on which they had come, the hawk circling above them in the air. Following the sound of its flapping wings, Chikuma Koshirou pursued them.

"You Iga baboon!" Hyouma shouted. "Wait for me!"

Koshirou turned and looked back. "Who are you?"

"Muroga Hyouma." Immediately after answering, Hyouma crouched low and sprinted forward. Behind and above him, in the place where he had spoken, the air ripped apart.

Both of these men were blind. Blind—but both ninja. However, Hyouma had been born blind, and he moved with greater accuracy and speed. His blade sliced forward and Koshirou barely managed to block the blow, parrying not with the blade of his scythe, but with the handle.

Hyouma's sword chopped the handle in two, which split apart in Koshirou's hands. Nearly cleaved in two like a pear, Koshirou leaped backward.

Hyouma began to close in on him again when he sensed

Koshirou sucking air through his pursed lips. In that moment of terror, Hyouma knew he could not avoid Koshirou's attack.

"Look at me, Koshirou!" he screamed in a ragged voice, and opened his eyes. Golden arrows of light shot forth.

Perhaps Muroga Hyouma already knew at this moment what his fate would be. Surely he had known that Chikuma Koshirou might be waiting to ambush them after they separated from Saemon. But perhaps the surprise of the attack had confused him. Or maybe Hyouma was confused because he could not see Koshirou. In any case, Chikuma Koshirou was still blind.

If Hyouma had been Oboro, he would not have been able to use his basilisk eyes on her either because she was also unable to open her eyes. Even so, at least Hyouma could open his eyelids and shoot his rays of death. That was why Saemon said that Hyouma was currently more powerful than Gennosuke. But against Chikuma Koshirou, whose face was wrapped in white cloth, those rays of death had no effect. Hyouma cried "Look at me, Koshirou!" but Koshirou could not look. Even a weapon that can kill nine out of ten opponents depends on the luck of the moment. Fate's cruel whimsy chooses the winner and loser.

Where Muroga Hyouma stood, the air fluttered before his sightless eyes and his face burst open like the flesh of

a pomegranate. He staggered and his sword plunged into
the dirt. His weight shifted forward upon the hilt of the
sword. There, standing in place, Muroga Hyouma died.

4

PERHAPS MUROGA HYOUMA HAD ACTED TO SAVE GEN-
nosuke. Perhaps he had chosen to die. But in any case, he
had been a leading figure at Kouga Manjidani. In contrast, Chikuma Koshirou had been merely a servant controlled by Yakushiji Tenzen. In other words, he was a foot
soldier. The worst possible fortune for a general is to be
killed by a common soldier.

But Chikuma Koshirou felt no excitement at his victory.
Even if he showed any reaction, it was covered in cloth
and not visible to others. He merely swiveled around,
seeking his next prey like a hunting bird.

At that moment, he heard a woman's voice in the distance.

"Koshirou! Koshirou—"

"Uh?"

Footsteps ran toward him as the voice cried his name.

"Koshirou!"

"Akeginu?" He recognized her voice, but he was startled. Akeginu and Oboro should still be at the inn at
Chiriyuu. But he could feel Akeginu's breath as she approached within four or five steps of him.

"The person standing there—"

"Yes. He died where he stood. That's Muroga Hyouma of Kouga."

"Ah, I see—"

"But what's going on with you? What happened at the inn in Chiriyuu? What happened to Oboro?"

"Ah, Koshirou . . . Kisaragi Saemon from Kouga attacked us. And Oboro, she—it was terrible!"

"What happened to Oboro?" Koshirou reacted as if jolted with electricity.

"They captured Oboro . . . They tortured her to death."

Koshirou staggered. For a moment, he could only tremble. His voice had died. At last, gathering his strength, he spoke.

"What about Tenzen? He told me he would kill Muroga Hyouma, but I killed Hyouma just now . . . I think Kisaragi Saemon must have adopted Tenzen's appearance in order to trick us and then attacked the inn. Damn you, Saemon! Just let me find you . . ."

"But, Koshirou—now that Oboro is dead, Iga has already lost."

"No, we can't lose. Can Iga lose to Kouga? Akeginu, what exactly happened when you saw them kill Oboro? You watched them kill her and then ran here?"

"No, no. They tied me up . . . I was able to escape and I ran out here to tell Tenzen—"

Chikuma Koshirou twisted in agony. Raising his face in

her direction, he roared, "I don't want to hear it! You should have died, too!"

"Koshirou, kill me!" Akeginu flung herself upon Koshirou's chest. He tore open her kimono, revealing her flesh. She writhed, her skin burning hot. Even her voice had changed: "Kill me! Kill me!"

Koshirou inhaled the gasping breath of the woman's lips. This was the first time that he had tasted the bittersweet breath of a woman. His intense, youthful mind was thrown into confusion.

"You should die! Die!" He turned his head away from her, howling the words, almost shrieking. The woman's chest and arms wrapped around Koshirou like a snake.

"Koshirou, I love you. Let's die together."

Growing up in the valley of Tsubagakure, Koshirou had thought of Akeginu as an older sister. A beautiful sister with pale skin, so cold and mysterious that she sent shivers down one's spine. Now she clung to him, boiling with passion. But he was not so surprised. During the trip, she had cared for him with such tenderness, and even spoke to him in a voice soaked with emotion. He imagined her breasts throbbing.

He thought of how Tenzen had assaulted Oboro—Tenzen would never have done such a thing back at Tsubagakure. Tenzen later claimed that he was only trying to lure Kasumi Gyoubu into attacking, but Koshirou felt certain this was a lie. What had happened to them? Had they all been driven insane by violence in the days after leaving Tsubagakure?

Now Oboro had been killed. Even if they went to Sunpu, what would happen? *Let's die together,* Akeginu had said. Or should they run off somewhere together? A tornado of self-destruction swirled inside his heart.

"Akeginu—" He squeezed her slender body. They stood in a road still slick with Muroga Hyouma's blood. He felt drunk from the scent of blood. No—he was drunk off of this woman's apricot-scented breath—

"Koshirou, let's die . . ."

The woman's voice filtered deep into his paralyzed brain. *This isn't Akeginu's voice . . .* By the time he realized that, Koshirou's spirit had already departed this world.

This young Iga warrior, incomparable in battle, ceased moving while in the arms of a woman.

Kagerou breathed heavily. Her face had an incomparable seductive power.

Ever since she clung to him, she had spoken with her own voice. Chikuma Koshirou hadn't noticed because his mind had already become paralyzed from her breath. In the beginning, a different man, standing behind Kagerou, had imitated Akeginu's voice. Later, he simply stood there and watched as Koshirou died.

The moon, hanging like a thread, shone down upon that man's face, expressionless as a Noh mask. The face belonged to Yakushiji Tenzen, but the voice had been that of a woman—a perfect imitation of Akeginu.

This man lifted his eyes and looked at Muroga Hyouma's dark shape, standing like a pillar. Gnashing his teeth, he mumbled: "If we had only known that Koshirou—"

But he broke off, looking up at the sound of flapping wings. As if unable to make a decision, the hawk turned irregular circles in the air. Suddenly it soared off toward the west.

"Well," he said, "according to Koshirou, Oboro is in an inn back at Chiriyuu."

Kouga Gennosuke approached the pair. Tenzen—or, actually, Kisaragi Saemon in the form of Tenzen—pulled a scroll from his kimono. He swiped Muroga Hyouma's blood from the ground and drew three lines on the scroll.

"Yakushiji Tenzen, Chikuma Koshirou, both dead . . . Hyouma was killed . . ."

His eyes closed, Kouga Gennosuke spoke gloomily. "Five ninja remain."

THE IMMORTAL PHOENIX
OF THE NINJA

A SUPERNATURAL BATTLE TO THE DEATH HAD JUST ended, and only the sound of wind remained in the Komaba plains. Where had the Kouga ninja gone? Throughout the plains, not a shadow remained. The white scythe of the moon sent silvery rays cutting through the waves of grass.

But, although none knew it, something strange moved in the shadows cast by the high grass. Could it really be described as moving? If you were to stare at it, you'd see nothing. But if you closed your eyes for a while and then opened them again, you would see that it had changed. But there were no bystanders to be startled by the sight. And even if someone had been there, no normal person could bear looking at that gruesome scene.

In the shadow of the grass, near the water, lay the body of Yakushiji Tenzen. Not long ago, hypnotized by Muroga Hyouma's catlike eyes, he had slashed himself diagonally from his shoulder to his waist. Kisaragi Saemon made sure he was dead by slitting his throat. This was Tenzen's corpse.

The corpse wasn't actively moving. Dried mud covered its face. Only the eyes were visible: white eyes without any shine to them, emitting a dull light. But . . . slowly, the injured neck and shoulder were changing.

When cut by a blade—even a thin blade—the skin will pull apart into a gaping hole that resembles leaves on a red willow tree. This occurs because of the pulling power of the skin. An immense amount of blood pours from a gash in the skin. Of course, blood soon clots. As blood clots, the blood oozes more slowly and thickens.

Although it would be difficult to see in the pale moon's rays, Tenzen's blood had turned a yellowish red color at his wounds. This was because the white blood cells, the lymphocytes, and cellulose had begun fusing with the clotted blood. But the fluids only act that way in live, healing bodies.

A wild rat ran through the grass and climbed atop Tenzen's body, licking at his blood. Suddenly, it became frightened and leaped into the water. The weird stench of fresh blood wafted upward, darkening the moon.

A bird's silhouette skimmed over the rusty surface of the moon.

The hawk swooped down, landing upon something standing in the road. That thing was Muroga Hyouma, who had died where he stood and looked like a guardian deva for the road. The hawk landed on his head.

Two shadows approached from the west. They saw the strange corpse upon which the hawk had perched.

"What is that?" one of them yelled. The shadow then ran toward another body, one crumpled upon the ground. *"Oh, Koshirou!"* She screamed as if a hole had been gouged out of her body.

Akeginu. The other one, wearing a woman's bamboo hat, was Oboro. They had remained behind at the Chiriyuu inn. Just when they had started to worry, the hawk that had left with Yakushiji Tenzen and Chikuma Koshirou for the Komaba plains had returned—alone. The two women followed the hawk and hurried toward the Komaba plains. Only Akeginu knew Tenzen and Koshirou had attacked the Kouga group that night. Oboro knew nothing. As they ran, Akeginu told Oboro about Tenzen's plan.

"Koshirou! Koshirou!" Akeginu wept. Ninja are trained to maintain silence, making no sound even at the death of parents or children. For the first time, Oboro witnessed Akeginu crying in agony like a woman.

Akeginu had thought of Koshirou as her beloved. He was her first love. Now, holding Koshirou's dead body, she forgot even that she was a ninja.

"But there's no wound!" she cried. "There's no wound!"

When Akeginu finally came to her senses, a cold chill ran through her spine. *Kouga is our enemy,* she thought, regaining consciousness. She lifted her eyes.

"You are the one who killed Koshirou!" she growled at Hyouma's body, climbing to her feet. His face had been torn open like a pomegranate, and he was clearly dead. Even so, Akeginu's shaking hand pulled out a knife.

"Akeginu," Oboro spoke, a shudder in her voice. "Who is it?"

"A member of Kouga . . . died. But he seemed to have killed Koshirou at the same time."

"So who—"

"Koshirou destroyed his face, so I can't tell who it is. It could be Kisaragi Saemon, Muroga Hyouma, Kouga Gennosuke—"

"Uh? Gennosuke?"

"No . . . His hair is pulled back in the samurai style. I'd guess it was Muroga Hyouma." With those words, Akeginu marched forward and jabbed her knife into the dead man's body. Hyouma fell to the ground.

"Akeginu!" Oboro shrieked, sensing Akeginu's movements. "Don't do such shameful things! It was inhuman the way that Yakushiji Tenzen stuck Kasumi Gyoubu into the ground at Sakai Bridge. Even if these are our enemies—even if he and Chikuma Koshirou did kill each other—humiliating his corpse will not bring Koshirou back!"

"There can be no mercy in a war between ninja," Akeginu answered. "Oboro—Oboro, when it comes to Kouga, your—"

She stopped halfway, staring at Oboro with a look close to hatred.

Oboro was blind and could not see Akeginu's glare. She spoke in a low voice. "No . . . I just mean that, we might become corpses, too . . ." Although blinded, she moved her head as if looking around. "What about Tenzen?"

"I don't see him. There's one Kouga corpse here. That means three of them remain. Perhaps Tenzen chased after them—"

"What if Tenzen has also been killed in battle?"

As if twitching, Akeginu's face smiled. "Well, if Tenzen was killed . . ." She laughed.

If Tenzen had been there with them, his greater ninja skills would have immediately sensed drawn weapons nearby. Akeginu finally sensed the enemy's presence and halted in midlaugh.

2

THE MOON HAD SHIFTED A LITTLE. YAKUSHIJI TEN-zen's corpse continued to change.

The liquids that had oozed from his body were undergoing a process known in pathology as granulation, the process of rebuilding flesh. In an ordinary person, it would take three days just for the edges of a wound to close. Tenzen's body completed the process in a few hours. And yet, he was dead . . .

But if one pressed an ear close . . .

Although he should have been killed when his throat was slit, a tiny, infinitesimal heartbeat remained.

Ah—an immortal ninja! Yakushiji Tenzen's talent would stun even those ninja with powers capable of terrifying the heavens.

This is why Yakushiji Tenzen could discuss his memories of the Iga Rebellion from forty or fifty years earlier with the elderly Ogen. This explained his comment that he had seen the 170- or 180-year-old zelkova tree in Kouga Manjidani as a sapling. This was the great secret behind his ability to reappear after Jimushi Juubei spit a spear through his heart and after Kasumi Gyoubu strangled him to death during the boat ride from Kuwana to Miya. And this was also the basis of his confident declaration, "We will defeat Kouga! We will definitely defeat Kouga!"

Tenzen still hadn't moved. His eyes were white and bulging. But the moonlight shining on his injury showed that the skin had smoothed together, swollen and shiny like silk. The wounds continued healing . . .

Wind blew through the plains. But strangely, in this one area, the grass drooped in a silence of stagnation and death. And yet there was noise. It sounded like the wailing of banshees. The eyes had been open and staring, but now the eyelids flickered—he had begun to move.

OBORO ORDERED Akeginu to dig a shallow hole in the thickets near the road. Akeginu dug using Koshirou's scythe.

"Koshirou! Koshirou!" She broke into tears again and again.

Oboro listened, her bamboo hat hanging low. She made no noise, but her heart cried out, "Gennosuke!" She feared more for the fate of her enemy, Gennosuke, than for her ally, Tenzen.

Akeginu's wails resounded like mountain echoes. In the shadows of the grass, Kouga Gennosuke grabbed the arms of his blood-hungry companions, Kisaragi Saemon and Kagerou.

They had been waiting to ambush Oboro and Akeginu. The battle was nearly won. Saemon had already adopted Yakushiji Tenzen's face. He intended to casually walk over to Oboro and Akeginu, and then whip out his sword and cut them down.

That was his original plan, but at the last second, he held back with a bitter smile. Saemon remembered that Oboro's eyes could overcome any ninja skill. As soon as he appeared in front of Oboro, his disguise would crumble. Saemon did not yet know that Oboro was blind.

But even if she broke through his disguise, so what? Only two women remained on the enemy side. Regaining his confidence, he once again prepared to attack. But then he heard Oboro rebuke Akeginu, ordering her to respect Muroga Hyouma's corpse. The bloodlust in Saemon's eyes froze and he hesitated. He listened to them—

"Tenzen must also be dead," Oboro mumbled. And

Saemon heard Akeginu respond with an unconcerned laugh: "Well, if Tenzen was killed . . ."

They didn't sound like they had much faith in Tenzen. That was clear. But why did they act so coldly about Tenzen's fate?

Kagerou, crouching next to Saemon, also became worried. "Are you sure that Tenzen died?" Kagerou whispered.

"Definitely," Saemon responded. But he looked away, into the hazy moonlit distance of the plains, as if sensing something there. "Don't be stupid . . ." he mumbled to himself. "All right! I'm going to grab those two women, force them to look upon Tenzen's corpse, and then kill them."

He started to stand, but Gennosuke grabbed him. "Saemon, wait."

Kisaragi Saemon looked back. Gennosuke's eyes were shut and a shadow of deep distress was carved into his face. Throughout the journey from Manjidani, the entire group had constantly worried about young Gennosuke's willingness to fight with Oboro.

Saemon glared at Gennosuke, furious. "So you are telling me not to kill Oboro."

"That's not what I'm saying," Gennosuke said softly, shaking his head. "People are coming here from the east. Not just a few. It's strange for such a large procession to be traveling in the middle of the night."

Having dug a shallow hole and placed Chikuma Koshirou inside, Akeginu collapsed alongside it, resting physically and emotionally. When she and Oboro finally noticed
its approach, the procession was already just 150 feet
away.

"What is that?" someone murmured at the head of the
procession.

Seeing four or five men approaching, Akeginu tried
to get into a fighting stance, but gave up. She and the
blinded Oboro had no energy to continue.

Those approaching were all samurai. They saw the
fetid corpse of Muroga Hyouma in the road and Akeginu
crouching nearby, holding a scythe. The samurai erupted
in shouts.

"Ah, robbers!"

"Everybody, be careful!"

Seven or eight samurai rushed forward toward Akeginu and Oboro.

Frozen in place, Akeginu watched them with wide
eyes. Regaining her strength, however, she leaped into
the air, running in front of Oboro to protect her. Akeginu
drew her sword and glared at the oncoming samurai. "We
are hurrying toward Sunpu at the order of the shogun,"
she said in a powerful voice. "Who are you and where are
you from?"

"What, the shogun?"

The samurai clamored in confusion. Finally, one of them
brazenly strode forward. "You are just a pair of women.

What use could the shogun have for you? Tell the truth now, what sort of people are you?"

"We are villagers from Tsubagakure in Iga."

Immediately, a commanding woman's voice sounded behind the samurai. "What did she say? Tsubagakure in Iga? Well, then—" A woman of apparently high rank stepped down from a carriage.

"So you must be the Iga members who are fighting with Kouga ninjas now that Hattori Hanzou has ended the ban on warfare, am I right?" She breathed hard.

Akeginu was startled. "You are—"

"I am the woman who raised Takechiyo, the future Tokugawa shogun. I am Ofuku." She sternly emphasized her name. Then she peered through the moonlight at them. "You must be Oboro and Akeginu, correct?"

The two Iga ninja were stunned. Why did a woman who had raised the future shogun know their names?

"Why did you say we are . . .?" Akeginu trailed off.

"Well, that's right, isn't it? Those are your names. You were both among the ten names that Ogen of Iga so proudly wrote on her scroll—have you forgotten? You are the precious ninja who have been selected on behalf of Takechiyo. This dead man here, who is that?"

"His name is Muroga Hyouma, from Kouga Manji-dani," Akeginu answered.

"Oh, he's from Kouga. So he's been killed! What about the other Manjidani ninja?"

"I think three remain—"

"So, then, where are they?"

"They are traveling toward Sunpu. But I think they are still here, somewhere in this field—"

Ofuku became startled. "Everyone, be on guard!"

She turned around. Immediately, a half dozen samurai spread out into the grass while the remaining soldiers formed a protective circle around her. There were about twenty men. Ofuku spoke in a shaky voice. "So, women of Tsubagakure, what happened to your other eight Iga fighters?"

"They died . . ." Oboro and Akeginu answered, their bodies frozen and unmoving. Ofuku's face got goose bumps, and for a while no one spoke.

3

OBORO HAD BEEN SILENT UP TO THIS POINT, BUT NOW she quietly asked, "What did you mean when you said that we are the precious ninja who have been selected on behalf of Takechiyo?"

"So you . . . have been fighting with Kouga and you don't even know why?"

Ofuku stared at the two Iga women with eyes tinged with fear. Then, solemnly and deliberately, she began explaining that the secret ninja war would decide the heir to the Tokugawa throne.

Ofuku would later become known as the Lady Kasuga.

In the *Ochiboshuu* of Daidou Temple, it is written: "The Lady Kasuga was returning from performing ritual ceremonies. She made a secret trip. Around that time, Kasuga came upon two women in the Hakone area, and they spoke at the pass. The Lady Kasuga wished to send the women to the temple of Ise. She firmly requested that Takechiyo become the next heir. She pressed them to help her accomplish this. Then Kasuga went forth." This section refers to what happened here. Ofuku should have been going to Sunpu, but she made a secret trip to the east. She had gone to pray at the Ise Temple that Takechiyo would inherit the throne. Those around her all knew about it, and the Kunichiyo faction learned about it later, so this trip was not the secret one referred to in the text. Actually, when Ofuku left Ise on her return trip, she had a secondary motive. She wanted to find out how the battle between Kouga and Iga was going.

Of course, the shogun had solemnly declared that neither the Takechiyo faction nor the Kunichiyo faction could take part in the deadly Kouga and Iga ninja war.

But Ofuku was a woman who could not bear watching fate be decided for her. This was not some spectacle of no importance. She could not merely watch and root for one side. If her faction lost, they would lose more than the entire kingdom—they would soon lose their lives. In fact, this wretched fate later befell the losing grandson. He was assassinated for the sake of his brother—or, more accurately, for the sake of the assassin's own political ambitions. The assassin was connected to the Lady Kasuga through his maternal line.

Many years before, Ofuku had been married to a leading official. She discovered that one of her husband's mistresses had given birth to a child. When her husband told her about it, she invited the woman and the child to visit and acted as if she didn't mind. But as soon as her husband left, she immediately stabbed both the woman and the child to death. She then fled her home in her own palanquin. She had broken rules before.

After explaining the reason for the ninja war, she came to a decision. It had turned out that slipping out of Sunpu was a great stroke of luck.

"Oboro, Akeginu, join my procession and travel with me to Sunpu, won't you? Actually, I command you to come with me."

She had concluded that these two, at least, must survive. She would rush them back to Sunpu, and then secretly use her influence to kill the remaining Kouga ninja. This was all she could think about.

Oboro was not excited to learn that the ninja war would decide the fate of the Tokugawa family. Instead, her silent face darkened with infinite resentment. "Let's go," she said.

Her decision to travel with Ofuku was not because she feared death. Right now, Oboro was recalling Gennosuke's words: "However, I do not like to fight. I also do not know why we are fighting. For that reason, I am going to Sunpu. I intend to ask the shogun and Hattori Hanzou their reasons." Now Oboro understood the reason for the war. But she intended to meet with the shogun and Hattori Hanzou and request that, upon her death, they reinstate the ban on warfare.

"Oboro," Akeginu shouted, "do you intend to just let the Kouga group get away, after all this?"

But it was Ofuku who answered. "We are not letting the Kouga group get away. However, I cannot allow you two to be killed."

Akeginu was silent. She did not mind sacrificing her life. But she thought of Oboro. She thought of how Oboro's blindness would be a hindrance to her. So she decided to watch over Oboro and make sure that she got to Sunpu safely. After that, she would definitely kill those who had murdered Koshirou!

The hawk soared into the air. The procession turned around and gradually picked up speed. Heading east—

When they disappeared over the horizon, three figures emerged from a thicket of grass. The soldiers searching the fields had, of course, failed to spot Kouga Gennosuke, Kisaragi Saemon, and Kagerou.

"So that's it . . ." Gennosuke mumbled sadly. He realized it was impossible to halt the fighting.

"It's to sort out the succession to the shogunate," Kisaragi Saemon said with a happy laugh. "Interesting."

The three of them set off eastward in pursuit of the

procession. In the excitement of learning the unexpected significance of the ninja war and because of the sudden involvement of Ofuku, they had completely forgotten about what Akeginu had said about Yakushiji Tenzen. It was the rare mistake of those who usually made none.

THE MOON went down, and a thick darkness spread over the predawn fields. Even the wind ceased.

Despite the absence of wind, the grass rustled in one spot.

"Ahhgahhh!"

It was a freakish sound, a little like the sound of someone waking from sleep with a yawn. In the depths of the darkness, something had arisen.

Yakushiji Tenzen. After shaking his head a few times, he crouched near the shore and splashed water against his face. As he washed, he stroked his neck and shoulders. Although nobody was there to see it, his wound had completely closed up. All that was left was a faint red mark. What sort of miracle was this—he had returned from the dead!

But what exactly had happened? What had happened was certainly astonishing, but it was not entirely unprecedented. If a crab's claw is torn off, it will regrow. If a lizard's tail is cut off, it will grow out again. If an earthworm is chopped in two, it will grow back to its original size. If the hydra—a small water organism—is chopped into little pieces, each of those pieces will grow into a new hydra. The lower animals frequently have the power to regenerate. Humans also have the power to regenerate parts of their body. Skin, hair, the mucous membrane, blood cells—all these and more can regrow. Embryos have an especially powerful ability to regenerate.

Regardless of whether Yakushiji Tenzen had the regenerative power of a lower animal, or if he simply maintained the regenerative power of stem cells even as an adult, even his heart muscles and nervous system had regenerative power.

In the faint light of dawn, his expressionless head lifted up. He grinned and ran to the east.

4

OFUKU HAD INTENDED HER TRIP TO BE A SECRET, AND so she had no set schedule. That is why Ofuku was traveling all night to get to Chiriyuu. But now she was hurrying back. Her procession spent the night in Okasaki.

This was the castle of the Tokugawa family's ancestors. It made no difference that her journey was a secret. Word quickly spread that the woman who had breast-fed Takechiyo was arriving. The head of the castle, Honda Bungonokami, sent forth a party of soldiers to meet them and kept a secret lookout around the inn where she stayed.

The next day, Ofuku's procession set off toward the east. The fact that there were now three palanquins being carried did not go unnoticed by the soldiers guarding them. A hawk often flew up into the sky above the procession, turning circles above it, as if it wanted to inform others of the location of its master, riding inside.

After covering sixteen miles, the procession reached Yoshida at nightfall. Barely an hour after they entered the inn, a man casually approached the seven or eight guards posted outside.

"Where are you going?" the guards demanded, glaring at him.

The man silently thrust his chin in the direction of the inn.

"Not possible," said one samurai.

"There's an important person staying here until morning. Go somewhere else," said another.

The man looked at the hawk, silhouetted against the dusk sky and perched atop the roof of the inn. "Who is the important person?" he asked.

"That's not something for you to know," said one of the samurai.

"Hurry up and get out of here!" the first guard said and tried to push him. Suddenly, there was a strange sound and the guard's arm hung limp.

The strange man grinned. His hair was pulled back in the samurai style, and his skin was white. His face was expressionless and feminine. Although young looking, he had maintained such perfect composure that the guards had not been ready. Now, however, after witnessing their leader's arm become paralyzed by some kind of magic, the samurai looked carefully at their attacker. Despite his elegant appearance, his purple lips gave off a mysterious, untamed air.

"Bandit!"

Two samurai drew their swords and charged from either side. Their target nimbly slipped between them like an escaping bat, and the two guards dropped their weapons. A knife had flashed as swiftly as lightning and their elbow joints were dislocated.

"Everyone! We're under attack! Come here!" one of the guards screamed as he leaped into the inn, tumbling through the doorway. A crowd of samurai raced out with weapons drawn. Among them—

"Ah! Tenzen!" a woman shouted. Akeginu stepped forward, holding the huge scythe. "It's all a mistake!" she said. "He's on our side. He's from Iga."

Although she had warned the guards that their ally, Yakushiji Tenzen, might follow them and show up at the inn, either the guards hadn't been paying attention or they hadn't believed her. In any case, the samurai wiped away the cold sweat of relief and sheathed their swords. They spoke in flustered voices.

"You should have said he was a friend!"

"In that case, hurry up and go inside!"

Tenzen did not even deign to glance at them.

"Akeginu, what's going on? I saw the hawk on the rooftop, so I knew that this was where you were. But who are those men?"

"They are the retainers of Ofuku, the woman who raised the next shogun, Takechiyo."

Tenzen continued to look uncomfortable. Perhaps it was the men outside. "Akeginu, where is Oboro?"

"She's fine. Tenzen, you should go meet with Ofuku as soon as possible. It would be better if you got the explanation from her. She can explain better than I the reason we traveled together."

"Speak with her about what? No, there's no time for that now."

"Uh? Why?"

"Kagerou of Kouga is now close to the Imure Bridge. It's a bridge to the east of Yoshida. I'll tell you more as we go there. I don't want anyone to hear except for you, and we've got to go as soon as possible."

"Kagerou!" Akeginu repeated, her eyes blazing with the white fire of bloodlust. Two or three samurai approached.

"What is it?" one asked. "Are the Kouga fighters around here somewhere?"

"If the Kouga fighters are here," said another, "let us handle it."

Tenzen cast a glance at the group of guards, who were still in confusion after he had dislocated two men's arms. With an icy sneer, Tenzen said, "I'm sure you can handle some things, but you are no match for them. Iga must win the glory of killing the enemy. We cannot leave it to outsiders."

Surprised, Akeginu hesitated.

"Akeginu," Tenzen said, "Kagerou is the woman who killed Koshirou. Are you coming?"

Jolted as if by an electric shock, Akeginu stared hard at Tenzen. "I'll go!" she declared. She then turned to the samurai. "Please do the following for me. Tell Oboro that Yakushiji Tenzen appeared and that I left with him to do something important."

She and Tenzen hurried off. Actually, they glided over the ground. The samurai watched, dumbfounded, as they rapidly disappeared into the sunset.

A mere thirty minutes later, a man casually approached from the west and stared at the roof of the inn. He approached one of the guards, whose mouth was hanging wide open. "I know that hawk—the one on top of the roof. I'm going to look around—"

With those words, he boldly walked inside. None dared stop him. That was because this man was the same man who had just vanished over the eastern horizon—Yakushiji Tenzen.

5

"YOU SAID THAT KOSHIROU WAS KILLED BY KAGEROU. How did that happen?" Akeginu asked questions as she ran.

"Didn't you see Koshirou's dead body at the Komaba plains?"

"I saw it," Akeginu said. "It was near Muroga Hyouma's corpse. I thought they had killed each other."

"Koshirou did kill Hyouma. But Hyouma didn't kill Koshirou. Kagerou did. That woman's breath turns to poison whenever she embraces a man. Perhaps you noticed that Koshirou's body had no wounds. Men fear Kagerou. That's why I need your help."

"I see. So then, Kagerou—?"

"I was locked in a back-and-forth battle with Gennosuke and Kagerou. At one point, I lost sight of them. I went searching for them and saw Kagerou alone at the western entrance to Yoshida. I followed her until she stopped at Imure Bridge, to the east of Yoshida. On my way through Yoshida, I spotted the hawk by accident, and so I knew that you two were in the inn. But since I was following Kagerou, I didn't have time to talk to you. But it looked like Kagerou had stopped at the bridge to wait for someone. She must be expecting Gennosuke and Kisaragi Saemon. I'll take care of them. But I want you to kill Kagerou. That's why I hurried back to see you." Tenzen said all this to Akeginu while running full speed. "But who are those men?" he continued. "What was that about the shogun's family?"

"We joined Ofuku's procession. Ofuku raised Takechiyo, the future shogun, when he was a child. Tenzen, do you know why Hattori Hanzou ended the ban on ninja warfare between Kouga and Iga? It's because our battle will decide whether the future shogun is Takechiyo or his younger brother Kunichiyo. Tokugawa Ieyasu could not decide between them, and so he has made Iga represent Takechiyo and Kouga represent Kunichiyo. Ten ninja are to fight for each side, and the side with more surviving members decides the future shogun. Ofuku was traveling on her way to pray for Takechiyo at Ise, and came across us by accident in Komaba. After she learned that we were Iga ninja, she told us not to fight them anymore and that she would use her own methods to kill the Kouga ninja—"

Akeginu began to look uncomfortable as she saw the cloud of displeasure forming on his face.

"Tenzen, we did the wrong thing, didn't we?" Akeginu said.

"Shameful!" Tenzen spoke as if spitting the words out. "Relying on someone else to kill Kouga ninja—what is that? People will look upon us and say that we weren't powerful enough to defeat Manjidani and needed others to help us win. You've dragged Iga's name through the mud, haven't you? Maybe it helps the Takechiyo faction to win. But their victory is not the same as a victory for Iga. After he wins and becomes shogun, Takechiyo won't feel that we won the battle. And anyway, why should we care whether Takechiyo or Kunichiyo becomes heir to the

Tokugawa family line? The only important thing is that the ninja of Tsubagakure must kill all of the ninja of Manjidani—without help. In his letter, Kouga Gennosuke said that he wanted to ask the shogun and Hattori Hanzou why they had authorized the ninja war. I guess he wants to know all about the infighting in the shogun's court. But even if he knew everything, how would that change anything? Idiot." Tenzen laughed mockingly. "Don't you think it will be much better for us if we fight Kouga and defeat them without help? Don't you want to kill Kagerou with your own hands?"

"You're right. I want to kill Kagerou with my own hands—I want to spray her with my blood. That's all I want. I shouldn't have gone with Ofuku." Akeginu sighed bitterly. "But, Tenzen," she said, "although I feel the same way you do, I was thinking that because Oboro is blind—"

Tenzen suddenly froze in place.

"What's wrong?" Akeginu asked.

"Nothing," he said. "Nothing at all. Um, so you were saying that Oboro is blind?"

"That's why I wanted to escort Oboro safely to Sunpu. I only agreed to travel with Ofuku to protect her."

"I see. Well, I guess we understand each other now." Although Tenzen's voice had become calm, his eyes were the opposite, flashing with a sudden, strange light.

Akeginu didn't notice.

"Tenzen, when will we reach Imure Bridge?"

"It's right over there. See it? She's still there!"

Far away, atop the bridge, they saw the figure of a woman looking absentmindedly at the water. The two of them soundlessly ran toward her. When she suddenly looked up, Tenzen was at the foot of the bridge.

"Kagerou, hasn't Gennosuke arrived yet?" he asked in a mocking voice.

"Tenzen and Akeginu," Kagerou said in a low voice.

"Where is Gennosuke?"

"I wasn't waiting for him. I was waiting for you two," Kagerou answered.

"What?"

Pushing Tenzen aside, Akeginu went forward—one step, two steps . . . As she did so, her left hand reached inside her sleeves and stripped off her clothes. Her breasts gleamed in the vast evening sky. Her right hand held the giant scythe that had belonged to Koshirou. Her actions contradicted her natural elegance and beauty.

The two female ninja faced each other.

"Kagerou—I will now kill the one who harmed Koshirou!"

"Ha—don't make me laugh! Come on!"

Akeginu suddenly swung the giant scythe at her, but Kagerou expertly flipped over it, leaping into the air like a soaring butterfly. Kagerou swiftly whipped out a small knife from her kimono. She slashed and it cut through the sleeve of the kimono that Akeginu had torn off and that was now hanging from her waist. Akeginu leaped backward. At that moment, a mist of blood gushed from her snow-white skin.

"Ah!"

Covering her eyes, Kagerou twisted away. In desperation, she climbed onto the handrail of the Imure Bridge. Her body was swathed in a spray of blood.

"Give my regards to the King of the Underworld! Now witness the ninja skills of Iga!" Akeginu prepared to swing the giant scythe in a final blow. But a hand squeezed her neck with a grip like iron.

"I saw it. It was entertaining."

The hand slid for a moment on Akeginu's blood, and she was able to look around. Her beautiful lips twisted in surprise. "Te-Tenzen!"

"Tenzen is dead! And so you can give regards to the King of the Underworld from the shape-shifter, Kisaragi Saemon!"

With her last bit of strength, Akeginu swung the giant scythe at Kagerou. It whistled through the air and struck the handrail of the bridge. When Saemon grabbed Akeginu, it slowed her down for a split second, allowing Kagerou to jump out of the way. Now Kagerou rushed forward and sank her dagger into Akeginu's breast.

"Soon Oboro will join you in the afterlife. You can spray your blood all over hell to welcome her!"

Kagerou pulled out the dagger. Akeginu tottered forward, collided with the handrail, and fell over it into the river. Kisaragi Saemon and Kagerou watched countless red rings ripple away from her body. Befitting the meaning of the name "Akeginu"—red silk—several dozen strings of red silk seemed to trail behind Akeginu as her body floated away in the current.

Kagerou wiped the droplets of sprayed blood from her face and smiled complacently. "You did an excellent job leading her out here, Saemon."

"It's this face. It wasn't hard to get her to come fight you."

"I appreciate it . . . by the way, Oboro must be alone now."

"Well, then, it's time to kill her."

Kisaragi Saemon's smile shone—in Yakushiji Tenzen's eyes. "Kagerou," Saemon said, "Oboro is blind. Her occult-piercing eyes are blocked."

OCCULT-PIERCING TIME

1

"WHAT'S THAT?" KISARAGI SAEMON LIFTED HIS HEAD and looked around. An extraordinary roar of footsteps and shouted voices was approaching from Yoshida. "Well . . ."

In the faint light of the street, he saw more than a dozen charging men. Among them were the silhouettes of spears and drawn swords. Saemon became nervous.

"I think Ofuku's retainers are coming," he said. "I was able to successfully lure Akeginu away, but it seems like something must have happened after I left. I don't think they have any way to realize who I really am . . . Kagerou, I must pretend to be Yakushiji Tenzen. If they see me standing here chatting with you, there'll be trouble. Hurry over to Gennosuke."

"What about you, Saemon?"

"I will slip into Ofuku's procession as Tenzen and get close to Oboro. If she really is blind, then killing her will be as easy as slitting a baby's throat."

Kagerou started to leave, but she stopped and her white face turned around.

"Saemon, you—you want to be the one who kills Oboro, don't you?"

"Yeah, I suppose."

Light from the water shone on Kagerou's beautiful eyes, turning them blue. "Me, too," she said.

"Well, then, I will call you over so that we can do it together. We'll stay at the inn tonight. Tomorrow, watch Ofuku's procession as we travel. If you see me—or, I should say, if you see Yakushiji Tenzen—that will be proof that I infiltrated their group. It will also be evidence that Oboro's occult-piercing eyes are blocked. Until that time, I have to win the trust of Ofuku's procession. Anyway, it shouldn't be that hard—they think that I'm their ally. Here's what I'll do, Kagerou—I will tell them I captured you and that I will take you back to Iga as my sexual conquest. So you have to pretend that you lost in battle to me."

"Your sexual conquest?"

"Ha, ha—yes, I know: any man that tries to make you his sexual conquest will lose his life. But the villagers of Iga don't know that. In any case, the important thing is that Oboro is blind, so there should be no problem."

Grinning and showing her white teeth, Kagerou nodded and hurried away. She moved like the wind, her footsteps making no sound. Within ten steps, her figure had vanished into the darkness.

Kisaragi Saemon folded his arms and adopted a stern look as he waited for the arriving samurai—Ofuku's retainers.

They came to a clamorous halt and stared at him standing atop the bridge. A few moments ago, he had decided to act arrogant and angry with them, but he decided that would be inappropriate. Instead he made a pained laugh, smiled, and walked over.

"I apologize for being so rude earlier. I grew up in the mountains of Iga, and we're all raised like monkeys there. I behaved rudely, and I am truly sorry."

A samurai wearing a foot soldier's helmet and a torn half-coat stepped forward.

"What happened to Akeginu?" the samurai asked. In the complete darkness atop the bridge, the painted lacquer surface of the iron helmet glinted with light reflected from the water. The helmet seemed to tremble.

"Akeginu just told me that you are on my side. I think you already know what's going on, so it won't hurt for me to tell it to you as well. Akeginu went chasing after the head of the Kouga group, Kouga Gennosuke."

"What?" the samurai asked. "Was Kouga Gennosuke here?"

"Yes—"

"So what happened to Gennosuke?"

"He was wounded, but he fought like a madman and escaped—"

"Isn't it dangerous for Akeginu as a woman to chase Gennosuke by herself?"

"Gennosuke was seriously wounded. And although you refer to Akeginu as merely a woman, remember that Ogen selected her as one of the ten greatest ninja fighters. Don't worry." Kisaragi Saemon laughed.

The foot soldier pointed at the bridge with his left hand. "So, what about that blood?"

It was the middle of the night, and Saemon had assumed that the retainers would not be able to see the blood. He became nervous.

"Uh—that's Gennosuke's blood."

"Oh, I see," the soldier answered, nodding his head. "Well, it sure stinks of blood. So this is where he was seriously wounded?"

Saemon relaxed as he realized that the soldier hadn't seen the blood; rather, he had smelled it. The soldier once again turned his helmet toward Saemon.

"So why did you stay here?" the soldier asked, moving closer.

But Saemon always had an answer for every question.

"I wanted to protect Oboro. There is still a ninja called Kisaragi Saemon on the Kouga side."

"Isn't there also another one left, a woman called Kagerou?"

"Ah, I've already tamed her."

"Tamed?" the soldier asked.

"Ha ha ha—I captured her at Komaba. I made Kagerou into my woman. Women are amazing things. She immediately betrayed Kouga. The next morning, it was none other than Kagerou who led me to find Kouga Gennosuke. She became frightened and ran away during the fight, but if that woman comes looking for me, just hand her over to me—Yakushiji Tenzen."

The soldier seemed to be impressed, and for a while he said nothing. "That is a real feat," he said at last. "I can see it would be better to have you as my protector than a million allies."

Kisaragi Saemon burst out laughing. "Oh, come on. I am not so perfect."

A million allies? He was about to kill Oboro.

"In any case," Saemon continued, "I want to meet with Ofuku and Oboro as soon as possible. Could you please direct me back to the inn?"

"Understood. . . . But I also want to say that we really appreciated your display of ninja skills earlier. In the flash of an eye, you dislocated four men's elbows and turned their arms into octopus tentacles. You said that you are embarrassed for acting so rudely; however, it was our first chance to see such frightful ninja skills. We were really impressed . . ."

"Oh, what I did could hardly be considered ninja skills."

"If we had known that you were Yakushiji Tenzen, we would never have acted so foolishly."

Kisaragi Saemon had gradually grown irritated with this never-ending conversation, but he needed to win the trust of Ofuku's retainers. He casually leaned against the handrail, allowing the night wind to blow against him. He barely listened to the soldier's words.

"Akeginu told us about your ninja skills," the soldier continued, sighing in curiosity and admiration. "You never die, no matter how many wounds you receive. An immortal ninja . . ."

Kisaragi Saemon froze in shock. An immortal ninja! This was the first time he had heard of such a thing. So Yakushiji Tenzen was immortal! He would never die, no matter how many wounds were inflicted upon him? Saemon had slit his throat at the Komaba plains. Was Tenzen still not dead? Could something so unbelievable be true? A cold shiver sprinted up his back.

"Akeginu told you such things?" Saemon groaned, clicking his tongue in disgust. Ninja did not reveal other ninja skills to outsiders. Saemon knew that Yakushiji Tenzen would act disgusted upon hearing the soldier say this.

Kisaragi Saemon was also overwhelmed with the urge to return to the Komaba plains and check Tenzen's corpse.

His interlocutor continued speaking, apparently unaware of Saemon's reaction: "I heard that you came back to life once after being killed by Jimushi Juubei and that you also came back to life after being killed by Kasumi Gyoubu. Apparently, unless your head is completely chopped off, you cannot be killed. Every wound you receive will soon heal, and you will return to life as if nothing had happened. I would love to see you perform that talent sometime."

Kisaragi Saemon suddenly hunched over like a shrimp. What had happened? Without any preparatory movement, the soldier had thrust a sword into his abdomen. The soldier had been holding the sword behind his back until then.

Saemon wrenched back and forth. His entire body twisted around his stomach. The sword had been driven through his body and nailed him to the handrail!

"Let's see you do it," the soldier said. "This wound must be no more than a fleabite to you. Are you upset, Tenzen? How are you feeling?"

The other foot soldiers seemed to have been waiting until now, but they suddenly charged. As he writhed in agony, Kisaragi Saemon's eyes bulged out of their sockets.

Through the darkness, Saemon saw it. The face appearing beneath the soldier's helmet was the same face as his. Saemon's adopted face was fighting through its dying moments, but a grin appeared in his opponent's almond eyes and twisted purple lips.

"Yakushiji Tenzen!" cried Saemon.

"So you are not Tenzen?" The speaker smiled coldly and twisted the handle of the large sword that had pierced Saemon. Gasping, Saemon stretched his hand toward his own sword.

"Tenzen, teach me!" said the guard, still mocking Kisaragi Saemon as if he were Tenzen. "In the Kouga group, the only ones remaining are Kagerou and Gennosuke. One is a woman and the other is blind. If you come back to life, please let me watch Iga win this war."

With his last bit of strength, Kisaragi Saemon drew his sword. But at that moment—

Tenzen laughed as four or five of Ofuku's guards drove their spears through his double, and Kisaragi Saemon's body was pierced with the spears as if by quills of a porcupine.

Saemon could not come back to life, and he met his fate because he had attempted to become Yakushiji Tenzen. A ninja who could change his appearance using death masks of mud used this technique to kill Hotarubi and Akeginu of Iga. But in the end, his ability to change his appearance caused his own death. His name had been eliminated from the ninja scroll.

Stitched to the handrail, the upper half of Kisaragi Saemon's body bent backward into an arc. Four or five spears stuck out of his body, shining in the night sky like the ribs of a giant folding fan. The sight was so gruesome that the soldiers who had rammed the spears into Saemon reflexively pulled their hands away.

But Yakushiji Tenzen paid no attention to Saemon. He looked eastward and stroked his chin as he thought. Although none could see it in the darkness—and there was no reason to notice it—the red mark on his neck had completely vanished.

"Kisaragi Saemon impersonated me in order to infiltrate the procession," Tenzen mumbled and laughed.

"So now I am Kisaragi Saemon. Apparently, Kagerou will

come to the procession looking for Saemon. But she will be just like a mayfly—a *kagerou*—flying into the flames."

2

WITH THE SOUTH WIND BLOWING SEA-SCENTED AIR upon them, Ofuku's procession continued down the Tokaido Road. Leaving Yoshida, it passed through Futugawa, Shirasuka, Arai, another two miles to Maisaka, and then to Hamamatsu. During that time, they traveled fifteen miles. Just as the sun was setting, a beautiful woman nervously approached the inn.

"Is . . . there a Yakushiji Tenzen staying here?" she asked.

The guards blocking the way had to suck in their breath upon seeing the woman's beautiful face in the light of the hanging lanterns. Finally, one of the guards gulped down his drool and spoke.

"Are you . . . Kagerou from Kouga?"

She did not answer.

"If you are Kagerou, then Tenzen is waiting for you inside. Please come with me."

"I am Kagerou," she said.

Throughout the journey from Yoshida to Hamamatsu, she had observed Yakushiji Tenzen, chatting and laughing with the retainers in Ofuku's procession. Confident that everything had gone smoothly, Kagerou went to visit him.

Even so, for a moment, she felt a strange shiver ripple up her spine.

She quickly relaxed and heaved a sigh of relief from deep in her chest. Everything had gone well! She smiled, as beautiful as a tree peony, and followed the guards into the inn.

Inside the inn was the last of her enemies, Oboro. Oboro was not only her rival in the ninja war—she was her rival in love. That was why Kagerou had demanded that Kisaragi Saemon—who had already successfully infiltrated the enemy and could kill Oboro at any moment—wait until Kagerou joined him before killing Oboro. Of course, Oboro knew nothing about what was going on. Kagerou's heart thumped with excitement. Only forty miles separated them from Sunpu, and by morning all ten ninja from Iga Tsubagakure would be eliminated.

"How did you know that I would be coming?" Kagerou asked the soldiers guiding her.

"Tenzen told us," said one of the guards. From the way their eyes gazed at her, she could tell they wanted to run their tongues over her face and body. These guards had heard that Yakushiji Tenzen had seduced her and convinced her to betray her own clan. Just as Saemon had promised, these men seemed to believe it. Kagerou thought it hilarious—and, at the same time, she felt boundless shame and fury.

"Where is Oboro?" she asked.

The soldiers exchanged glances.

"I need to pay her my respects," Kagerou explained.

"First, you should meet with Tenzen," one of the guards said, refusing her.

Apparently, they still don't completely trust anybody from Kouga, Kagerou thought. And, in fact, the soldiers surrounded her so tightly on each side that they could have carried her.

She entered a strange room with a thick wooden door that was closed behind her. Yakushiji Tenzen was sitting on the floor. Thick iron bars blocked the window.

"Kagerou?" Tenzen's grin shone through the light cast by a kerosene lamp.

Kagerou ran toward him and collapsed at his feet. "Saemon!" she cried.

"Shhh . . ." Tenzen hissed. He signaled with his eyes. "Kagerou, come here. They are eavesdropping on us."

Kagerou shuffled closer. "But why? You're Yakushiji Tenzen—"

"Of course I am. Everyone trusts me. Anyway, they seem to trust me. The problem is they don't trust you."

"Because of Oboro?"

"No, that girl is as gullible as a baby. It's Ofuku."

"She doesn't believe that a member of Kouga would turn traitor and support Iga?"

"She's a very suspicious woman. I said that I had tamed you when I seduced you, but she thinks that I've probably fallen into your trap instead."

"So, then, why did her retainers bring me here?"

"They half believe and half doubt my story. Anyway, we're not going to be able to do it tonight. Let's travel with the procession for a while. Sunpu is still forty miles away—about three days' travel. We'll definitely have a chance to kill Oboro. I can almost taste the victory . . ."

Kagerou placed her hand on Tenzen's knee and looked up at him. She had never before adopted such a position with Tenzen—that is, Kisaragi Saemon. Even now, she did it unconsciously. She had put herself in the midst of countless enemies. Yet she felt protected by the presence of Kisaragi Saemon, who could take on the appearance of any of those enemies. The thought of it stirred sexual desire inside her.

"First, we need them to trust you," Tenzen whispered, his hand stroking Kagerou's white chin. "We need to show them that you have become my woman. They are probably eavesdropping on us outside that door. Or maybe even peeking through a hole, watching us."

He spoke directly into her eardrum using a special ninja vocal technique, but even so, his voice was faint.

"Come to me, Kagerou. Let's do something for them to watch."

"What?"

"Let's prove to them that you have become my woman."

"Sa, Saemon . . . !"

"I lied when I said that I slept with you at the Komaba

plains. But, the truth is that I want to have sex with you, even just once——"

Kagerou's eyes bloomed wide open, like two black flowers in the dark. Tenzen seemed overcome with madness. Out of control, his hands slid onto her breasts and he pulled her against him. Her breasts burned with fire under Tenzen's fingers. Silent, Kagerou gazed up at Tenzen.

It was a life-or-death moment for Yakushiji Tenzen. He had called Kagerou to him in order to kill her. But as soon as he saw her—that body could hypnotize the world—he changed his plan. He could kill her at Sunpu. Until then, she would believe that he was Kisaragi Saemon, and he would enjoy the pleasures of this beautiful female ninja.

Kagerou, however, had begun to doubt that this was Kisaragi Saemon. Kisaragi Saemon knew about her poisonous breath. He knew that any man who made love to her would immediately die. Saemon would not talk to her like that—this man was not Saemon! Waves of fear and surprise slithered beneath her skin.

Was it possible? Could Yakushiji Tenzen still be alive? Could it be that instead of Saemon pretending to be Tenzen, this was the real thing? And yet—

"Sa-Saemon!" she said. "My breath——"

"Yes, I can feel your gasps! Your breath tastes as sweet as flowers. Kagerou, scream out loud, let the people listening hear us!"

Kagerou made her decision. This must be Yakushiji

Tenzen. The only explanation was that he had murdered Saemon.

I have to kill Tenzen, she thought.

Tenzen thinks that he has outsmarted me and led me into his trap! Those Iga fools! I will outtrick his trickery. He has already fallen into my deadly trap. I will kill Tenzen first and then Oboro. I don't give a damn whether her eyes are open or shut, I will slit her throat and complete the mission.

Even as the thoughts roiled her brain like a violent squall, Kagerou twisted her body seductively and accepted Yakushiji Tenzen's caresses.

Yakushiji Tenzen tore open the collar and hem of Kagerou's kimono. The light from the oil lantern fluttered as it was buffeted by the wind, emphasizing the woman's snow-white skin. Kagerou dropped her head back, her breath coming fast. She had arched her slender body, allowing Tenzen to run his hands over her.

"Kagerou. Kagerou . . ."

Tenzen had forgotten Kagerou was his enemy. He had even forgotten that he was pretending to be Kagerou's ally. His ninja senses had clouded and his mind had devolved into the mind of a mere beast, focused only on having sex with this beautiful woman.

Equally in anguish, Kagerou wrapped her legs around Tenzen's waist and coiled her arm around his neck. Her wet, half-open lips approached his mouth, releasing gasps of air as if unable to control her desire. Her bittersweet apricot scent enveloped Tenzen's nose and mouth. Insane with lust, she devoured his lips, her tongue delving into his mouth.

One breath—two breaths—Yakushiji Tenzen's face became flushed with blood. Kagerou tasted death on his lips and she immediately flung aside his arms and legs. She pushed his body aside and stood up.

Kagerou grinned as she looked over Tenzen's body. She withdrew Tenzen's sword and carefully slit his throat from left to right. Then, the bloody blade in her hand, she walked away from his corpse. She ignored her disheveled kimono. Half-naked and carrying a bloody sword, she had an incomparably gruesome beauty.

Where was Oboro?

She automatically went to open the wooden door. A spear thrust through it. She twisted out of the way and snatched the base of the spear. But a second spear stabbed through the door, and this time there was no chance to dodge it. The spear pierced her thigh.

"Ah!" she screamed and dropped the sword. She collapsed to the ground and grabbed for the sword even as a huge angry roar erupted on the other side of the door. It burst open with a splintering crack, and eight soldiers rushed in upon Kagerou like an avalanche.

Not everything Yakushiji Tenzen told her had been a lie. Samurai had been eavesdropping on them. Despite Tenzen's carefully explained trap, Ofuku—ever cautious— did not trust his plan to lure a Kouga ninja into the inn.

Her samurai had watched through a knothole in the door as Kagerou consented to Tenzen's sexual advances.

The scene they watched astounded them. The blood rushed to Tenzen's face and his body slumped so quickly that before they could whisper "So that's her trick," Kagerou had already slit Tenzen's throat. In a panic, they stabbed their spears through the door, side by side.

"Ya—Yakushiji!"

A few samurai ran to cradle him, but he had already died.

"Terrible news!" shouted their leader. "Yakushiji Tenzen has been killed by a woman from Kouga!"

Even before he finished speaking, two women had appeared behind the line of samurai, apparently drawn by their commotion.

"This must be Kagerou from Kouga?" Ofuku said, looking upon Kagerou, who was pinned to the floor. Then she turned her eyes toward Yakushiji Tenzen, outstretched in an ocean of blood.

"Didn't I say that something like this would happen . . ." she said with a snort. Soon she turned around. "Oboro, kill this woman."

Kagerou stared up through her disheveled hair. Sure enough, standing behind Ofuku was Oboro. A hawk perched upon her shoulder. Although Oboro had heard that Tenzen was killed, she did not rush into the room. That made sense, because—as Kagerou could see in the dim light of the lantern—Oboro's eyes were shut. So

Oboro really was blind. Upon seeing Oboro, Kagerou—despite being wounded and held down by about five samurai—writhed with resentment.

"Oboro," she screamed, "don't you feel ashamed to rely on others during a war between Kouga and Iga?"

Oboro did not speak.

"I don't care if they hide you behind an iron wall," Kagerou screamed. "Don't forget that Kouga Gennosuke is after you! Gennosuke will definitely kill you!"

"Where is Gennosuke?" Oboro asked.

Kagerou laughed. "You idiot. Do you think a woman of Kouga would tell you that? To reveal anything to you would make my mouth filthy. You'd have to kill me first."

"Oboro, hurry up and kill her," Ofuku ordered again.

Oboro remained silent for a while, and finally shook her head lightly. "It would be better not to kill her."

"Why?" Ofuku questioned.

"If we make this woman our prisoner and continue our journey, Kouga Gennosuke will come after us. We don't have the ninja scroll, and this woman isn't carrying it. So Gennosuke must have it. By the time we reach Sunpu, we will kill Gennosuke, take back the ninja scroll, and declare victory in the ninja war . . ."

In truth, Oboro could never kill a woman from Kouga. And she continued hoping that Gennosuke would kill her before she reached Sunpu.

3

OFUKU'S PROCESSION HURRIED THROUGH THE RE-
gions of Mitsuke and Fukuroi. The procession had carried three palanquins until Yoshida, but now there were
four. Akeginu was gone. Ofuku sat in one sedan chair,
Oboro rode in another, and the third carried Kagerou,
tied up with ropes. A fourth palanquin trailed behind.

They covered sixteen miles and spent the night in
Kakegawa.

Two of the palanquins were placed in a single room.
The innkeeper started to object, but changed his mind
upon learning that the procession belonged to the woman
who had raised the shogun's son.

Later that night, Kagerou—inside one palanquin—
gazed at the mysterious palanquin placed in the corner of
her room. The drop curtain to her palanquin had been
raised, but her companion palanquin's curtain hung low.

"Who is inside that one?" Kagerou asked.

She had one snow-white foot protruding from the
palanquin. A bearded samurai was wrapping the foot in
cloth while a young samurai peered at her with bloodshot
eyes.

These two samurai had been ordered to stand guard
as night watchmen. At first, they pretended not to hear as
Kagerou moaned about her bloody foot. Finally, the older
one said, in an artificial mumble, "Well, we'll be in trouble
if we let her die."

That was how things got to this point.

The two men did not notice that, even as she extended her beautiful leg to them, Kagerou's eyes flashed. She knew that they had been ensnared within her web of seduction. But who could blame them? Even Manjidani ninjas with powerful self-defense instincts were often helplessly lost within her seductive spell.

Neither Oboro—who was much more beautiful than Kagerou—nor Ofuku understood Kagerou's power. Oboro had prohibited the guards from harming Kagerou. But after just one day of traveling, the samurai had become so hypnotized by her beauty that they would be unable to kill Kagerou even if Oboro ordered it. Kagerou had secretly been entrapping the men in her cobweb of seduction. According to plan, the two watchmen had abandoned their duties in favor of her beauty.

The guards felt secure in the knowledge that the prisoner was tightly bound. But those ropes wrapped tightly around her flesh only increased her power. She was hellishly seductive. They had tied her up just after she'd had her clothes torn open by Yakushiji Tenzen and after the samurai had pinned her to the ground. Ropes bit into exposed flesh. One full breast hung loose, and alongside it was her smooth, glistening belly. Her breasts, belly, waist, legs—every part of her flesh and skin writhed faintly, paralyzing the two men and causing them to boil with desire. The bearded samurai wrapping white cloth around her thigh turned dizzy. And yet he was one of those who had witnessed Kagerou slitting Tenzen's throat!

"Wha—What was that?" the guard asked. He had been unable to focus on her question.

"Who is in that other palanquin?" she repeated.

"It's . . ." He looked back, and saw that his young partner was staring at him with hate-filled eyes. Flustered, he looked away. "Young lord, pardon me, but could you go over there and get my medicine case?"

"For what?" the young samurai answered.

"I want to rub some more medicine on this woman's leg."

"Go get your own stuff," the younger one snapped.

The bearded one glared at him. "What?" Then he laughed foolishly. "Ha ha—you just want to make me go get medicine so you can try to seduce this woman."

"You old fool! You're the one who tried to get me to go there in the first place!"

Kagerou smiled at their childish argument.

"Could one of you bring me a glass of water?" she asked. "My throat is so dry."

"Oh, well, I'll go." The bearded samurai hurried off.

Kagerou gazed at the young samurai. He tried to look away, but the more he tried the more he became absorbed in the woman. Trembling and in a husky voice, he asked: "Would you like to run away?"

"I want to run away," she said.

"Y-you want to run away with me?" he asked.

The young samurai's breath came in broken gasps. He had become drawn into Kagerou's eyes.

"Yes," she said.

When the bearded samurai came back, a teacup of water in his right hand, he did not see his partner. He looked around, bewildered—and suddenly, someone leaped from the shadows of the second palanquin. An arm constricted his neck. The teacup shattered on the ground. The bearded man was strangled to death atop the spilled water without ever making a sound.

"Yes"—that was all this woman needed to say. The younger samurai—who caused his partner to be strangled—had hurriedly cut through Kagerou's ropes with his knife. He drooled as he panted over her.

As soon as Kagerou was free from the ropes, she had torn off her clothes, and then flung her naked body onto the palanquin as if exhausted. Nervous, the young samurai hugged her body, shaking her. "Can't you stand up? We need to hurry."

"Come here," she said. "My throat is dry—"

The lips on her uplifted face had parted like a blooming flower. Her soft arms twisted around the young samurai's neck.

"Let me drink your saliva," she said.

The young samurai completely forgot about fleeing. Their lips touched and he immediately stiffened. Kagerou, holding him tightly, silently twisted her body and caused him to thump to the floor. The samurai's feet and hands had become the color of lead.

"Idiot," she cursed him, spitting the words.

After killing the two guards, Kagerou picked up a huge sword. Bloodlust blazed in her eyes as she left the room.

She would kill her way to Oboro!

Kagerou did not think even for a moment about the fact that Oboro had saved her life. Kagerou thought nothing of obligations or mercy. She cared not whether she lived or died. Her ninja training made her burn with the urge to kill every enemy in the inn. Naked, her skin snow-white, a huge sword clasped in her hand as she crept forward—this Kouga ninja shone like a heroic beam of light.

Finally, Kagerou found Oboro's sleeping quarters. She opened the sliding screen door a sliver and spotted Oboro sleeping in the darkness. Like a female panther, Kagerou prepared to pounce—but at that moment, a hand seized her from behind.

When she looked around, Kagerou screamed.

The man's smile spread so wide that it formed the shape of a sickle. He had returned to life, and had left his palanquin to follow her—Yakushiji Tenzen.

THE NEXT day, signs were posted at every town, from Kakegawa to Fujieda—including Nissaka, Kanaya, and on the opposite bank of the Ooi River at Shimada:

KOUGA GENNOSUKE, WHEREVER YOU HAVE FLED:

KAGEROU HAS BEEN CAPTURED BY US. AFTER SHE TASTES IGA TORTURE FOR A COUPLE OF DAYS, WE WILL SLIT HER THROAT.

IF YOU ARE THE LEADER OF KOUGA MANJIDANI, COME OUT OF YOUR HOLE AND SAVE KAGEROU. DO YOU DARE TRY TO SAVE HER? IF NOT, THEN COME BEFORE US HOLDING UP THE NINJA SCROLL. WE WILL SPARE YOUR LIFE AND BRING YOU AND KAGEROU AS OUR CAP-TURED PRISONERS TO SUNPU CASTLE.

OBORO OF IGA
YAKUSHIJI TENZEN

But Kouga Gennosuke was blind and could not read the signs.

From Kakegawa to Sunpu, twenty-four miles and three towns remained. Two ninja remained on each side. The secret ninja war had become a nightmare for all involved.

THE FINAL BATTLE

1

THEY HAD TRAVELED FROM THE INN AT KAKEGAWA through six miles and twenty towns to reach Kanaya, then crossed an additional two miles to reach Shimada, where they crossed the Ooi River. After Shimada, they traveled four miles and eight towns to reach the inn at Fujieda.

Here, in the midst of mountains, there was an open expanse and a small town.

If you went beyond it to the north, you would find a patch of high ground, home to an abandoned temple. Right below was the rear courtyard of a large inn. A thick clump of trees blocked the view. But in the middle of the night, when the houses had all turned off their lanterns . . . In that barren temple where nobody should be living, all sorts of lanterns were flickering.

As fog settled over the land, the lanterns became blurry. Eventually they were overwhelmed by the sheer blackness of the night.

A candle, hazy in the fog, stood in the center of a broken prayer table. On top of the dust, droplets of wax built into irregular mounds. Nearby, a naked woman had been tied spread-eagled against a thick pillar. The rope that bound her arms and legs was stretched taut and knotted tightly on the other side of the pillar.

Something strange glittered on the woman's snow-white solar plexus. With each flicker of the candle, silver *kanji* glittered on her belly. The character for "that"—*I*—was as large as her breasts. Below it, somewhat smaller, was the character for "add"—*ka*.

Nobody came near her, and yet her body undulated, spasms rolling through her. Her screams were blood-curdling.

"Kagerou." The voice came from about ten feet away. "Gennosuke is not coming."

Yakushiji Tenzen. He sat in the center of the abandoned temple's inner sanctuary and was drinking from a cup. He smirked as he watched Kagerou writhe in agony.

"Even if he is blind, he should have heard rumors on the street about the signs I posted everywhere. I wrote that you would taste Iga torture, and that tomorrow I would slice your slender neck. And yet your Gennosuke does not come. The leader of Kouga Manjidani knows that a companion's life is in danger, and yet he doesn't care enough to come save her. He's a coward."

After Tenzen spoke, he held something to his mouth and blew it. A narrow, silver object shone as it flew through the air. Kagerou writhed and screamed as it struck her stomach. She did not respond to Tenzen's comments.

"He he he he he," Tenzen laughed. "I can hardly bear watching your hips wriggle. I want to be inside of you. If I was closer to you, I'd become overwhelmed with the desire to hold you—and if I did that, I would die. Ah, two days ago in Hamamatsu, you surprised me. I had always wondered what your special skill was. So your breath turns to poison! Even a ninja as great as I was slain by your charms . . ."

Even in the midst of her suffering and distress, Kagerou felt a lingering sense of surprise many times greater than what Tenzen had felt when he died kissing her lips. On that night in Hamamatsu, she was confused and startled to discover that Tenzen—who should have been dead—had instead taken the place of Kisaragi Saemon. But she killed him herself using her poisonous breath—and for good measure, she had sliced through his carotid artery. And yet Tenzen had reappeared in Kakegawa; this terrified her beyond all measure.

By the time she had learned Tenzen was immortal, she had already been captured. But even if she had known about his talent ahead of time, was there any way to completely kill Tenzen? Right now, she was unable to act on any of the ideas that sprang to mind, but even if her body were free from these ropes, she couldn't imagine any way to kill him. That was why Kisaragi Saemon had met his death. He could continue disguising himself behind the faces of the enemies he killed—but when one of those who should have been dead came back to life, Saemon's game was over. Kagerou too recognized defeat. Defeat not only for herself, but for the entire Kouga group. For a woman from Kouga Manjidani who had never recognized the possibility of failure, acknowledging the defeat of her clan was more devastating than any physical beating Tenzen could deliver.

Tenzen licked pleasurably at his sake cup.

"Even though I know I would die if I approached you, I still want to caress you like I did two nights ago. I may not be Oboro, but like her I also regret the constant warfare between Tsubagakure and Manjidani. If it weren't for this war, I would let myself die again in your arms. I wouldn't mind dying a few times in order to make love to you."

Tenzen again puckered his lips and blew. A streak of silver darted from those lips and struck Kagerou. She strained forward against the ropes. But she was tightly bound in the spread-eagle pose and all she could do was struggle.

"Ju-just kill me now!" she screamed. Her hair was disheveled and her mouth hung open.

"Oh, I'll kill you," Tenzen said. "I don't want to, but I will follow your wishes and kill you. But not yet. I need you alive until tomorrow. Tomorrow we enter Sunpu, you see? From Fujieda to Sunpu—it's only eleven miles. We still have to cross some mountains and a large river, but even at a slow pace, we'll get there by evening. Your name will not be eliminated from the ninja scroll until the Iga ninja enter Sunpu Castle."

A silver thread darted forward. Underneath the *ka* on Kagerou's belly had appeared the character for "moon"—*tsuki*.

"If Kouga Gennosuke does not show up by tomorrow morning, I will tell the shogun that he fled out of cowardice. The thing is, I want that ninja scroll! Gennosuke has the ninja scroll. I want to kill him—the last of the ten Kouga ninja!—and cross his name from the scroll. Then Iga will have complete victory!"

Another flash of silver. Kagerou screamed in otherworldly agony.

It was a small dart blower. Sitting at a distance, Yakushiji Tenzen blew darts, one at a time. He spelled words on her body using the needles.

Just the needles alone would be a hellish torture. However, Tenzen had coated the needles with a special poison. The agony was so severe that Kagerou—a ninja who wouldn't scream even if her own arm had been cut off—was bellowing in anguish like some beautiful dying beast. She had already received a deep thigh wound while fighting Ofuku's guards back at Hamamatsu. She repeatedly passed out from the pain of her injuries. But each time

Tenzen's needles pierced her skin, the pain brought her back to her senses and she made new bloodcurdling screams.

"I have to do this to bring Gennosuke here," Tenzen said. "He's blind, of course, but I'm sure that he will hear news of those signs we posted. After that, he should certainly learn that Ofuku's procession is in Fujieda, staying at the inn below us. If he got that far—"

Tenzen shot another poison needle. A line across the bottom of *tsuki* changed the character from "moon" to "eye"—*me*.

"Tenzen." The soft voice came from behind Tenzen. It was the voice of someone unable to bear the situation any longer. Standing in the shadow of the broken-down altar, Oboro spoke up. "You've done enough. I cannot stand it."

The temple was empty except for Tenzen, Oboro, and the captured Kagerou. Tenzen had posted signs along the main roads in order to lure Gennosuke into his trap. But Ofuku worried about the rival Kunichiyo faction. If samurai from the Kunichiyo side saw those signs and heard that Iga ninja were traveling in her procession, they would accuse her of meddling and the shogun would punish her. Tenzen had suggested that they travel separately for a while. Ofuku and her retainers naturally had complete faith that Tenzen would emerge victorious—after all, he was an immortal ninja.

Oboro had returned with food and wine from the inn, as Tenzen had requested. But she froze in place when she heard Kagerou's screams. Tenzen looked at Oboro with disgust.

"You can't stand it?" he asked. "Oboro, eight members of Iga have already been killed and are gone from this world forever. Are you really telling me to let Kagerou go?"

Oboro was silent.

"She also killed me once, and she was on her way to kill you."

"If you must kill her . . . at least show some mercy and do it quickly."

"Ninja have no use for mercy," Tenzen answered. "Anyway, I need Kagerou's screams for my trap."

"Why?"

"Well, Gennosuke should come to the inn searching for her. He will hear her screams and be lured to the temple."

Gennosuke! Stay away!

Both of the women—friend and enemy—wanted to scream in horror as Yakushiji Tenzen blew another needle. *Me* turned into *kai*, the character for "shell."

When the characters *ka* and *kai* are read together as a single word . . .

The bobbing silver needles stretching from Kagerou's abdomen to her solar plexus spelled out two syllables— "Iga"!

This is what Tenzen meant when he wrote that Kagerou would suffer "Iga torture." Yakushiji Tenzen had come up with the incomparably cruel torture of carving the word "Iga" upon a woman from Kouga. A single drop of blood had formed at the base of each silver needle, creating a ghastly, beautiful image upon her snow-white skin.

"Oh, I understand now . . ." Sneering, Tenzen tossed aside his sake cup and seized Oboro's hand.

"Wha-what are you doing?"

"Oboro. Kagerou breathes poison. But her breath can't be poisonous all the time. If it was, she couldn't travel and live alongside the members of Kouga. It seems her breath only becomes poisonous at certain times. And I think I've just realized when it is that her breath turns deadly . . ."

"When?"

"It's only when she becomes sexually excited . . . that—"

"Tenzen, let go of my hand."

"No, I won't let go. I want to try something. If I try to have sex with Kagerou, I will die. But I want to force her to watch me make love to you."

"Tenzen, stop it!"

"No, this should be interesting. Oboro, have you forgotten what I said to you while we were traveling by sea from Kuwana to Miya? I'm still thinking of that right now. You and I are the only ones who can pass on the bloodline of Tsubagakure. Ogen selected ten Iga ninja. The only ones left are you and me."

His eyes looked drunk. He crushed Oboro in his arms.

"There's nobody left who can stop us now," Tenzen

said. "Tomorrow we'll enter Sunpu as husband and wife."
Tenzen grabbed Oboro and wrestled her to the ground.
"Kagerou! Watch us reach sexual ecstasy! And I'll watch
you while I do it—and see if that moth circling the candle
dies from your breath!"

He glanced back once, but Tenzen soon became crazed
with sexual lust. He became as ignorant of his surroundings as the moth, which had already dropped into the
flame of the candle. Tenzen crawled on top of Oboro.

Just then, the candle went out.

Yakushiji Tenzen instantly recognized that this was not
the result of ground tremors or wind or Kagerou's breath.
He rolled off Oboro's body.

It was dark. Tenzen snatched his scabbard and climbed
to his feet, staring into the darkness. One minute . . . two
minutes . . . he dimly recognized a figure standing in front
of the round pillar. But it was not Kagerou. Cut free from
her ropes, she had collapsed into an unmoving heap at the
base of the pillar.

Tenzen shouted, "Kouga Gennosuke!"

2

KOUGA GENNOSUKE WAS STILL BLIND.

His heart wandered in darkness as well. After sending
the letter of challenge to Iga, he and his four followers departed Kouga. He wanted to know why the shogun had
lifted the ban on ninja warfare between Manjidani and

Tsubagakure. He also knew that the Iga ninja would attack him. And, in fact, a group of seven pursued him.

During the journey, his group killed Mino Nenki and Hotarubi at Seki, and on the ocean journey from Kuwana, his ally Kasumi Gyoubu killed Amayo Jingorou. Yakushiji Tenzen and Chikuma Koshirou died at the Komaba plains. On his ninja scroll, only Oboro and Akeginu remained. But as the number of enemies decreased, his torment grew closer.

Oboro. Detestable Oboro. But . . . what if he had to cross blades with her?

He had gnashed his teeth and shook off the waves of fear and confusion. But his followers were perceptive and could read his mind. Kasumi Gyoubu, for instance, had left the group and traveled alone; he killed Amayo Jingorou but was killed in return. And Muroga Hyouma had saved him at the Komaba plains by dying in his place. Including his, only three names remained on the Kouga side of the ninja scroll.

But Kisaragi Saemon and Kagerou had left him behind. Perhaps they couldn't wait to attack after they learned that the final two enemies were both women. Or perhaps they thought his blindness would be a hindrance. No—he knew the real reason. They had seen how confused and blind he was when it came to Oboro, and they had left him in disgust.

Lacking self-awareness or purpose, Gennosuke had wandered along the Tokaido Road. He expected Saemon and Kagerou to return, singing victory songs. It should be a happy song for him, too—but anguish gripped his soul. Would Gennosuke have to cross Oboro's name from the ninja scroll with his own hand?

But—

On the western banks of the Ooi River, Gennosuke came across a crowd discussing a strange sign.

"Kouga Gennosuke, wherever you have fled . . . Kagerou has been captured by us. After she tastes Iga torture for a couple of days, we will slit her throat. If you are the leader of Kouga Manjidani, come out of your hole and save Kagerou . . ."

He listened with rapt attention to the voice reading the sign.

Then came the names of the enemy: Oboro and Tenzen.

So apparently Akeginu had died on the enemy side, and his friend Saemon had also died. But Gennosuke's jaw dropped when he heard the name Yakushiji Tenzen. How had Tenzen survived?

If he wanted to learn the truth, he had to figure out where they had gone. Gennosuke lifted his blind face toward the evening clouds and walked forward.

AND NOW, in the darkness of the disintegrating temple of Fujieda, Kouga Gennosuke faced off against the very much alive Yakushiji Tenzen.

Tenzen laughed softly.

"Finally, you are caught in my net, Kouga Gennosuke."

Abandoning his usual caution, Tenzen strode forward. Gennosuke slipped away to the side. An ordinary person watching Gennosuke's movements would not imagine that he was blind. But Yakushiji Tenzen could see that his eyes were still closed.

"Tenzen," Gennosuke said, speaking for the first time. "Is Oboro there?"

"A-ha-ha-ha-ha-ha!" Tenzen could not hold back his laughter. "So, Gennosuke, your eyes really have been destroyed. Oboro is here. Just now we were taunting Kagerou by having sex in front of her. It was as wonderful as a dream, but then you arrived. It's too bad your eyes are ruined, or I'd force you to watch."

Oboro remained where she was. She didn't speak. Her body seemed to be bound in ropes.

"And worst of all is that you won't be able to see Oboro's smiling face as your final image in this world when I kill you."

Yakushiji Tenzen thrust his sword forward, but Kouga Gennosuke escaped to the side. It was as if Gennosuke really could see. But Tenzen was a ninja, and he was not deceived. He saw the confusion in Gennosuke's footsteps.

"Are you trying to flee, Gennosuke?" Tenzen roared with pleasure. "I thought you came here to die!" His blade flashed. Gennosuke evaded most of the blow—but a thread of blood flowed on his white forehead. He reached the edge of the veranda and leaped backward, flying into the courtyard.

Even in the dark, Tenzen could see the blood running on Gennosuke's forehead. He rushed after Gennosuke's shadow and reached the end of the veranda before freezing in terror.

The courtyard was a swamp of fog. Even ninja who had become accustomed to seeing in the dark cannot see through swirling fog. For a moment Tenzen stood still, but then—

"The ninja war between Kouga and Iga will be decided right here!" he screamed and kicked the veranda.

Perhaps fate had its own plans: The boards that Tenzen kicked were rotten! As he swung his sword toward the shadow fleeing into the fog, the boards gave way and the sky revolved. Tumbling, Tenzen touched the ground toes first, and as he looked up he saw the shadow—coming from the depths of the fog—running forward and rising up. It was a thrown sword—it struck into his neckbone, and made a loud crunch as the vertebrae were cleaved in two.

Yakushiji Tenzen took five steps. His neck hung from a single sliver of skin, drooping down his back like a hanging sack. In place of his head, a geyser of blood exploded.

Kouga Gennosuke kneeled on one leg and took a deep breath. As he listened, he heard the sound of Yakushiji

Tenzen thumping to the ground. His eyes blinded, in the midst of the fog and the darkness—his desperate strike had drawn on something outside his five senses. It came from his enlightenment as a ninja.

The blood spray from Tenzen's neck mixed with the fog and gradually fell onto Gennosuke's face. As if waking from a dream, he stood up.

There was no sound in the abandoned temple. He approached the veranda.

"Oboro," he called. "Are you still there?"

"I'm still here, Gennosuke."

How long had it been since Oboro responded to Gennosuke's call? If one counted, only eight nights had passed since Gennosuke left the palace of Ogen of Iga. But those eight days had been so long that they seemed to exist within another world. And Oboro's voice had lost the cheerful lilt that had resembled the song of a little bird. Now her voice was dark and low, barely human.

"I killed Tenzen," Gennosuke said. "Oboro, do you have a sword?"

"I don't have any weapons," she answered.

"Get a sword. Fight with me."

In contrast to his bright, challenging words, his tone was gloomy, as if the fog that encircled them had entered his voice . . .

"I have to kill you," he said. "You have to kill me. You might be able to kill me. I'm blind."

"I am also blind, Gennosuke."

"What?"

"Before I left the valley of Tsubagakure, I blinded myself."

"Wh—why? Oboro, that was—"

"I couldn't stand to watch a war with Manjidani."

Gennosuke swallowed. Those words were all he needed to hear. He knew instantly that she had not betrayed him.

"Gennosuke, please come kill me. I was waiting for you to come." For the first time, some joy had entered her voice. "Iga has been reduced to me alone."

"I am also the last one of Kouga."

Their voices again sank into the depths of the fog. Fog and time spread endlessly.

The silence was broken at the foot of the temple. A scream.

"Did you hear that?"

"Yeah. That must have been Tenzen's final scream."

"Hey, it's the Kouga—!" This voice came from the inn below the temple. The cries of samurai sounded as they raced each other up the hill.

"Nobody is left to see the end," Gennosuke mumbled slowly. The word "nobody" referred to the eighteen ninja of the Kouga and Iga who had killed each other in battle. "Oboro, I'm going."

"Uh? Where?"

"I don't know where." Gennosuke's voice was hollow.

He suddenly knew that he could not kill Oboro. "I don't need to fight you. We are the only two who know what happened. No one else knows . . ."

"I know," said a voice at Gennosuke's feet. A crawling hand sank its nails into Gennosuke's leg. "Gennosuke, why can't you kill Oboro?"

3

THE VOICE CAME FROM A NAKED WHITE BODY STAINED with drops of blood—Kagerou. Although Gennosuke and Oboro could not see it, the shadow of death had already descended upon her face.

"Ge-Gennosuke . . ." Kagerou gasped, "have you for-gotten that when you were at Seki, you swore to me that you would definitely kill Oboro?"

Her trembling hand shook Gennosuke's leg.

"I-I allowed my body to be abused, I was wounded, I was tortured, and now I am dying because of the people of Iga . . . but I feel no bitterness . . ."

"Kagerou," Gennosuke moaned. He could say no more. He felt like a nail had been driven into his lungs.

"I-I did it all for the sake of Kouga, for the sake of Manjidani . . . Gennosuke, are you turning your back on that same Kouga, that same Manjidani?"

"Kagerou . . ."

"Le-let my eyes see Kouga victorious. Kill her—"

Her cries came from the ground. Kagerou gradually

clawed her way closer. Gennosuke picked up Kagerou and held her.

"Let's go, Kagerou."

"No, not like this. Without seeing Oboro's blood, I will never retreat. Gennosuke, use Oboro's blood to cross off her name for me—"

Gennosuke did not answer. Holding Kagerou, he walked toward the veranda. One of Kagerou's hands, shaking, wrapped around Gennosuke's neck. Her eyes stared at Gennosuke's face. Her hollow eyes began to burn with a strange blue fire. Gennosuke, blind, could not see it.

A strange smile ran across Kagerou's face. And then— she breathed into his face.

"Ah—Kagerou!" he cried.

Instantly, he turned his face away and dropped Kagerou. But it was too late. Gennosuke staggered to one knee, then slumped to the ground. He had inhaled Kagerou's deadly breath.

For a long time, Kagerou did not move. But she finally lifted her head a little. Her dying expression contained a bone-chilling mixture of ecstasy and evil. Perhaps this beautiful and terrifying woman's sexual desire was unique in the world. Her fingernails dug into the floorboards, scratching through them as she dug her way toward Gennosuke.

"If you're going to hell, ta-take me with y-you."

Kagerou wanted Gennosuke to take her with him on the road to the underworld. Perhaps she wanted to fill him with another lungful of her poisonous breath to make sure he really died.

Like a dying white snake, Kagerou slithered toward Gennosuke's body. She heard another woman's voice.

"Gennosuke—"

Lifting up her head, Kagerou saw bright shining eyes.

They were the eyes of Oboro, seeing through the dark. Her talents aside, those shining beams of light were mesmerizing. At that moment, Kagerou's breath lost its venom.

"Gennosuke!" Oboro cried and ran to him.

Her eyes were wide open! The Seven Days of Blindness potion had already reached the seventh day, and its powers had finally faded away.

Oboro saw the fallen Gennosuke. She also heard footsteps rushing up the steps to the temple's mountain gate. Oboro didn't look at Kagerou's body. Instead, she lifted up Gennosuke and held him, at the same time examining her surroundings. In the shadow of the altar, she saw the wooden chest used for holding sacred texts. She dragged Gennosuke toward it.

Kagerou saw everything. She had touched Gennosuke's body and knew from his body heat that he was not yet dead—he had only blacked out. But Kagerou couldn't speak or move. In front of her face, a single spider dropped down on a thread. Its legs immediately shriveled up and it died. At that same moment, Kagerou's head landed with a thud on the ground.

"Hey, what's this?" shouted a voice.

"It's Tenzen!" cried another.

Startled voices swirled in the garden. Oboro pushed Gennosuke into the chest, and shut the lid with its peeling red paint.

In the courtyard, samurai were shouting to each other—

"Kouga ninjas were here!"

"Where is Oboro?"

Grasping pine-tar torches, the samurai ran into the main hall. They found Oboro sitting silently on the chest, her head drooping.

"Ah! There's a dead woman here!" one shouted.

"Oboro is uninjured," said another.

"Oboro, what happened?"

Eyes shut, Oboro shook her head. The voices continued.

"Did Kouga Gennosuke come here?"

"Or did Tenzen and this woman kill each other at the same time?"

Despite their clamor, Oboro responded like an infant, only shaking her head. Maybe it meant they were mistaken, maybe it meant that she didn't know the answer to their questions. In any case, they thought she was blind, and they didn't push her to talk.

A woman's voice sounded in the garden. "Don't worry— this Tenzen is an immortal ninja. Last night we thoroughly explained this to you."

It was Ofuku's voice.

"The wound that this man received will quickly heal up, and the places where his skin was cut will build back up. You will be able to see the talents he boasted of so much right now. Someone pick him up and carry him. And hold his head in place."

The soldiers hesitated.

"What are you afraid of? The fate of Takechiyo—and that means me and all of you—depends on you doing this right now."

Five or six men gathered around Tenzen's corpse.

Startled, Oboro got up from the chest and went to the veranda.

In the garden, the pine torches glittered and sent up oily smoke. The red flames shone upon Tenzen's body as the samurai collected both the body and the head that dangled from it. The eyes, open and distended, gazed out toward her.

The men holding Tenzen's body, the men taking his arms, the men supporting the head—all trembled. In the background, the broken-down mountain gate floated against the night sky. It looked like soldiers of hell were escorting the dead.

Tenzen saw Oboro. Oboro saw Tenzen. The length of time that separates life and death is a moment and an eternity.

Oboro's eyes opened wide, sparkling, and they stared

at Tenzen. Those eyes filled with tears. Everyone there was more focused on Tenzen than on Oboro. But little did the soldiers know of the magical spark in the air, linking the living light that shone through her tears and the dull glow from the dead man's dark, muddied eyes.

Oboro cried because her occult-piercing eyes were slicing through the last threads of life to which Tenzen—her ally—clung. She was snuffing his burning desire to remain alive. Kouga, Iga—who lost, who won—she cared less about these things than about saving Kouga Gennosuke.

In the light of the torches, Tenzen's eyes blazed like fire. These were not the eyes of a dead man, whose neck was almost completely severed, held in place by a mere strip of skin. These eyes burned with infinite anger and hate and suffering. But suddenly that light faded and the color ebbed from his face. His eyelids once again closed.

Her energy exhausted, Oboro also closed her eyes.

It was then that Tenzen's head spoke. The lead-colored lips on the severed head bellowed like a water buffalo, "Kouga Gennosuke . . . is in the sacred chest."

Tenzen's lips stretched into a frightening death smile that extended to the tips of his ears before it hardened in place. Tenzen turned into a statue. The eternally reborn phoenix finally flew away.

As she watched the samurai rush past her, Oboro blacked out and collapsed.

4

IT WAS THE EVENING OF THE SEVENTH DAY OF THE fifth month of the nineteenth year of the Keichou era. In Osaka, Tokugawa Ieyasu's rival Toyotomi Hideyori had been performing endless rituals in honor of his Great Buddha statue. On this day, Katagiri Katsumoto traveled to Sunpu, and informed Ieyasu that he could now seize Osaka.

Osaka, the last city holding out against the Tokugawa family, had at last fallen under his control. Ieyasu chuckled to himself. But he did not know about the duel to the death that would occur that same evening, west of Sunpu Castle, near the Abe River. That duel would decide the fate of the Tokugawa family, but the message did not go to Ieyasu. Only Hattori Hanzou, leader of the ninja, was informed of the duel.

The secret urgent messenger from Ofuku had arrived at Hattori's quarters, the seventh floor of Sunpu Castle. At that moment, the setting sun burned brightly as it disappeared, turning the waters of the Abe River the color of dusk.

Upstream and on the other side of the river, there was a space of white sand surrounded by tall reeds. Within those reeds crouched several dozen of Ofuku's retainers. They surrounded the spot where Ofuku met with her invited guest, Hattori Hanzou. Ofuku quickly summarized everything that had taken place.

She didn't lie, but neither did she tell the whole truth. The way that Ofuku told the story, it was as if she had accidentally stumbled upon the duel. She handed the ninja scroll to Hanzou.

Hattori Hanzou had heard rumors of strange Iga signs posted all along the Tokaido Road from Kakegawa to Fujieda. *Well, what should I make of this,* he had thought. He closed the scroll. The scene he was about to witness caused him to shiver reflexively and to release a deep sigh.

"The ten warriors of Kouga and the ten warriors of Iga must now fight each other to the death. On the final day of May, the survivors shall bring this scroll back to Sunpu Castle." This was written on the scroll. Although Hanzou ranked as the leader of the ninja clans, he had not expected the lightninglike speed with which the ninja bloodbath had neared conclusion. Instead of the final day of May, they were only at the seventh day. Barely ten days had passed since the war had commenced. Furthermore, when he looked at the list of twenty ninja from Kouga Manjidani and Iga Tsubagakure, eighteen had already been crossed out in lines of old, crusted black blood.

"The only ones remaining are those two," Ofuku said, her face a mask.

Hattori Hanzou had thought her secret trip to Isei was suspicious, but he could not interpret this woman's expressionless face. Anyway, it didn't matter if she wanted to influence the ninja war because outsiders and normal soldiers rarely had any impact upon ninja.

"I just happened to witness this scene," Ofuku explained. "I knew that if the Kunichiyo faction got wind of this, some of their more thoughtless members might think I had influenced the result and they might want to get revenge on me. I also didn't want to break the shogun's rules. For that reason, I took the precaution of guarding the perimeter, to make sure that nobody comes and influences these two fighters. But I worried that someone might think that I was involved and the gossip might spread. So that's why I called you, the leader of the ninja. I want you to be a witness and see for yourself that I did not interfere in any way in this final duel."

Ofuku had traveled a mere eleven miles from Fujieda. She had been waiting for Kouga Gennosuke, who had passed out, to awaken. One reason she had waited for him to awake was that Oboro had asked her to do so, but another reason was to have Hanzou serve as a witness.

"If I kill a Kouga ninja while he is unconscious, it would not honor Iga," Oboro had said. Ofuku's reasoning was different, but reached the same conclusion: She wanted Hattori Hanzou to personally witness the magnificent victory of Iga over Kouga.

Magnificent? Ofuku knew that Kouga Gennosuke was blind. She also knew that Oboro's eyes were open. She was confident that Oboro already had the victory in her hand.

"As you can see," Ofuku explained to Hattori Hanzou, "the Kouga ninja's eyes are closed."

"What?"

"Apparently, the Iga ninja blinded him. Hattori, that's simply part of ninja warfare."

Hattori Hanzou stared at Kouga Gennosuke, standing in the reeds. "Of course," Hanzou answered.

Ninja warfare did not recognize the concept of shame. Any trick or handicap was fair game. The laws of war do not fit into the world of ninja. Surprise attacks, assassinations, killings through trickery—all of these were simply options from which to choose in the mercilessness of war.

"Kouga Gennosuke!" Hanzou called. "You have no objections to this duel with Oboro?"

"I will do as you wish," Gennosuke answered calmly. He had traveled to Sunpu to demand answers. But now that he was here, Gennosuke had not one word of bitterness toward Hattori Hanzou.

"And you, Oboro?"

"Ready!"

The hawk rested on Oboro's shoulder. Something was flowing down her lovely cheeks.

The day before, while being questioned by Ofuku, Oboro had seemed resolute about killing Gennosuke. Perhaps she was resigned to her fate. Or perhaps, at this final moment, the blood of Ogen of Iga had surged once more within her veins.

Hattori Hanzou, unaware of the thoughts of the two opponents, also felt gloomy. Many years earlier, he had visited Kouga and Iga, and he had met with Kouga Danjou and Ogen. At that time, the two he had seen were a young man and woman full of youthful energy. Now, looking at these two, his eyes could hardly believe that they were ninja. They were so beautiful and young. These two had been hounded to the border of death by his schemes—even if they were made at the order of the shogun—and now Hanzou looked back with regret upon what he had done.

"Well, then, I will observe," Hattori Hanzou shouted decisively. "You two may begin." He ran onto the sand with the secret scroll, placing it between the two.

The hawk suddenly soared up into the air. In contrast to Hanzou, scurrying back to his position, Kouga Gennosuke and Oboro silently walked out upon the white altar of battle.

THE EVENING wind came out. The reeds rustled. Cold waves seemed to extend within the flowing darkness, just as if it were autumn.

Kouga Gennosuke and Oboro held their swords and faced each other.

This image would long remain burned on Hattori Hanzou's eyes. Here were the son and daughter of the archenemies, Kouga and Iga. Looking upon this scene and told only that four hundred years of hatred would culminate in death, who could have guessed what was really in the man's and woman's hearts?

Only ten days earlier, in a spot a little distant but also along the Abe River, their grandfather and grandmother had sighed and said these words: "The fate that befell us will now befall Oboro and Gennosuke. Too bad their stars are crossed!" Those two had fought each other and died together. But did anybody know?

In the west, the remaining sheaths of red light slowly faded. With time, they shifted and became blue. The two figures stood there in silence, without moving.

Unable to stand it, Ofuku angrily roared: "Oboro!"

As if carried along, Oboro walked forward. One step, three steps, five steps. Gennosuke remained still, his sword hanging limply in his hand. He did not adopt any defensive posture.

Standing directly in front of him, Oboro raised her sword to Gennosuke's chest. And then, at that moment, something unexpected occurred. The blade twisted around until it pointed at her. The sword jabbed into her abdomen, under the breasts. Without a sound, she collapsed to the sand.

From the midst of the reeds, there came an incomprehensible scream. Ofuku's face changed color. She didn't understand what had happened or why. She drew in her breath, held it, and then went crazy. "Someone! Kill Kouga Gennosuke!"

She had completely forgotten about Hattori Hanzou, whom she had invited to attend. Oboro had lost! Oboro's defeat was the equivalent of Takechiyo's defeat, and it was her own defeat as well! And those defeats meant her faction would all be killed.

Samurai rushed forward, their blades shining and confused amidst the Japanese pampas grass. When they closed to within fifteen feet of Kouga Gennosuke, a nightmarish scene erupted. The samurai began hacking at themselves with their own swords.

Ofuku watched the clouds of misty blood like a vision of hell. In the light of dusk, Kouga Gennosuke still held his sword limply, standing alone. But he had opened his eyes and gold light was shining.

He began to walk in her direction. Ofuku was petrified from terror. But Gennosuke merely took the scroll and opened it. Then he walked to Oboro's side and, standing there, silently looked at her. "Oboro . . ."

His voice shivered and vanished with the wind blowing through the reeds.

Gennosuke was the only one who knew the truth. Oboro had died before he had opened his eyes.

For a while, Gennosuke held her, and then he carried her body to the water. Opening the scroll, he dabbed his fingertip in the blood on her chest, and crossed out the two remaining names. Although none would know it until later, he wrote the following in blood beneath the list of names: "The last person, writing these words, is the ninja Oboro of Iga."

Gennosuke rolled up the scroll and threw it into the air. Until now, the world had been soundless, but suddenly there was the beating of wings. The hawk snatched the scroll in its talons.

"Iga won. Go to the castle," Kouga Gennosuke shouted. Then he took Oboro's sword and ran it through his own chest. He fell into the water. He held tight to Oboro, already floating there, and the two bodies drifted silently in the current.

In the remaining light, the hawk turned a few low circles and then followed the current. Beneath the gently flying hawk, the young pair of ninja became one, and flowed away in water without waves.

In the blue moonlight of the Suruga waters and the open sea, the black hair of the corpses tangled together as they floated. The hawk had followed them this far, but now it turned and flew north again, its talons holding the scroll. But the twenty greatest ninja from Kouga and Iga were all gone.

ABOUT THE AUTHOR

FŪTARO YAMADA was born in Japan in 1922. He published his first detective novel in 1947 while in medical school. In 1958, he published *The Kouga Ninja Scrolls*, the first in a series about supernatural ninjas. The immense popularity of the series led to numerous adaptations, including the manga series Basilisk and the 2005 movie *Shinobi*. Fūtaro Yamada received numerous awards for his ninja and detective novels, including the Fourth Annual Japanese Mystery Literary Award in 2000. He passed away in July of 2001.

ABOUT THE TRANSLATOR

GEOFF SANT is a Japanese and Chinese translator living in New York. He received an MA in Japanese and Chinese literature from Columbia University, and translates Japanese for the East Asian Department. Sant's other translations include the 9/11 Oral History Documentation Project, in which he translated interviews with Chinatown residents. His original writings, in Chinese and English, have been developed into a radio program in Taiwan and selected for an anthology of the year's best Chinese-language essays.

Basilisk

ORIGINAL STORY BY FŪTARO YAMADA
MANGA BY MASAKI SEGAWA

THE BATTLE BEGINS

The Iga clan and the Kouga clan have been sworn enemies for more than four hundred years. Only the Hanzo Hattori truce has kept the two families from all-out war. Now, under the order of Shogun Ieyasu Tokugawa, the truce has been dissolved. Ten ninja from each clan must fight to the death in order to determine who will be the next Tokugawa Shogun. The surviving clan will rule for the next thousand years.

But not all the clan members are in agreement. Oboro of the Iga clan and Gennosuke of the Kouga clan have fallen deeply in love. Now these star-crossed lovers have been pitted against each other. Can their romance conquer a centuries-old rivalry? Or is their love destined to end in death?

Mature: Ages 18 +

Special extras in each volume! Read them all!

VISIT WWW.DELREYMANGA.COM TO:
- Read sample pages
- View release date calendars for upcoming volumes
- Sign up for Del Rey's free manga e-newsletter
- Find out the latest about new Del Rey Manga series

Basilisk © 2003 Fūtaro Yamada and Masaki Segawa / KODANSHA LTD. All rights reserved.

THE EPIC FILM BASED ON THE 'KOUGA NINJA SCROLLS'

S H I N O B I
HEART UNDER BLADE

"*Masterpiece*"
— *Toronto After Dark Film Festival*

2 Discs – Bonus Disc includes:

VFX Behind the Scenes   Storyboards   Artwork at Manjidani
Weapons Introduction   Behind the Scenes at Sumpu Castle   Original Trailers & TV Spots

OFFICIAL SELECTION OF THE   Official Selection Seattle International Film Festival 2006   TORONTO AFTER DARK FILM FESTIVAL torontoafterdark.com

ON DVD SPRING 2007
Check www.shinobithemovie.com for more information.

L O V E   I S   W A R

P.O. 0005283858 202